Editor: S.G. Thomas

Cover photo: © CanStockPhoto.com

Cover Design: by Sommer Stein with Perfect Pear Creative

ISBN: 1492351024

Chapter 1 – Four Months Ago Drayton University

He slams me against the door, his lips meeting mine urgently. His hands search my body and I wrap my right leg up around his, moving my dress higher up my thighs.

His lips move to my tear-stricken cheeks, where lines of mascara still cover them. He makes his way to my neck and then my ear, lightly nibbling around my earlobe and I know at that moment, I need this.

"Make me forget," I whisper.

"Oh believe me, you will forget your name when I'm done with you," he says, grabbing my ass, forcing my legs to wrap around his torso.

He carries me across the room, his lips on mine, thrusting his tongue deeper in my mouth with every step. My arms are tight against him, keeping him close. The feeling of safety is what I crave.

He throws me on the bed, our eyes never leaving one another. Pulling on my legs, he brings me to the edge of the bed and takes off my heels. His hands inch up my legs until his fingers are wrapped around each side of my black thong. He slides it down my legs, tossing the tiny piece of material onto the floor before returning to push my dress up, exposing me to him. I hear the breath hitch in his throat before he starts unzipping his dress slacks and pushing them down. He shuffles over to the nightstand and seconds later, he is on top of me.

"I have been waiting so long to have you," he says, entering me hard and rushed. "Oh...so worth the wait."

I remain quiet, trying to push all thoughts out of my head. When his hands reach my ass, pulling me harder against him, the pleasure increases and everything disappears. He thrusts forcefully into me, whispering how good I feel. He may not have as many moves as others and he talks too much for my liking, but I'm enjoying how well-endowed he is.

The feeling builds inside of me; I love this part. All I feel is his touch while he pumps into me. As sweat starts slicking between us, I flip him over, straddling his body. I can no longer wait for him. He is going way too slow and I crave my release. Isn't this what it's all about?

"That's what I'm talking about!" he says and smirks as I slide him back into me. I want to stick a sock in his throat. His talking is making it harder for me to find my relief.

He grabs my hips, trying to move me to his rhythm, but I pick up his hands and place them on my breasts so I can control the speed and rhythm. Five minutes later, my body shudders and I sink down on top of him.

"Fuck, Sadie. You're awesome." He moves to kiss me, but I climb off his body, pulling my dress back down.

I stand up to put my heels back on, but he grabs me from behind, bringing me closer to him. "Stay with me tonight," he says, wrapping his arms around my waist.

"Okay," I agree, crawling back on the bed. It is better than being alone. I hate being alone; it only makes me relive my mistakes.

He wraps his arms around me and I can smell the alcohol on his breath as his mouth rests close to my neck. The feeling of safety surrounds me and I drift off to sleep.

The next morning the light wakes me up, streaming into the small room and I find myself alone in a strange bed. I look around, trying to remember where I am and what I did. The dirty clothes overflowing in the hamper and the sports team paraphernalia on the wall tell me that I'm most likely in a frat house...again.

I tiptoe to get my shoes, hooking them in my hands. I slowly open the door, peering right and left down the hall. I see no one, so I quietly make my way down the stairs. It seems like the front door is a mile away and I can't get through it fast enough. Just as my hand reaches the knob, I hear talking in the next room.

"I wouldn't brag, Soren, I had her last week." A deep voice laughs. "Actually, you might be the last to have her."

"She a great lay though," Jeff Soren says in return.

"I told you she was," the other male agrees. "Ever since...the incident, she has become the college slut."

"I know. It's kind of sad though." Jeff's voice actually sounds concerned. "I wish..."

"Dude. You can't save girls like that, you just enjoy what they give you," the other voice replies back.

I close my eyes, taking a deep breath. I catch a glimpse of myself in the mirror. Mascara is stained in long lines down my face and my long, honey-colored hair looks like a bird made its home there. My lips are swollen red, and I can't help but think I resemble a hooker on the corner waiting for her next trick.

I turn the knob to the door slowly, hoping Jeff and his buddy don't hear me. I sneak out, walking across the street to my sorority house. I'm happy to find that everyone is either still asleep or out. When I crash into my bed, I take the picture out of my drawer that's been hidden away since last year. I clutch it hard against my chest while sobs escape my mouth. Curling up into the fetal position on my twin bed, I can't help but think how I have disappointed him. I need to change the direction of my life. Make him proud of me.

Chapter 2 – Present Day Western College

I have never felt so out of place. If it wasn't for my roommate, Jessa, I would have never known this place even existed. She told me we were coming to a bar, but this looks like a rundown house that drug addicts inhabit. When she told me to park along the street, I thought we were going to the bar across the way. Not this old white house we stand in front of now. The paint is chipped away, exposing the wooden frame, and dark colored sheets cover the windows.

"Come on Sadie, it looks worse than it is." Jessa tugs on my arm, pulling me toward the door. Girls and guys file into the bar that resembles a house, sporting different hair colors and more piercings and tattoos than I have ever seen. I can count on one hand how many people I know who have a tattoo and no one I know has a piercing other than their earlobes.

Of course, Jessa fits in with her short blonde pixie cut and tongue piercing. I notice the guys giving her a once over before turning to me, questioning and judging why I'm here. How different this feels, to be the one judged. I suddenly regret every glare I've ever given someone who is different than me.

"I don't know, Jessa. Maybe I should just go back to the dorm, you can text me when you need a ride home," I say, starting to back step to the safety of my car.

"No you don't, Sadie. I won't leave your side, just give it a try. The music is really good." She grabs my hand and I reluctantly follow her to the opening door.

A bald guy with a reddish, long-haired goatee and tattoos stretching over each arm puts his hand out to us. Jessa takes out her five dollar cover fee out of her back pocket, while I fumble through my purse, handing him a fifty. He cocks one eye at me, then hands me my change back in five dollar bills. I stuff them in my purse and clasp it shut.

Jessa grabs my hand and leads me into what I envision as the living room. There are couches along every wall and chairs strewn around. All the furniture looks like it should be in a landfill and it shocks me that people are actually comfortable relaxing on them.

Walking a little further into the bar/house, a band is playing in the far corner, which I assume was the kitchen at one time. It sounds like they are banging on their instruments rather than playing them while the lead singer screams into the microphone. I can't understand one word coming out of his mouth but Jessa's head keeps up with the beat, bopping from shoulder to shoulder, making me wonder what I'm missing.

Thankfully, Jessa positions us against the wall out of the way and buys two beers from some guy in the corner. I'm happy when they're unopened, since he pulled them out of a cooler one usually takes camping. I reluctantly take a sip and wince from the taste. Quickly, I smile over toward Jessa to reassure her I like it, but she's already distracted by the music, jumping up and down.

I take my time to observe my scenery. Almost every girl has looked me up and down in disgust and guys skim over me curiously. It's a one-eighty from what I'm used to. Until recently, I have never been a girl guys notice. Not until after Theo. I didn't handle the attention very well, but it felt nice to be desired.

I left that Sadie behind though. I'm going to reinvent myself. No more letting boys lead me to their bedrooms at the end of the night, or waking up in strange beds in the morning. No more out of control shopping trips, or parties until dawn. I will make the Dean's List and be the child they miss. I promised I would no longer be the screw-up daughter who did nothing but disappoint them.

Lost in thought, I'm surprised when I turn to my right and see Jessa making out with a short, dark-haired guy with "Rebel" scripted into the back of his neck in big, black lettering. His ringed fingers grab her ass, pulling her closer to him and she doesn't seem to be pushing him away. This is my time to escape.

"Jessa, I'm going to get going. Call me if you need a ride." I tap her shoulder. She stops kissing the dark-haired rebel.

"No Sadie...stay," she begs, while Rebel continues to kiss and suck on her neck.

"Really, I need to go." I start getting my keys out of my purse.

"Okay," she relents, nodding her head with disappointment on her face. "Don't worry, I'll get a ride."

I wave my hand to her and walk toward the front door. I hadn't realized how packed full of people the bar/house became. I weave in and out between clusters of people, trying to make my way to the door. I couldn't imagine if a fire broke out. Surely this is not a legitimate business establishment, but rather a permanent house party.

I'm almost back to the bald man when someone bumps into me. My feet fumble and I try to catch myself before I fall straight back on this disgusting floor, or worse, into a group of people. My purse flies off my arm, spilling its contents when it crashes to the floor. I put my hands out behind me ready to catch myself when an arm wraps around my waist, pulling me back.

"Whoa girl," the stranger says. He tries to straighten me up, placing both his hands on my hips.

"Thank you," I respond, not looking his way. I kneel on the ground and hurriedly pick up my items, shoving them back in my purse.

"Here you go." That same voice has my keys in his hand. When I go to grab them, he shuts his hand. "I don't think you need them."

I look up at a set of caramel eyes staring back at me. His brown hair is short, but slightly turned into a small Mohawk in the middle. Although he isn't my usual type, he is absolutely stunning. He isn't wearing khakis and a polo. His hair isn't trimmed and cut to perfection. He is nothing like what I am used to, but still I can't tear my eyes away.

I stand up and glance down at his hand wrapped around my upper arm and then back up to his face. He smirks at me. "Why are you holding me up and can I have my keys now?" I demand.

"Sorry, I don't let people drive drunk." He puts my keys in his pocket.

"I'm not drunk," I spit out.

"That's what they all say," he deadpans.

"What do you want me to do to prove it? Walk a line? Say the alphabet?" I ask, irritated that this man is keeping me from my lonely night in my dorm room. "Z, Y, X..." I start to rattle off the alphabet backwards.

"You really aren't drunk?" He holds his hand up to stop me from continuing.

"No, some jerk knocked me down," I tell him.

"Really?" He looks deeper in my eyes for some sign of alcohol. "Sorry, I just assumed since you were fumbling backwards." He looks me up and down. "I figured you swayed over from the frat party down the street."

"No, I was here with my roommate, I had a couple sips of a beer and if you could hand me my keys, I would like to leave now," I request, keeping my eyes on the ground.

"You're leaving before the final band?" he asks, still not giving up my keys. Not that I would mind going after them myself.

"Yes, I have an early morning," I say with my hand out, impatiently waiting for my keys.

"I will give these back to you on one condition." He digs them out of his worn-in jeans, dangling them in front of me.

"How about you just give them to me and call it a night?" I suggest.

"What's the fun in that? I want you to stay for the last band. It's my band, The Invisibles." He smiles down at me.

"Listen..." I pause for his name.

"Brady. Brady Carsen," he discloses.

"Listen, Brady. I'm not the kind of girl you are looking for. So I thank you for stopping my fall and helping me pick up my things, but why don't you just give me my keys. You can go up and play and I will go home."

"Kind of girl I'm looking for?" He raises his eyebrows. "Just stay and afterwards we can get to know each other better." There's that phrase, 'get to know each other', which clarifies to me again that I'm not the girl he wants. I figure the easiest way to get him to leave me alone is to agree to his terms.

"Alright, I'll stay," I agree, already deciding that I will leave once he starts playing. He finally hands me my keys and I keep them placed in my hand, planning my escape.

"You're going to love it," he says and grabs my hand, tugging me back the way I came.

He stops me at a spot on the right-hand side at the corner of the kitchen/dining room. "Stay here. I'll come back for you after the show," he whispers in my ear, since the band before him is still playing. He turns away from me, but quickly turns back around.

"I never caught your name."

"Sadie Miller," I spill out before thinking I should have given him a fake name.

"It's nice to meet you, Sadie. Enjoy the show." With a turn of his heels he walks away from me.

Five minutes later, the one band has taken off their equipment and I'm guessing the three other guys up on stage with Brady are the remaining members of The Invisibles. When they are all ready, Brady looks my way. He winks at me before he jumps off stage and walks toward the back hallway.

Abruptly, the whole place gets quiet and people push their way through the crowd to get as close as possible. I see now why Brady positioned me here; no one will be able to push me around and I can still see the stage clearly. All the lights go off and then colored lights beam down from the ceiling. I'm surprised they only do this for The Invisibles. What about the other bands? Why don't they get this special treatment?

A guy who is older than me by ten years or so stands up to the microphone. His hair is in a long Mohawk with different streaks of color throughout. He introduces The Invisibles and Brady leads his band members up onto the stage. Brady takes the microphone off the stand and the drummer starts beating his sticks in the air. The guitarist and bassist stand in a wide stance, holding their instruments, anticipating the start.

Brady's presence on stage demands attention and the crowd gives it willingly. He is probably just over six feet or so. Strong build but not overly muscular. His old school band t-shirt molds tight across his shoulders and it rises up when he raises his arms, exposing the small ripples of his stomach. Brady in jeans and a t-shirt is the most incredible vision, but I wouldn't mind seeing him without them, too.

His voice carries throughout the bar/house. At first it is slow and steady but quickly builds into a faster beat. He appears completely enthralled in the moment, shutting his eyes from time to time, as though he feels every word. It is the sexiest thing I have ever witnessed and I know I can't stay. This will only end one way, me in his bed and him ignoring me tomorrow. *He is looking for a fast lay Sadie, nothing more*, I think. Too bad I didn't meet him last year. Pretty sure he could have showed me a thing or two.

I wait two songs and start making my way through the crowd, hearing the groans and protests for having inconvenienced them. When I get to the front door, bald man is no longer there. I hear Brady's voice turn sultry and sexual while the music moves to a slower beat. This is my cue; if I hear it, I won't have the self-control to walk away.

I open the screen door and step onto the street, trying to stay on the straight and narrow. My parents deserve it and Brady Carsen would veer me off the course of a trouble-free life.

That Monday I'm walking back to my dorm after a long Algebra course. I hate math; it is by far my worst subject. I have to find a tutor if I'm going to pass it. I make a mental note to check that out tonight. Digging into my messenger bag, I realize I forgot my iPod back in my room. Since the math building is clear on the other side of campus, it's going to be a boring walk. It leaves me alone with my thoughts and there is nothing I hate more than that.

A half hour later, I grab my keys to open the dorm building. The quad is filled with laughter and jokes from students. A couple of girls sit in the corner and stare at some of the guys horsing around. Checking my mail, I'm not surprised to see the mailbox empty. I glance at my watch and notice it's only three o'clock, making me relieved that Jessa has another hour before she has to leave for class. I hate being in that room by myself. It is the sole reason I decided to go into the dorms instead of getting an apartment.

When I open the door to my room, I see Jessa sitting on her loft bed. Our room is small so we opted for two loft beds. We set up chairs and a table under one and the television under the other. Our small refrigerator sits next to the television with a microwave on top. Our dressers line the walls on either side. It is close quarters, to say the least.

"You had a visitor today," she says, beaming over at me.

"Who?" I question. I don't know very many people here.

"Well, I'll give you two hints." She starts climbing down from her loft. "He is fucking hot and two, he is fucking hot. What else matters?" She grabs a water bottle out of the fridge.

"Okay. I don't know any hot guys, so I'm at a loss." I plop my bag down and grab a bottle for myself before sitting in my chair.

"Think really hard," she says, sitting next to me. "He left something for you. I put it on your dresser." She motions with her hand.

I stand up and lying on my dresser is my iPod with a sticky note attached.

"May I say, he is so beyond fuckable, Sadie. If you don't jump on that, I will," Jessa continues talking as I pull the note off.

Since you left without seeing my show,

I'm leaving you to your own private listening pleasure.

- B

"Brady Carsen?" I question, picking up my iPod. I thumb through the albums and spot The Invisibles listed. "How did he know where to find me?" I whisper to myself.

"You should have seen how upset he was you weren't here. He hung around for a while, but said he had somewhere to be," Jessa reveals, coming up behind me.

"Huh," I mumble to myself. I grab my ear buds and climb up to my loft.

A couple minutes later, I hear the door shut and Jessa is gone. I curl up on top of my blankets listening to Brady sing to me. Surprisingly, there are quite a few love songs. I assumed they would mostly be loud and fast. I love how you can hear Brady's breath suck in at the end of the lyrics. A particular slow song comes on and Brady's soft voice starts singing, *I thought I would be enough but I guess I was wrong. I never thought it was possible to miss someone for so long but you just keep walking away.* When it gets back to the chorus my eyes start drooping and eventually I'm lulled to sleep with Brady's voice filling my ears.

Chapter 3

In the last two days, I have listened to The Invisibles at least thirty times. It plays when I walk to class, when I study at the library, and when I fall asleep. Brady Carsen's voice has an effect on me that I have never felt before. Even the faster songs bring a calming sensation over me.

Even though I know nothing about him, he consumes my every thought. I find myself doing a double take with every guy that sports a small Mohawk, checking if it's him. I don't even know if he is a student; he could very well be trying to make it to stardom as a musician.

I curse myself when my stomach fills with butterflies just imagining his face when he winked at me on stage that night. As much as I tell myself he's trouble with a capital T, I can't stop the thoughts. I know I should change my music, take The Invisibles off my iPod, but every time my finger hovers over that delete button it chooses cancel instead.

Since today is Thursday, I have a three hour gap between classes.

Jessa had company when I woke up this morning, so I decide to head to the library instead of the dorm. I need the quiet study time anyway.

I walk through the doors of the library and make my way directly to the elevators. I ride the elevator by myself up to the sixth floor. I select my spot at a table for four in my usual area, close to the bathroom and elevator. Then I notice a guy sitting a few seats over by himself with his laptop out, typing so hard it sounds like the keys are going to pop off the keyboard. I debate leaving for a second, but decide I'm going to fight for my spot. I found it the first week of classes and I'm not giving it up easily. I put my ear buds in and turn my music up loud with the hope that it will annoy the angry typist.

Five minutes later my plan worked, except he now stands on the other side of the table from me. I pretend to concentrate on my book in front of me, but I see his pressed khaki slacks out of the corner of my eye. I don't look up, but he gives me no choice when he taps his pen on the page I'm reading.

My eyes follow the blue pen that is held by long lean fingers, up to the tanned forearms, followed by the strong shoulders until I meet a pair of blue eyes staring down at me. A smile appears from his lips showing his perfect white teeth. When I realize he is talking to me, I pull the white cord from my ear bud out.

"I'm sorry, what?" My voice displays a hint of annoyance to it.

"Is that The Invisibles?" He points to my ear bud resting on my book.

"Yeah." I look down and back up to him. I notice his smile has faltered. "Do you like them?" I ask.

"They're okay," he says, shrugging his shoulders up and down. His reaction confuses me. He must like the band, how else could he pick them out from hearing it from my ear bud?

"Do you mind turning it down?" he asks.

"I will turn it down if you are a little nicer to your keyboard," I jokingly respond.

"Deal," he laughs, putting his hand out for me to shake. "Grant Bishop."

"Sadie Miller." I shake his hand back.

"So Sadie, what year are you?" He pulls a chair out from the table.

"Senior. I don't want to be rude but I have to finish reading this." I point to my book, praying he doesn't sit down.

"How come I've never seen you around?" he asks and a loud sigh escapes my lips when he sits down.

"Do you know the entire fifteen thousand student body?" I sarcastically ask.

"No, but since roughly sixty percent are female, I only really need to know nine thousand. Regardless, I would never forget a face like yours." His flirtatious lip turns up to the right.

"Nice line," I chuckle.

"Thanks," he laughs. I'm happy to see he knows how cliché his line is. "Seriously, I have been coming up to the sixth floor since my freshman year and I have never seen you," he states.

"I just transferred from Drayton University," I reveal. I doubt he knows anyone from there.

"That would explain it," he says, staring at me for a few seconds before standing up. "Welcome to the sixth floor. You won't be bothered since it's the Entomology area; there aren't many people that come up here unless they are biology majors," he advises me.

"Thanks," I respond and put my ear bud back in, turning down the music.

My stomach growls an hour later and I realize I haven't eaten since the banana this morning. I stand to pack up my books, deciding I should grab a bite to eat before heading to Clinical Psychology. Slinging my messenger bag over my shoulder, I see Grant is still typing, or in his case finger pecking on his computer. Right as I'm about to press the elevator button to go down, Grant puts his finger up in the air to me. "Hold on, Sadie. I'll ride with you." He quickly shoves his computer in his backpack and jogs over to me. I press the down button and we wait in silence together.

Once we enter the small confines, Grant turns my way. "Are you off to class?" he asks.

"Um...yeah." My voice hesitates, sounding unsure. Damn, I can tell he knows I'm lying.

"For some reason I don't believe you," he says, cocking his eyebrow.

"Well, I'm going to grab something to eat and then I have to head to Wright Hall," I admit.

"Psychology?" he questions.

I nod in affirmation.

"I usually don't do this, but you want to go grab a coffee or something?" he asks and suddenly the elevator is traveling way too slow.

I bite my lower lip, stalling in hesitation. Grant's eyes stay firmly on me, anticipating my answer. Last year I would have said forget the coffee, where's your dorm? But I'm not that Sadie any longer. A wave of relief envelops me when the elevator beeps and the doors peel open. Unfortunately, my relief only lasts a second, when a set of familiar caramel eyes meet mine.

Brady Carsen looks delectable. He's wearing a black hoodie paired with charcoal jeans and a set of black Chuck Taylors. His hair is pushed to the side today, making him appear less like a rocker than Saturday. But it's his smile that absorbs me first. A warm safe feeling blankets me as we stare at one another.

"Sadie Miller," Brady states.

"Brady Carsen," I mimic his tone.

He smiles widely at me, but it dissipates when he looks to my left.

"Grant," he nods over to him. I look back and forth between them, surprised they know each other. Their appearances would suggest they hang out in different circles.

"Brady," Grant nods back.

Brady quickly disregards Grant, focusing his attention solely on me. "So, did you get my note?" The dimple in his right cheek indents further when his lips turn up.

"I did," I say, returning his smile.

"What did you think?" He nervously rocks back on his heels. "I mean it wasn't the live version like I would have preferred." He raises his right eyebrow to me, informing me I should have never left Saturday night.

"It's alright," I jokingly shrug my left shoulder.

"Just alright," he says softly. His lips turn down in a disappointed frown.

"Hey." I playfully hit his shoulder with my hand. "I'm just kidding. Just ask Grant who I was listening to a few minutes ago when I was studying." I point toward Grant, who seems completely disinterested in our conversation.

Brady's eyes perk up at me. "Really?" He honestly sounds surprised that I like his band.

"Yes really. Tell him, Grant." I motion with my hand to Grant, who is standing with his hands in the pockets of his khakis.

"Yeah...she was," Grant mumbles and his attitude makes Brady smile even bigger. "Listen, I have to go. See you around, Sadie." Grant starts to walk away before I can respond.

"Bye, Grant," I call out but he's too far to hear me.

Brady's eyes follow mine to Grant's back. "Do you have time to get something to eat?"

"Sorry, I can't." I stare at the ground, not wanting to look into his eyes.

"Can't or won't?" He dips his head down, trying to see my face.

"Won't," I answer softly right before my stomach grumbles. My face instantly reddens.

"I was on my way to get something to eat. Walk with me to the Student Center." He motions with his head. "We can sit at different tables if you want," he teases.

"I thought you were waiting for the elevator?"

"Plans change. I heard your stomach and now mine's reacting. Come on." He shrugs his shoulder forward to follow.

"Don't get any ideas Carsen, my stomach made this decision." I walk in line next to him.

"I wouldn't dream of it, Sadie Miller." He wraps his arms around my shoulders before I squirm out of it. "Sorry, I had to take a chance." He laughs and I try to conceal my grin from him.

Brady doesn't touch me for the short walk across the campus to the Student Center. When we enter through the doors, tables are filled with students reading and talking.

"What are you in the mood for?" Brady asks me as his eyes roam across the different fast food places.

"I don't know." The last thing I want to do is eat in front of him, but I will never make it through Clinical Psych without something in my stomach. "I think I'm going to get a bagel sandwich." I point to the bagel place.

"Sounds good." He puts his hand on the small of my back, leading me that way. His hand radiates a wave of heat throughout my body so I start walking a few steps faster.

"You don't have to get anything from there," I tell him, assuming he wouldn't enjoy it.

"What are you trying to say? A guy can't like a bagel sandwich? Do you think I should stuff my face with fries and burgers?" His face shows no trace of humor.

"No, that's not it. It's just..." I try to backpedal.

"I'm kidding, Sadie. To be honest, I have never tried this place but you have piqued my interest." We stand away from the shop to look up at the menu. "So, what do you usually get?" he asks.

"The veggie de lite."

"Are you a vegetarian?" he inquires, sounding like it could be the worst thing in the world.

"Is that a deal breaker for you?" I ask.

"Deal breaker?" he scrunches his eyebrows, confused.

"You know, something you find out about someone that makes you not want to date them," I answer.

"What's yours?" he asks.

"I asked first. If I was a vegetarian, would that be a deal breaker?"

"I'm not sure anything I find out about you would be a deal breaker, but to be honest, I don't understand vegetarians."

"Hmm." I turn around to give my order to the cute red head behind the counter who can't keep her eyes off Brady.

"You never answered. Do you eat meat?" He comes up behind me.

"No, I'm not a vegetarian. I just like the sandwich," I honestly reply. "I'll have a veggie de lite with low fat cream cheese," I say to the girl. Usually I get the garlic and herb spread, but I'm not about to talk to Brady with garlic breath.

"What can I get you?" The red head looks Brady up and down while her co-worker starts to make my sandwich.

"Same, but garlic and herb cream cheese." He smiles over to me and I'm sure awe fills my face. I'm half tempted to change my order. "I hate that low fat shit."

"They have meat, you know," I tell him.

"I know. I want to experience why you like it so much." He scoots next to me and my heart races when his hand brushes against mine. I quickly make my way down the line away from him.

When we get to the cash register, Brady pulls out a twenty before I can even get in my messenger bag, adding chips and drinks to our meals.

"Don't pay for me!"

"Why not?" Brady looks around, seeing a few students peering our way after my outburst.

"This is not a date," I confirm.

"Hey, just because I decide to buy you lunch or dinner or whatever this meal is, doesn't mean it's a date." He softens his voice, getting closer to me.

"It's just...things get implied with dates." I'm desperate to compose myself. I don't want to owe him anything.

"Relax, Sadie. I'll make you a deal." He grabs our tray and leads us to a table.

"What?" I take a seat, happy he picked a table in the back.

"You can buy me a meal tomorrow." He smirks up at me.

"Nice, Carsen."

"A meal for a meal, then we're even." He takes both straws and pounds them on the table until the wrappers fall down. He puts one in mine and the second in his own drink.

"When are your classes tomorrow?" I ask.

"Well...I live off campus and I don't have classes on Fridays, so it will have to be later." He takes a bite of his sandwich.

"Later, when?" I ask before I take a bit of mine.

"This is really good, you don't even miss the meat," he says, lifting his sandwich. "After my show," he answers my question.

"I told you the sandwich was good. After the show, what?" I take a sip of my soda.

"I have a show tomorrow night. We will get something after I'm done," he casually says while he continues to eat his sandwich.

"Sorry, but I'm not going to that bar, house or whatever it is from last week." I shake my head back and forth.

He laughs. "Good, because we are playing at Aces. I'll pick you up."

"Um...no. Let me just give you the money." I dig through my bag and get the ten dollars out, placing it on the table.

"That's not the deal. A meal for a meal. Just so you know, after a show I'm so hungry you might get the raw end of this deal," he jokes.

"I think I already got the raw end. I can't go to your show tomorrow or out to eat," I say, putting my sandwich down, suddenly not able to finish it.

"What do I have to do?" he asks me before he pops a chip in his mouth.

"Nothing. I don't date."

"Okay, it won't be a date. A friend coming to another friend's show and then grabbing something to eat. I will even invite my band if it makes you feel better." His eyes are begging me and I have to admit I want to go after listening to him sing the last few days.

"Fine," I sigh. "But I'm bringing my roommate, Jessa, with me,"

"Great, the more people the better. I'll pick you both up." He picks his sandwich back up, happier than before.

Chapter 4

Brady texted me this afternoon, saying he would pick us up at seven. Jessa was going to the show anyway so she agreed to come with me and Brady. I don't think she understands why I don't want to go with him by myself and I'm not about to tell her how much he scares me. I wouldn't have picked him out of a lineup two years ago. Sure he is attractive, but not my usual well-groomed type. My dad would have a coronary if I brought him home. With all of that said though, I can't remember feeling so relaxed with someone. He looks at me differently, like I matter. As though what I have to say is important. My guard falls every time he is around and that is the last thing I need right now. I have to keep remembering the promise I made to myself. I will go to his show and pay for his meal. Then that will be the end of Brady Carsen in my life.

At seven on the dot my cell beeps; it's Brady telling me he's outside. I take one more look in the mirror. I straightened my hair, so it falls a couple inches past my shoulders and my eyes are smoky with dark eyeliner and mascara. Since I recently swore off red lipstick, I opted for a nice soft shade of pink lip gloss. I smooth out my blue blouse over my dark skinny jeans. Sometimes I still don't recognize myself in the mirror. Closing my eyes, I tell myself it will be okay. Relax and have fun, Brady has no expectations.

"You look great. Let's go." Jessa smacks my ass, walking to the door.

"Thanks, so do you." I grab my phone and lip gloss, shoving them in a small cross body purse. I don't know how Jessa goes without a purse every time.

She is giddy with excitement as I follow her down the hall. Her short skirt with checkered tights and Doc Martens makes her look so much sexier than me. A twinge of jealousy sweeps over me, that Brady might prefer Jessa over me. Who wouldn't?

Brady is leaning against a midnight blue Camaro with two white racing stripes down the middle when we walk outside. He smiles up at me, pushing his body off the car to open the passenger door for us.

"Hey," I say, my eyes barely looking at him.

"Hey," he returns, motioning with his hand for us to get in.

"Brady, you remember Jessa." I signal my hand out to her.

"Yeah, hey Jessa." Brady shakes her hand.

"Hi, Brady," Jessa responds and I see her lips turn up in appreciation, eyeing him up and down before she gets in the back of his car.

Right before I bend down to get in the car, Brady reaches around my waist and pulls me in for hug. "You look incredible," he whispers in my ear and my face immediately starts to blush.

"Thank you. You look pretty good yourself." I quickly sit in my seat before he notices how red I've become.

"God Sadie, what did he say?" Jessa eagerly asks from the backseat while I watch Brady make his way around the car to the driver's side.

"Shh...I'll tell you later." I wave my hand at her.

"You better." She relaxes back into her seat and secures her seatbelt.

Brady eases into his charcoal-colored fabric seat. He's wearing another band t-shirt that looks as old as the band displayed. When he starts the ignition, I notice a couple of black leather bands around his right wrist.

"We Built this City" by Starship blares and Brady hurriedly turns it down before pressing a button on the radio. "Sorry, must have come on after the song I was listening to before," he quickly comes up with an excuse.

I remain silent. I don't mention that I saw him press the button, switching it from CD to radio. I most definitely don't mention my appreciation of eighties music as well.

"It sounds like your music, Sadie," Jessa chimes in from the back seat. I can't turn around to give her a dirty look so I stay quiet. Brady looks my way and grins, waiting for me to say something.

"I'm pleading the Fifth." I slightly smile and stare ahead, trying to ignore him staring at me.

"Me too." He smiles and turns back toward the road, putting the car in drive.

Aces is an actual bar, not like the place I saw The Invisibles play last week. The stage is situated to the right and booths line the wall along the windows. Tables fill the floor with a small bar in the corner on the left.

Brady grabs my hand and leads me to a circular booth off to the right of the stage, motioning for me to get in. The bar seems empty except for a few middle-aged men sitting in the stools around the bar and a few couples occupying the tables.

"We have to get everything set up. Do you want something to drink?" Brady asks, staying on the outside of the booth while Jessa and I scoot in.

"No, I'm fine. Thank you."

"Alright. It won't be long," he says hesitantly, standing by the table.

"Jeez. Just go. I'll take care of her," Jessa impatiently tells him.

Brady grins and turns around to head down the hallway.

"Be nice, Jessa. He's just being polite," I tell her.

"That *was* nice. I could have told him to go get his fucking equipment and give you some damn breathing room," she responds, straight-faced.

"God, Jessa," I sigh.

"Well, he can't stop staring at you. It's making me sick. Just look now." She motions her head to Brady, who is walking back down the hall holding a large, black square box. His eyes are set on me the whole time. When our eyes meet, he winks.

"Whatever." I ignore her comment. I'm in his direct line of vision.

Three other guys follow Brady up on stage. The first has a guitar swung over his shoulder, carrying a piece of the drum kit. He has spiky black hair with an eyebrow ring and a huge tattoo that covers his elbow. After he places the drum down, he glances our way and his stunning blue eyes set me back. One side of his mouth turns up in interest, staring between Jessa and me.

The next guy has another guitar instrument across his back and symbols fill his arms. He is shorter than Brady and has dreamy blue eyes, but his body is completely rock hard. His shirt is so tight you can almost make out every curve and crevice in his chest and shoulders. Buzzed brown hair covers his head and I don't see any piercings or tattoos on him, but black boots cover the bottom of his black jeans.

The last band member lingers a few steps behind holding two drums, a pair of drumsticks sticking out of his back pocket. He is wearing a black tank top, but you would think it was a full shirt with all the tattoos covering his chest and arms. His hair is tucked behind a baseball cap that rests backward on his head. His appearance intimidates me, showing me again how out of place I am in Brady's world.

"Holy shit. Check out his band. I would take any one of them." Jessa gawks up at the stage with wide eyes, like it's a buffet.

"Haven't you seen them before?" I inquire.

"Just last week and I was a little occupied," she says with a smile.

"Oh yeah, Mr. Rebel," I utter in disgust, reminded of her tongue down his throat.

"I'm getting all hot just thinking about him," she says, waving her hand rapidly across her face.

"I sure as shit hope you are talking about me." The dark, spiky-haired guy sits down next to Jessa, his eyes roaming across her body.

"Um...no." She turns her whole body my way, putting her back toward him.

"Give me five minutes and you will be," he responds to her back. Jessa remains quiet which surprises me. In the month I have known her, she has never once held her tongue. She transferred here as well which makes me wonder if there's something in her past she's running from, but I never ask her and she never asks me. It works for us.

Jessa hits my hip with her hand, pushing me to get out of the booth. For some reason she wants to get away from him and I don't know why. "Come on Sadie, let's go get a drink."

Brady takes a seat next to me, trapping us in the booth. "Don't worry, Roni will come over," he says to Jessa. Her face is red and I swear I can hear her heart beating.

"So, this is Rob," Brady says, pointing to the spiky, black-haired guy, "Trey," pointing to the drummer, "And the muscle man is Hulk. Guys, this is Sadie and Jessa." I feel their eyes on me. They are judging and evaluating me. From the expressions on their faces, I assume Brady has already spoken about me, which terrifies and thrills me at the same time.

"Hulk?" Jessa questions.

"Actually it's Dex. These dipshits think it's funny to call me Hulk. They're just jealous because I could kick all their asses." He smirks up at us.

"It's nice to meet all of you," I tell them.

"You too," Trey replies back sincerely, and Dex nods his head in agreement.

Rob's eyes travel from my chest back up to my face and I notice the disappointment. He shrugs his shoulders but nods toward me, informing me he heard me. He already knows I shouldn't be with Brady. As his friend, he senses my baggage and doesn't approve.

In the meantime, Jessa is sitting hip to hip and shoulder to shoulder next to me, making me move closer to Brady, who only smiles and rests his arm behind me. Shivers roll off my back as his thumb accidentally touches my neck.

A waitress, most likely in her late thirties, comes by. Her hair is piled high in a ponytail and she's dressed in a pair of jeans and an Aces t-shirt with a name tag that reads Veronica. She pulls out her pad of paper and pen looking down at us.

"What will it be tonight, boys?" Then she notices me and Jessa. Rob starts to give his order but she interrupts him. "Whoa. You have ladies with you tonight. Have some manners, they go first," she exclaims, staring over at me and I don't know what I should order. I feel Brady looking at me and Rob seems disgusted for having to wait.

"Vodka tonic with a lime, please." My voice is so soft, I'm surprised she can hear me. Rob rolls his eyes, waiting for his turn.

Jessa surprises me by ordering the same instead of her usual beer. All the boys order a round of beers except for Brady, who orders his usual and Trey asks for a shot of tequila with his beer.

"Thanks, Roni," Brady says before she leaves to fill our order.

Roni comes back with our drinks and she places a glass of ice and a bottle of water in front of Brady. I look up at him, shocked.

"I don't drink before shows." He shrugs.

"Don't let the preacher boy fool you, he never drinks," Rob shouts over and Brady's eyes give him a warning to shut up.

"Are you a recovering alcoholic?" Jessa leans forward across my shoulder, directing her question to Brady.

"I drink, just not very often and never before I have a show," he answers her, pouring his water into the cup, not looking at any of us.

"I think that's awesome," I softly tell him so the rest of the table can't hear. He turns his head toward me and our lips become so close they could touch if either of us moves an inch.

"Thank you." The corner of his mouth turns up and my eyes fixate on how pink and wet his lips are from drinking the water. There's a drop of water resting in the center of his pouty bottom lip and I have an immense urge to lick it. His hand cups my shoulder holding me in place, ready to pull me closer as I lick my lips in anticipation.

"Cut that smoochy shit out. It's time to go up." Rob throws the napkin between our faces, bringing me back to reality.

I blink and Brady's soft brown eyes peer back at me. Our moment is over and disappointment fills me. What was I thinking? I told myself that this was not going to happen, but oh how I wonder how he tastes.

"Enjoy the show," Brady says, looking from Jessa to me. "Please stay this time," he whispers in my ear before he scoots out of the booth, jumping on the stage.

"Holy crap, Sadie. What was that?" Jessa asks, right after he leaves.

"What? Nothing." I shake my head, still trying to figure it out myself.

"It was like you two were in your own world. Like the rest of us weren't here," she says, finishing her drink before flagging the waitress down.

I ignore her comment. I don't know what to think about that. Brady has this pull over me, making it incredibly hard to keep my promise to myself. *Just stick to the plan*, I tell myself. Show, dinner and no more Brady after tonight.

Roni brings Jessa her drink and then the lights go down for The

Invisibles to start playing. Aces has filled up in the time we have been sitting down. There is a line outside the window, waiting to pay their cover charge to see the show. I relax in the booth and the vinyl sticks to my arms. Thankfully, Jessa has moved over from me now that Rob is up on stage.

"Are you ready out there?" Brady's voice fills the bar and Trey starts hitting the drums. Everyone cheers and rushes up toward the stage.

Surprisingly, my body starts moving to the beat. Every song he put on my iPod is embedded into my mind. It's adorable the way he glances from the corner of his eye to make sure we're still here. When the edges of his lips turn up at me, I melt into the sticky vinyl. The crowd around the stage jumps up and down while their heads bob back and forth to the beat of the music. Brady's eyes divert back to them, showing them he's there for their enjoyment and wants them to have a good time. He looks down to an eager girl right up front and smiles. She raises her hand and he reaches down in return, grasping a few of her fingers. A sudden pang of jealousy consumes me.

I can only see her black, short hair from the back. She has a smaller, more petite frame than me. Then the crowd engulfs her in around them and I can't locate her anymore. But there was something in her body movements that makes me believe that she and Brady either have or had something in the past.

An hour later The Invisibles finish their set. Brady's soaked grey t-shirt clings to his body, revealing all the creases around his muscles. He holds up his finger to me, telling me to give him a minute. I couldn't keep count how many times he looked over during the show to see if I had deserted him like last time. The smile that absorbs his face when he knew I was still there was enough to make me want to jump on stage into his arms. He brings feelings out of me I didn't think I possessed, or could exist inside of me.

Brady leaves the stage and the dark-haired girl follows him down the hallway and I wonder what is going on, but quickly remind myself it is none of my business. I will be out of his life after tonight anyway.

"Who's the girl?" Jessa asks next to me.

"I don't know," I respond, stirring the small straw in my drink. I watch the nearly dissolved ice cubes spin around.

"Oh my god. You try to act all cool like he doesn't make you all wet but look at you now." She hits her shoulder to mine.

"What are you talking about?" I ask her, still staring at the nearly nonexistent ice cubes twirling around in my cup. I feel like them, nonexistent to the world. I no longer matter to anyone, or have any one important person in my life.

"Are you ready?" Brady waits on the outside of the booth with his hand out. He has changed his shirt to a long-sleeved blue Henley. "Or do you want to stay for the next band?" I glance up at him and all those thoughts that just filled my brain vanish when his perfectly straight white teeth gleam down at me. For some reason he makes me feel alive again.

"Who was that girl?" Jessa asks before I can answer him.

"Who?" Brady's eye scrunch. He honestly appears to not know who she is talking about.

"The one that's eye fucking you over there." Jessa points to the dark-haired girl. Now that I see her face, she looks a few years younger than us. Her black bob hair cut has a few dyed strips of red. A cute striped dress that ends mid-thigh covers her tight black leggings. The way she's staring over at Brady's ass tells me for sure she wants him.

Brady turns around and then back to us. "That's Kara. She's a...family friend," he stutters, making me think he's lying.

"Oh." Jessa rolls her eyes, matching my thoughts.

"So, what do you want to do?" He gazes down to me.

"Um...I don't really care. Whatever you want is fine."

"Then let's go. I'm starving and you owe me a meal." He smirks, holding his hand out for me to take.

"Alright." I grab his hand without a second thought. "Are you coming?" I turn around to Jessa, still sitting in the booth. The other Invisibles make their way over and Rob scoots in next to her.

She looks at him and then back to me. I raise my eyebrows questioning her. Before the band's set she couldn't get away from Rob fast enough and now she is debating whether or not to stay with him.

"I'll take her home," Rob says, his eyes not leaving hers.

"Are you sure, Jessa?" I ask, concerned.

"Yeah, see you back at the dorm." She waves her hand toward me, keeping her eyes locked with Rob. I swear she is so confusing.

"Alright, if you're sure," I respond cautiously.

"Just go W.A.S.P. I've got her." Rob raises his eyebrows.

"What the fuck, Rob? Step back," Brady hollers at him.

"It's fine. Let's go." I start to walk out of Aces, not looking at Rob.

"Rob, we will be talking later," Brady tells him before coming up behind me.

"I'm sorry about that." He grabs my hand and turns me around to face him.

"It's fine. I'm used to it...well...not really, but I know I don't really fit in here," I say quietly, keeping my head down as I shuffle my feet back and forth on the cracked cement sidewalk. The truth is I am or was a wasp. Before I came to this school, I attended the finest college on the eastern shore. My parents are wasps, my friends are wasps, and their parents are wasps.

"Hey, Rob's an asshole. Don't let him get to you." He places his finger under my chin, bringing me up to meet his face. "You owe me a dinner and I plan on making you pay." He grabs my hand and leads me to his car.

Fifteen minutes later, we are off campus and downtown at some dive diner off the highway. When we enter there are a few older men at the counter, but all the booths are open. Brady lets me pick the table so I choose one in the back corner. A waitress in her fifties with her hair pulled back in a bun and wearing a pink and white dress and an apron comes over, handing us menus.

"Hi, Brady," she says, glancing from him to me. "Who is your friend?" she smiles.

"This is Sadie," he answers, holding his hand out toward me. "Sadie, this is Jacks."

"It's a pleasure to meet you, Sadie." She puts out her hand for me to shake and I oblige.

"It's nice to meet you too," I concur, noticing her name tag actually reads Jackie. Brady seems to shorten everyone's names.

"So, you two, what will it be?" Jackie asks, taking out her pencil and paper.

"Do you mind if I order for you?" Brady questions, shy and hesitant, so I nod. "Thanks," he responds. "We will have two of my usual, Jacks." He grabs our menus and hands them to her.

"Sounds good," Jackie says before walking away.

I have never been to a diner in my life. The decorated black and white vinyl booths with red piping flows nicely with pictures of vintage cars and past actors and actresses from a time before I was born. The older men are engrossed in their own conversation regarding some sports game, leaving Brady and me to ourselves.

"So, what did you think of the show?" Brady relaxes back into the booth, stretching one arm along the top of the booth and his other arm out resting on the table.

"It was good," I answer, smiling over at him.

"How about awesome or incredible? How about you couldn't keep your eyes off the lead singer?" he jokes.

"You are a really good singer," I admit.

"That's it? That's all you have to say?" He leans forward in his seat, eager to hear more.

"Well...I do have one question." I tap my finger to my bottom lip.

"Yeah?"

"Is the drummer single?" I grin up to him.

"Oh man, I think you just broke my heart." He puts his hand over his chest, sighing.

"Seriously though, how come you didn't play any of the love songs from the album you gave me?"

"First of all, I have never written a love song. Second, our band has a certain reputation and that doesn't include the slower...more...emotional songs."

His response confuses me. Those songs were about losing someone and being left alone. Did he just lie to me again? That would mean two times in just a few hours.

"I think your fans would like your slower songs. I fell completely in love with them," I confess.

"Really? That means a lot." Brady appears surprised by my reaction to his music. "I don't usually share..." He stops when Jackie interrupts us with our food.

"Here you guys go." She sets down two chocolate milkshakes, two cheeseburgers with fries, and a plate full of nachos in the middle.

"I'm never going to finish this," I tell him after she walks away.

"Wait until you taste this food." He pops a fry into his mouth and smiles from ear to ear.

After the meal, my stomach is so bloated I think the button of my pants might pop off. Brady tells me how he's been coming here since he was little. He grew up in this town and has lived his whole life here. I keep him in the dark regarding my past, telling him I went to Western Colorado and my family resides there as well. I can't fault him for lying since I am too.

I go to the bathroom after the meal, leaving Brady to chat with Jackie about someone they both know. I stare at myself in the mirror, applying the lip gloss that the food and shake rubbed off. My hair has fallen limp and straight so I pull it back in a low ponytail. Straightening my blouse out, I venture back out to the booth. Jackie's gone and Brady is doing something with his phone.

"Did you enjoy the meal?" He puts his phone away and peers up to me.

"I did. I can't believe I ate that much," I declare, observing my half-eaten burger with no fries left and an empty milkshake.

"I might have overdone it with the nachos," he admits, chuckling. "Are you ready?" He scoots out of the booth, waiting for me.

"Where's the bill?" I grab my purse, scooting out myself.

"Oh, I took care of it already." He grins up to me.

"I was supposed to pay," I exclaim, narrowing my eyes.

"Sorry, I forgot." He jokingly shrugs his shoulders. "I guess you will just have to treat me another time. Actually, twice now." He laughs.

"Brady Carsen, did you set me up?"

"Maybe." He raises his eyebrows up to me. "It's not in me to let a lady pay."

"Goodnight, you two," Jackie says, waving from behind the counter.

"Bye, Jacks. Thanks for everything," Brady responds and waves back.

"Nice to meet you, Jackie," I say in return.

"You too, sweetie," she replies.

Brady opens the door for me and I watch him make his way to his side of the car. He is so different than what I'm used to as are the feelings he invokes in me. I'm at ease with him, as though I would walk away from the life I know and be content to spend my remaining days with him. *Holy Shit, what the hell, Sadie?*

When he settles in the car, he looks over at me and I see it on his face. His desire is clear as he gazes at my eyes and then my lips and back up to my eyes again. I see his hand moving up to my cheek. Oh I want this, I want nothing more than his lips on mine. He leans in, closing the gap between us. Just as he licks his lips, I abruptly turn around toward the window. I close my eyes as I continue to face the passenger window, ignoring what just happened.

Brady sighs before he puts the key in the ignition and drives out of the parking lot. I don't think I have to worry about him pursuing me further; I'm sure I just put a stop to that. I did the right thing, right? Could I have stopped at just a kiss? I have never stopped there.

He pulls up outside my dorm and I open the door before he can put the car in park. I can't face him; I'm embarrassed how I reacted. It was just a kiss. I didn't have to do anything I didn't want to if got more heated.

"Sadie," he yells over to me. I'm already at my dorm doors.

I ignore him and walk through the doors. Some guy comes out as I go in and I hear Brady ask him to hold the door, which the guy does. *Thanks a lot buddy.*

"Sadie, hold up," Brady calls out, catching up to me at the next set of doors.

"What?" I ask with my back turned to him, staring at the ground.

"Look at me," he requests softly. Lucky for me no one else is around. I'm sure they're still out enjoying their Friday night.

"I can't," I whisper.

He walks up to face me, putting his hands on my arms. "Please," he begs.

I reluctantly look up through my eyelashes and see that he isn't mad that I didn't kiss him. Only concern fills his eyes and face.

"Why are you running away from me? I thought we had a pretty good date."

"I'm sorry, Brady. You shouldn't waste your time on me."

"Tell me you feel this. Tell me it's not just me."

"Brady," I sigh. "You don't understand. It doesn't matter what I feel. I can't do this." I shake my head.

"Don't walk away from this, Sadie." His eyes bore into mine. "I know we look different from the outside, but it's the inside that counts," he argues. He thinks I don't want to be with him because of our outward differences, but the truth is he's too good a person for me.

"I don't care about that, Brady. There are things about me you just don't know and once you find out..." I continue to shake my head, putting my key in the door.

"I could give a shit about your past. Hell, we all have pasts, Sadie. I refuse to let you throw this away."

I hold the door open with my back, my eyes fixed to the ground. "Goodbye, Brady," I say to him, walking through the doors.

"No, Sadie." He grabs my arms, pulling me to him. "Goodnight... not goodbye." His lips brush across my cheek. "I won't give up. If you're not going to fight for this...I'll do it for the both of us." He releases me before letting the door shut between us.

I make my way up the stairs and open the door to an empty room. I walk over to the ladder of my bed, shedding my flats as I go. Crawling up to my bed I close my eyes, willing the tears that are escaping to stop.

Why am I so fucked up?

Chapter 5

Jessa's key turning in our lock wakes me. She stumbles in the doorway, wearing what she wore last night. The smile on her face is evidence of her good time with Rob. Staring over at my clock, I notice it's ten in the morning.

My stomach is still full from the meal at the diner, which brings visions of Brady to mind. I sit up in the loft, watching her try to be quiet, tip-toeing around the room to change.

"So, where have you been?" I shout down and she jumps back.

"Jesus, Sadie. You scared the shit out of me," she screeches, holding her hand over her heart.

"Please tell me how you go from wanting to get the hell away from him to coming home the next morning from his bed?" I climb down from the loft.

"I don't know." She appears to be contemplating something in her head. "I never told you this but..." She hesitates and I realize she is about to tell me her secret but I'm not ready to share mine.

"You don't have to tell me, Jessa," I declare, shaking my head.

"I want to," she assures me. "Don't worry, you don't have to tell me yours, until you are ready," her voice sympathetic. "Rob reminded me of my ex. To say we ended things on bad terms is an understatement. We were dating for a couple months when he asked to take pictures of me while we were having sex. I fully trusted him; he gave me no reason not to. We continued to date for about two weeks after that." Her head is down, reliving the moment things went bad.

"We were out at a party," she continues. "I saw an old boyfriend and was talking with him. Nothing big, just catching up with one another. What we had been up to in the years since we had seen one another. Jason, that was my ex's name, became furious. He started busting tables and throwing things around until his friend took him outside to cool down. Honestly Sadie, it was an innocent conversation. I didn't even hug him hello or good-bye." She seems adamant that I believe her. "Anyway, he wouldn't talk to me. Just kept calling me a whore. I was in tears, practically begging him to forgive me, for what now I have no idea, but at the time I just wanted him to stop being mad at me." She takes a deep breath, letting it out slowly before continuing.

"The next day when I woke up, my phone had fifteen missed calls and twenty texts from my friends. He posted the pictures online and had his friends send it to his friends and so on. Everyone from my childhood friends to my college friends saw the pictures." A tear rolls down one of her cheeks, but she swipes it away quickly. "After that, all the guys thought I was easy and the girls thought I was a slut. I have never regretted anything more and the thing was, I couldn't do anything to stop it. My parents were embarrassed in front of their friends and family, not being able to ignore what I had done. That was last January. I dropped out of school and ran away from everything I knew. My parents are the only ones who know where I am. They didn't even tell my sister, afraid she would slip at some point." The grief and distress is evident in her voice.

"I'm sorry, Jessa," I say, knowing it's not enough. I know first-hand that sorry isn't enough.

"When Rob first sat down, it was all I could think of. But after the show started and I saw him up there, I was able to see the differences between him and Jason. My therapist has taught me many coping techniques to be able to start trusting people again. Of course, those two vodka tonics didn't hurt," she jokes, but her laugh is empty.

"Where is Jason now?" I ask her.

"Back home. Working as a mechanic, fixing up cars. Hopefully enrolled in a wonderful anger management class," she jokes again, but it's not her true laugh and there is a twinge of unsettled fear in her.

"What an asshole," I confirm.

"Yep. Speaking of assholes, what is a wasp?" she asks.

"It's a term to describe privileged white kids with money. The actual phrase is White Anglo Saxon Protestant. Jokes on him, I'm

Catholic," I laugh, mine as empty as hers.

"I don't know what his problem is with you. I hope you aren't mad I slept with him." She puts her hand on my knee.

"No, I've handled worse than him."

"Don't worry. I think Brady was ready to pounce on him when he came home this morning." Jessa goes to stand up. "When Rob was leaving to drive me home, Brady was pulling up in the driveway. He stuck his head in the window and told Rob to get the fuck back because they had to talk about last night."

"Brady didn't get home until this morning?" I swallow the large lump in my throat.

"Well... yeah. Wasn't he with you?" She answers her own question when she notices the shocked expression on my face. "Oh...I'm sorry, Sadie. I just assumed," she says. Her eyes display her empathy to my pain.

"It's okay. I'm going to go take a shower," I say, fumbling to grab my robe and shower caddy before I cry in front of Jessa. I should have known he was like all the others. I didn't let him sleep with me last night so he found someone else, most likely that Kara girl from Aces.

After my shower, Brady is washed off my body. I will no longer let him fill my head with his words, or my heart with his songs. I have to admit he played me well. At least I never acted like I wanted more than their body when I only wanted sex from someone.

Jessa is asleep when I get back in the room. She is so much braver than me to share her story. She brought up going to a therapist and I wonder if that is what I should do. My parents said it would do us no good and we didn't need to reveal our dirty secrets to strangers. I can't help but think that me sleeping with every male at Drayton wasn't exactly dealing with it.

I quietly get dressed and pull my wet hair back in a bun. I grab my messenger bag and sling it over my shoulder. I stop by the cafeteria to grab an apple and yogurt before heading to the library. As it's Saturday, the library is vacant of people, making me hopeful that the sixth floor will be unoccupied today. I try to shrug off the memory of Brady when I get to the elevators.

When I get to the sixth floor, there is no one around except the librarian assistant down the hall, making me happy to have a quiet place to concentrate on my Algebra. I put my bag down and pull out my book. I take my ear buds out since I need all the attention I have to absorb this information.

Going back and forth between the problems I have to solve, I shove my notebook across the desk and rest my head on the table. This is beyond me and I feel like such a major idiot that I cannot understand it. I really should have investigated the different colleges to make sure a year of math wasn't a mandatory requirement for Psychology majors.

"What? No music today?" Grant stands next to me, grabbing the notebook before it falls to the ground. He is wearing a pair of running pants with a matching jacket. I wonder how he ended up here at Western; he would have fit in at Drayton, no problem.

"No, I need to focus, but it's not working," I whine.

He looks at the notebook. "If you're a senior, why are you taking Algebra 101?"

"My last school didn't have a requirement of math for psych majors. Since I transferred, I have to fulfill this year of math if I want to graduate," I admit, embarrassed.

"Do you want some help?" He motions to the empty seat. I'm pleased he asks permission this time.

"If you can get me to understand this, I will buy you lunch."

"Deal," Grant agrees and sits down across from me. He takes my book and notebook, reading the instructions.

An hour and a half later, Grant has done the impossible. I actually semi-understand what he is talking about, even solving the problems on my own.

"Now you owe me lunch." He stands up, going for his bag.

"Yes I do. Thank you, Grant. You are a lifesaver." I pack up my bag, slinging it over my shoulder.

"Can I talk you into dinner instead? My treat, of course," he requests.

"Sorry I can't, but we can head over to the Student Center now if you want."

"I will take what I can get," he agrees.

Grant and I take the elevator down and it's empty of Brady when the doors open on the main level. I walk with him across the courtyard to the Student Center. We grab a couple of sub sandwiches and sodas and sit down at a table. Just like Brady, Grant doesn't let me pay. I find out that he is a senior business major and is in a fraternity.

"Do you mind if I ask you a personal question?" Grant takes a sip of his soda, glancing over to me.

"Depends. What is your question?" I ask, hesitant to talk about my personal life.

"How come you didn't ask Brady for help in math?"

"Um...I don't know. Why would I?"

"Don't you know?" He looks at me, surprised. "I assumed you guys were friends."

"We are...were. It's complicated. What don't I know, Grant?" I ask.

"He's an engineering major. Top of his class, Dean's List. He's even a teacher's assistant in a couple of the undergraduate classes," he reveals before taking a bite of his sandwich.

"I really just met him last week," I declare. I realize the only things I know about him are that he's the lead singer of The Invisibles, drives a Camaro, and makes my stomach fill with butterflies when I hear his voice.

"Just be careful, Sadie. There is a lot about him you don't know," Grant says.

"Thanks for your concern, Grant." I force a smile up to him. Even though I'm mad at Brady, it infuriates me that Grant is talking about him like this. It is none of his business what is happening between Brady and myself.

"It wasn't my intention to get you mad, Sadie. It's just…"

"None of your business," I finish his sentence.

"Sorry." He puts his head down, finishing his sandwich.

"It's alright. Let's just agree to not talk about him," I try to compromise.

"Sounds good," Grant agrees.

We finish our lunch and leave the Student Center. I say goodbye to Grant and head toward my dorm.

I'm just past the library, walking up the hill to my dorm when I notice a homeless man lying asleep on the bench by the basketball courts. He is wearing brown corduroy pants and a plaid, flannel, button-down shirt. His brown loafers look old and worn-out, his grey beard looks unkempt, and he is in desperate need of a shower. I dig in my messenger bag, grabbing half of the sandwich I didn't finish and a water bottle. I take twenty dollars out of my wallet and tuck it inside the sandwich wrapper for him to find. Placing it on the bench next to him, I'm thankful he doesn't wake up and I continue my walk down the sidewalk to my dorm.

Chapter 6

Brady has called me twice and texted me three times since Saturday afternoon. I have ignored every one of them. Jessa stayed in with me Saturday night and we watched some movies and made popcorn. I was close to telling her my secret, but I just didn't have the guts to do it. Luckily, she seems okay with it.

I walk down the stairs from Alcove Hall, excited that I understood Algebra today thanks to Grant, when I hear a familiar laugh. Looking down the steps, I see Brady to the right, talking to a couple guys. I glance behind me, wondering if there is another way out, but I have no idea where. Reluctantly, I make my way down the opposite side of the stairs, hopeful he doesn't notice me. A smile spreads across my face when I get to the last step, assuming I'm safe.

"Did you really think I wouldn't notice you?" I startle when he comes up alongside me.

"Hopeful is more like it," I spurt.

"Why are you dodging me?" He keeps in step with me.

"I don't know what you're talking about," I lie.

"I called you this weekend. You never called me back."

"I'm sure you found someone else to keep you company." I continue to stare straight ahead while increasing my speed.

"What is that supposed to mean?" His steps speed up to match mine, while his eyes never leave the side of my face.

"Did you really think I wouldn't find out?" I shake my head. "It doesn't matter anyway, but next time try not to make a girl feel so damn special if all you want to do is get in her pants," I blurt out, turning toward the courtyard.

"Sadie, you lost me." He shakes his head.

"Brady. It's not like we were dating; it just irritated me that it was right after you left me," I lie. The image of him sleeping with another girl tears me apart.

"Sadie. Just fucking tell me what you are so pissed at," he demands, his voice rising another octave.

"Well Brady, let's see. The fact that *you* pursued *me*. Tricked me into going to your show and to dinner. Made some plea that there is something between us you have never felt before, but as soon as I don't give it up, you find someone else to get it from. Did you think Jessa wouldn't tell me you came home the next morning wearing the same clothes? The funny thing is that she thought you came from being with me," I reveal, noticing my mistake. I led us to the field that separates the dorms from the academic building, leaving us alone.

"Fuck!" Brady screams, taking his head in his hands. "When are they going to stop fucking with my life?" he murmurs.

"Listen. It's been nice. Bye, Brady." I turn around, walking up the hill toward my dorm.

"SADIE!" he yells after me, but I ignore him. He jogs up to me, grabbing my elbow. "Just come with me. We need to talk." His eyes are mixed with determination and agony at the same time. I have been here before. He is going to tell me it is something else and then I will put my heart on the line, and in a couple months I will find him in bed with someone else.

"No, Brady. Sorry, you had your chance but I can't risk it," I respond.

"You're kidding, right? You never gave me a chance," he says, upset.

He's right, I truly never did. It's just too much. He will break my heart if I allow him in.

"Please Sadie, give me an hour. If nothing changes your mind, then we will part and I won't bother you again," he requests. I can't say no to those gorgeous eyes, so I give him a small nod.

"Thanks." He releases a deep breath. "Let's go." He takes my hand, leading us the opposite way toward Daffodil Hill. I love this area of campus. It is part of the original campus before the college expanded. It is shaped like a bowl with one of the hills filled with daffodils that blossom in the spring. Since fall is already on its way, the grass is green but dry.

Brady sits me down at the top of the hill, keeping us hidden by the trees and buildings. "This is my favorite spot on campus. I have been coming here since I was a kid." I look around and see Shubert Hall, the music building, behind us.

"It's a nice spot," I say. You can watch students making their way to classes below, but no one really notices this secluded area.

"I was up here about three weeks ago. It was one of our last hot days and I was just about to pack up and leave," he starts talking. He looks over at me and I see something in Brady's eyes I have never seen, insecurity. "I saw this blonde-haired girl walking down the path." He points to the open field below us where the streams of students now walk. "Her head was down as she walked down the path, as though she didn't want to be noticed. There was something about her, something I couldn't explain. All of a sudden, I felt this pull inside of me. A sudden urge to run down the hill, throw her over my shoulder, and run away." He opens his backpack, searching for something.

"Before I could get down the sidewalk to make our paths cross, she had disappeared. I lost sight of her. I assume she must have snuck into a building." He continues to look in his bag and I wonder why he is telling me this story of some girl he is obviously infatuated with. "I came back to this spot every day at that exact time, but I never saw her again. All I had to remember what she looked like was this." He pulls out a sketchbook and there's a drawing of a girl with her long hair flowing along the side of her face. Her face is turned down toward the ground, staring at her feet. The girl appears sad and lost in the drawing and a pang hits my stomach; this is how people see me. How could Brady want to be with someone so absent and disoriented?

"It's beautiful, Brady," I say, admiring his sketch of me. He was able to portray exactly what I feel every day in only a glimpse of me walking across a field of grass. What can't Brady Carsen do?

"*You're* beautiful," he whispers in my ear, leaning over me to stare at the sketch. My heart races and chills cover my body. Oh I want him, how did he do this to me? He made me go from hating him to wanting to jump him in a matter of fifteen minutes.

"And then I saw you that night at Billy's which, by the way, that's the name of the house you first met me at. It is a house that they gutted to have parties and bands play. We usually don't play there, but we were filling in for another band that cancelled last minute. When you walked in with Jessa, I have never been more thankful for anything in my life. You appeared so shy and intimidated standing against the back wall. I didn't have the nerve to go up to you for fear you would turn me away. I was frozen, watching you from across the room. When you waved goodbye to Jessa, I couldn't let you out of my sight again."

"So you knew I wasn't drunk?" I ask him and he grins.

"Yeah, I knew you were sober. I didn't knock you down though. That was just luck on my part," he chuckles. "Then you were there by my side, and I had to go up on stage to play. There has never been a time that I didn't want to perform more than that night. I told the guys we were going to cut it short. When I finished the second song, I saw you had left and it was all I could do to finish the set. I was so pissed at myself for allowing you out of my sight again."

"Why are you telling me this?" I ask him.

"I need you to trust me." He grabs my hand, placing it in his lap. "I can't tell you where I was Friday night, at least not yet. But believe me Sadie, I wasn't with anyone else. You're the only girl who consumes my thoughts, my dreams, and my mind. Please trust me when I say there is no one else," his voice is desperate, saturating his soft brown eyes.

A big part of me believes him. My thoughts go to Jessa and how she now trusts guys again after what her ex-boyfriend did to her. I need to move on with my life; it's been over a year and I still harbor all of the hurt and remorse. If I don't start living my life, it is going to pass me by. Brady's right, I never gave him a fair shot.

"I believe you," I whisper, still unsure of my decision to give this a chance.

"Thank you, Sadie." He releases the deepest breath in relief. "Now I have one more favor." He peers over at me, continuing to hold my hand.

"What, Carsen?"

"Go on a date with me. A real date, just you and me from beginning to end," he asks, squeezing my hand.

I close my eyes, willing myself to allow me to have this. Give myself the possibility to have happiness and accept the consequences. "Yes," I answer him.

He picks up my hand and spreads it open, kissing my palm to his lips, and I wish he would continue that kiss up my arm.

"I'll pick you up tonight at six," he instructs.

"Tonight? It's Monday," I counter.

"I'm not waiting a whole week, Sadie." He shakes his head and releases my hand, placing the sketchbook back in his bag.

"Alright," I agree.

"Let's go, I'll walk you back to the dorm." He holds his hand out to help me up and then keeps it firmly in his for the entire walk.

"I have a question." I look over to him.

"What?"

"How did you know where I lived?"

"Hey, I've got to keep some secrets to myself." He smirks over to me, squeezing my hand again.

"You aren't some stalker guy who is going to murder me tonight, are you?" I question seriously.

"I promise you, I'm not a stalker and I'm not going to murder you. Kidnap maybe, but not murder," he laughs.

As we get closer to the dorms, there are more students around. A group of girls relax out in front of the dorm when Brady and I walk up. They are talking about some boy band and who is hotter, but they fall quiet when they see us. I see the question in their eyes. The same question I saw in people's eyes at the bar last week. Except this time, it is why I'm with him instead of the other way around. The girls resemble my friends from only a few short months ago. Shallow and vain. Although they probably are drooling over Brady, they would never date him. Most likely, they believe his car isn't expensive enough and his clothes aren't designer enough.

Brady walks me up to the door and I notice his car in the parking lot.

"Why is your car here?" I ask him.

"Oh," he looks back and laughs. "I swear I'm not a stalker, but you wouldn't answer my calls or texts." He holds up both his hands in defense. "I've been chasing you around this whole campus all day. I kept missing you."

"I'm glad you found me," I divulge.

"Me too. Don't ever hide from me again," he demands.

"Looks like you got a ticket." I point to the yellow envelope on his windshield.

"Oh, I can take care of that." He waves it off like it doesn't matter.

"See you tonight, Brady." I get my keys out of my bag.

"Sadie?"

"Yeah," I answer and turn around. When I shift my head in his direction, he is so close, my heart skips a beat. "I just want to warn you. I'm going to kiss you tonight," he whispers in my ear and then turns around and walks toward his car.

Chapter 7

When I open my dorm door after taking a shower, I find a bouquet of different colored daisies on my dresser. Jessa smiles over at me through the ladder of my bed, studying my reaction.

"When did these come?" I ask.

"While you were in the shower. The florist delivered them." She's beaming more than me.

I grab the note from the bouquet and my name is scripted in guy's handwriting.

You deserve something beautiful, but they aren't nearly as beautiful as you. I'm anxiously counting the seconds until you open the door and I see your gorgeous face. See you at six. — B

I hold the card to my chest, sighing. "Do I even want to know?' Jessa holds her hand out for the card.

"It's private," I giggle, keeping it close to my chest.

"Come on, Sadie," Jessa pleas.

"Fine." I hand it over to her and she reads it. "Should have known a singer would write some romantic crap." She hands it back to me. "Are you sure you want to go through with this?" She still believes he was with another girl Friday night.

"Yeah, I'm sure," I say with a smile, reassuring her. I put the note in my top drawer and go over to my closet to find something to wear.

"Where is he taking you?" Jessa asks, putting her book down and turning on the television.

"He never said," I answer, continuing to sift through my hangers. I finally decide on a red dress that flares out at the waist in a series of pleats, paired with black heels.

I get in my matching panties and bra. Even though Brady will not be seeing them tonight, they make me feel sexy. I curl my blonde hair in waves that travel down my back, pinning the front part off my face. My make-up is a little darker than Friday, but I still don't use the dark red lipstick. I will never use it again.

It's five forty-five and I'm already dressed and ready to go. I sit down next to Jessa while she flips through channels and wait for Brady's call. Suddenly there is a knock on the door. Jessa and I share a puzzled look and she gets up to open the door where Brady stands on the other side with his hands in his pockets, rolling back on his heels.

I might have actually stopped breathing for a moment. He is wearing a pair of dark jeans with a red sweater and black leather jacket. His hair is loose and free of gel, pushed to the side. He smiles over to me, making me melt in desire.

"You look even more amazing than I imagined," he says to me while I get up and walk toward him.

"Thank you. You look great, too." I smile back.

"Shall we?" He holds out his hand.

"Please, before I throw up," Jessa answers my question, walking back to her seat in front of the television.

"Bye, Jessa," I say, grabbing my clutch from the dresser next to the flowers.

"Bye, guys." She waves her hand, not looking our way.

"See ya, Jessa. Hey, Robbie wants you to give him a call," Brady shouts toward her before he shuts the door.

"Whatever," she remarks.

When we enter the hallway I notice a couple girls milling around, obviously trying to check out who Brady is here to pick up. They quickly scurry like rabbits when we start walking down the hall, whispering to each other. Brady puts his hand on the small of my back and leads me through the door. His Camaro is parked outside with his hazards on, probably trying to not get another parking ticket.

"You could have called, I would have come out," I tell him while he opens the door for me.

"Sadie, this is a date. I'm not about to be some shmuck who waits in the car for you to hop in." He closes the door once I'm securely in the seat and I admire him walking around the front of the car before he settles into his own seat.

"So, where are we going?" I pull my dress closer to my knees. It seems completely too short now that I'm seated.

"It's a surprise." He leans over to me. *This is it. He is going to kiss me now.* Stretching his arm over me, he grabs my seatbelt, bringing it across me, and pushes it in the clip.

"Sorry, I forgot," I embarrassingly admit.

"Don't apologize. I quite enjoyed it." He winks at me and starts the car.

I can't stop my grin while trying to roll my eyes at him.

I notice we are driving into the city, away from campus. Being so close to two different cities had been a major perk for me when I decided to attend. Brady has a CD in that I have never heard of, but his fingers hit the steering wheel to the beat. His wrists are empty of the black leather bracelets tonight.

"Do you like tapas?" He asks me, bringing my attention back to the conversation.

"Truthfully, I've never had them," I confess.

"Really? That surprises me," he exclaims.

"Why does that surprise you?"

"I just figured I would have nothing new to introduce you to. That you have pretty much experienced...everything," he responds, making me believe he had a hard time planning this date.

"You would be astonished what I haven't experienced."

"I think you will like tapas," he assures me.

"I'm sure I will." I smile over at him.

We pull up to a small and intimate restaurant. There are only about fifteen tables and a bar along one wall. The hostess seats us in the corner by the window, handing us the menus. Brady pulls out my chair and then takes his seat across the table.

A guy about our age comes over with two waters, informing us that his name is Sergio and he'll be our waiter. He suggests we have sangria so I order one and Brady does too, but non-alcoholic.

"Do you see anything you like?" Brady asks me, perusing the menu.

"I think I will take your lead on this. How about something with shrimp?"

"You pick three things, I will pick three things, and we can share," he compromises.

I pick a shrimp and two vegetables and Brady picks three meat tapas. After my first sangria, I switch to water.

As we sit back in our seats waiting for our food, I start drilling Brady with questions.

"So tell me, do you plan on making a go of it with The Invisibles?"

"Um...no." He leans back, hesitant to answer the question. "I love music and I will miss it, but I don't want it as my career."

"Do the others know that?"

"Yeah, Trey and Hulk are enrolled in school, too. It's only Robbie who seems to want to pursue the dream of rock 'n roll. He left school last year with only a year left, and I have been trying to get him to enroll again for spring semester."

"What is your major?" I ask him since he never told me, Grant did.

"Engineering. Yours?" he asks in return.

"What kind of engineering?" I dodge his question.

"Civil. *Again*, what's yours?"

"Why Engineering?" I spit out another question.

"I love to build things. Always have," he answers. "Now, what is your major?"

"Guess," I say.

"Hmm..." he contemplates. "Education. No, that's not it." He thinks some more. "Design, no not that either." He puts his finger to his lip, smirking over to me. "How about Psychology?" He smiles as though he already knew the answer.

"How did you know?" I ask, shocked.

"My secret. I don't know what you want to do with it though." His tone becomes serious again.

"I haven't decided. I hate the idea of being in school anymore, but I would love to counsel people," I reveal.

"So, you haven't applied for graduate school yet?" He seems concerned.

"No, I decided to take a year off."

"Where did you say you are from again?" he asks innocently.

I can't decide if I should lie or start telling the truth. I'm not ready to tell him yet, but I don't want to lie either. I'm thankful the food comes just as I'm about to spit the truth out. But Brady can't be detoured. After Sergio leaves the plates and we start picking at the food, he asks me again.

"Um...I don't care to talk about my past," I honestly answer.

"I understand, you tell me what you want. If I pry too much, let me know. But Sadie?" He waits for my full attention. "At some point I want you to trust me enough to tell me everything, okay?" he says and I nod.

"I'm from Maryland," I reply, divulging the truth.

"Huh," he says, remembering I lied previously to him, but he lets it go. "Did you leave both parents behind?" He cuts up his meat.

"Yes, my parents are married, living in Maryland, and wondering what the hell I'm doing down here," I confess, making this seem too easy to reveal my past.

"Why did you leave school with only one year left?" I can tell he knows this is a bad question, but he is trying to figure out how far he can dig.

"Too much prying," I inform him and he nods his head in confirmation. "What about you?"

"Let's see. As you already know, I've lived here my whole life. My parents are divorced. My mom lives in Florida and my dad is still around. I live with Robbie, Trey, and Hulk off campus. That's about it." He pops a shrimp in his mouth, smiling.

"You make it sound so simple." I admire him.

"Oh believe me, my life is anything but simple," he admits.

We lighten up the conversation after that, talking about music and movies. Besides eighties music, the only thing we have in common is that we both love horror films.

After we finish the dinner, Brady pays the bill and escorts me out of the small restaurant. Butterflies fill my stomach when he grabs my hand outside and leads me back to the car. We only drive a few miles down the road to an area where bars fill each side of the road. He parks in one of the vacant lots, paying the man his parking fee. When he opens the door for me to get out, he pulls me into him.

"I'm really betting that when you pleaded the Fifth, it was because you enjoy eighties music." He turns me around to face the bar across the street where a big sign across the entrance reads "Monday – Eighties Night".

"I guess we will have to see, won't we?" I smirk over at him and he wraps his arms around me, pulling me in closer. *This is it; he's going to kiss me.* His mouth draws closer to mine and I suck in a breath, licking my lips in anticipation. Right as I feel them brush along mine, he slowly moves to my cheek.

"You have no idea how much I want to feel your body against mine." He kisses my cheek and grabs my hand, leading me into the bar. I stagger behind him as my heart picks up another beat.

We enter the bar and I'm pleased to find it's a mix of different ages, not just the usual drunken college kids. Brady guides me past a couple of tables, taking one right next to the large dance area. There are still a lot of empty tables, but the dance floor overflows with couples. I don't notice any groups of a single gender huddled together, but rather everyone seems to be half of a couple. "Total Eclipse of the Heart" by Bonnie Tyler plays over the speakers while the couples dance, holding each other close.

Brady motions for me to sit in a chair and then takes the seat across from me. His smile hasn't faltered all night and I'm enjoying how easygoing his personality is. The waitress comes by, looking him up and down, but he only looks at me until I give my drink order. He gives his order and then thanks her. Either he is oblivious to women checking him out, or he has the courtesy not to look when he is on a date because the waitress is young and attractive.

The tall brunette brings our drinks and I take a small sip of my vodka tonic while Brady drinks his water. Since I have met him, he hasn't had one drink. This spurs a red light for me. Is he a recovering alcoholic like Jessa asked?

"How come you never drink?" I wonder if he'll lie to me.

"I do but I'm driving tonight. Anyway, I would never put you in harm's way." He glances over and then turns back toward the dance floor. I can't help but feel he is keeping something from me.

"One drink wouldn't hurt," I offer.

"That's what a lot of people think." His voice goes cold and I know I struck a chord.

"I'm sorry, I didn't mean to offend you," I say softly, swirling the straw around my drink.

"You didn't. It's just everyone always asks..." he says, trailing off and then abruptly, he scoots out of his chair. "Let's dance." He holds out his hand.

"Footloose" by Kenny Loggins plays over the speakers while the men swing their partners around. Suddenly, I'm incredibly nervous. With only a couple sips of my drink, I'm entirely too sober to dance, especially in front of Brady. I press my heels to the ground in front of the wood planks and shake my head at Brady, but he grins and pulls me harder. I reluctantly follow, dragging my feet while Brady walks to the center of the room. We are more camouflaged here and I start to feel more comfortable. I move side to side, displaying my lack of dance skills. As much as it scares me to be close to Brady, I would rather be slow dancing than show my lack of ability to follow a beat.

Brady wraps his arm around my waist and rests his hand on the small of my back, drawing me into him. I hold my hand in his and he leads us around the dance floor in a smooth form of the box step. A calm feeling absorbs me and I start enjoying myself before he pushes me away from him. When he pulls me back to him, I smack into him and both his hands fall to my waist, catching me. We both laugh. As much as I hate to admit it, I think he just discovered I can't dance. But instead of letting me go, he pushes me out again and this time I attempt to come back more gracefully.

We dance for another three songs before we make our way back to the table. My cheeks hurt from the constant smiles and laughs. He holds the chair out for me like the gentleman he is, while I tuck my dress under me and take a seat. My drink is completely watered down, and since we were gone from the table, I don't really want to drink it. The cute brunette comes by and asks Brady if we want something else, never glancing my way. He looks over at me for an answer, forcing her eyes to follow his. I tell her I'll take a water and Brady asks for the same.

A couple minutes later, she brings bottles of water and two glasses of ice. Brady twists my cap off and pours it into the glass for me. "Your mom raised you well," I compliment his chivalry skills.

"Actually, it was my dad. He always told me to treat a girl the way you want your daughter to be treated." One side of his mouth goes up while he places my bottle down and picks up his own.

"Sounds like a wise man".

"Yeah." He stares off toward the dance floor again. I'm starting to think Brady Carsen could have more secrets than me.

"Where do The Invisibles play next?" I try to divert the topic.

"Are you going to come?" He turns his head my way and smiles as though there wasn't an awkward silence a moment ago.

"I don't know. Their music is okay but the lead singer is so incredibly...what's the word?" I jokingly look up at the ceiling and scrunch the side of my mouth up.

"Hot?" Brady asks.

"No, that's not it," I say, still pretending to think.

"Talented?" He smirks over at me.

"Nope." I smile.

"Amazing?" He laughs.

"He's kind of...kind of a stalker," I joke, trying to conceal my giggle.

"From what I hear, he sees what he wants and goes after it," he confirms.

"What do you think he wants?" I question.

"I heard that he is completely infatuated with this incredibly beautiful girl. Hold on...I know her name...just give me a minute." He taps his finger to his lips as though he's thinking hard.

"What a lucky girl".

"I know, right? I mean Brady Carsen is like the best catch." He uses his best girl voice. "I think her name is Sadie. Yeah, that's it, Sadie Miller. Do you know her?" He leans over the table toward me.

"Yeah, I do. What on earth would he see in her? They are so different, surely his friends would disapprove?" I continue to joke, but Brady's face drops.

"Are you kidding me? Sadie walks into a room and every guy turns. From what he told me, she is not only gorgeous but smart and funny. The complete package with an amazing body to boot. As far as his friends, he could give a shit what they think and he wishes she would, too." His brown eyes seem to have gotten a little darker as they pierce into me from across the table.

I don't know what to say. Thankfully, "Lady in Red" by Chris de Burgh fills the room and Brady takes my hand.

"The last song of the evening and how fitting it is...my lady in red." He nudges his hand on my back and leads me to the dance floor. He wraps his arms around me, resting his hands on the small of my back. I don't know where to place my hands, so I ultimately rest them around his neck. We sway back and forth to one of my all-time favorite songs.

Brady holds me close to his chest and my eyes automatically close, letting the beat of the music move my body. He softly sings the words in my ear as he leads me around the floor. His cheek presses against mine as though we are the only two people in the room. My heart beats out of control with his warm hands around me and his soft breath on my neck. I swear I feel his lips graze slightly against my neck and I ache for them to meet mine. I want him...I want him to be mine.

As the song comes to an end, Brady doesn't sing that last line, telling me he loves me. Instead he hugs me tightly, lifting my feet from the ground. "Thank you for the most incredible date I have ever been on." He kisses my cheek again before he releases me.

We leave the bar and surprisingly, the waitress looks at me as well as Brady and tells us to have a good night. The car is silent on the way home, but Brady holds my hand, rubbing his thumb across my finger. When he glances over at me, we exchange smiles. The ride back to my dorm feels too short. I don't want to say goodnight to him, but I will never ask him to stay. The thought of him leaving me tomorrow after I sleep with him is unbearable.

Brady parks the car in front of the dorm and his eyes move my way. For a brief moment, I think he is going to ask me to go home with him, but he opens the door and steps out. I watch him as he walks around the car before he opens my door. My body protests leaving the safe Camaro cocoon with him, but I get out and accept the hand he offers. He entwines our fingers and we slowly walk toward the doors. Emptiness fills my stomach with every step.

When we get to the door, Brady asks for my keys. I hand them to him and he opens the dorm doors, motioning for me to enter before him. He turns me into the mail locker alcove to conceal us from passers-by. He leans me against the cold metal mailboxes and stretches his arm above my head. *This is it; he is finally going to kiss me. I should have popped a mint in my mouth.* His other hand moves up toward my face and his thumb lightly brushes over my lips. I stare into the caramel eyes, filled with desire and want. He tips his head down to me and before I have a chance to lick in preparation, his lips are on mine. He cups the side of my face and captures my bottom lip with his soft and gentle ones. I allow his tongue access after he slides his tongue between mine, asking to enter. We taste one another as our tongues mingle together. He tightens his hand against my cheek and draws his body closer to me.

Brady slowly stops the kiss but continues to give me short tender kisses before he ultimately pulls away, leaving me numb.

"This date keeps getting better," he says softly and grins down at me.

I smile back. I can't think of a good come-back because I just want to beg him to do it all over again. I lean forward from the mailboxes and Brady puts his arm around my waist, leading me down the hall.

The halls are empty since it is Monday night and almost everyone has class tomorrow. I don't hear Jessa on the other side of the door, so I assume she is asleep. The pull to have him come in and climb into my bed with me is fierce. But I can't take the chance he won't be there tomorrow. That he will use me like the others.

"Thank you, Sadie. I had a great time." He leans me up against the door again, encasing me with his arms.

"Me too," I agree, "thank you." I hold the doorknob behind my back with my hand and stare up at those eyes that could make me do some very bad things.

He gives me a chaste kiss on the lips. "I will definitely be dreaming about you tonight." His eyes roam my body, as though trying to burn the image in his head.

"Goodnight, Brady." I open the door before I beg him to come in.

"Goodnight, Sadie. Sweet dreams," he responds.

I shut the door and lean against it, releasing the breath I have been holding. I'm in so much trouble. Brady Carsen just carved out another piece of my heart.

Chapter 8

The next morning, my stomach flutters every time I think about the dance with Brady. That's nothing compared to when I think about the kiss. My whole body actually covers in goose bumps: in the shower, on my way to class, and eating lunch. He has consumed my thoughts every minute to the point that I have to finally stop listening to his music on my iPod.

After my second class, I head back to the dorm and stop by the mailboxes. As I stand there, I can almost feel Brady's lips on mine. I shuffle through the junk mail and land on a pink rectangle envelope. My fingers go weak and it almost drops to the ground. I can't believe with everything going on, I forgot.

I toss the junk mail in the nearby trashcan and make my way to the chairs in the common area. Resting my bag on the chair next to me, I carefully open the card. Star confetti drops in my lap as I pull the card out of the envelope. The card has a picture of a cake and the title says

"To a Special Daughter on her Birthday". My mom signed the card with love from her and my dad, instructing me to call soon but I know they don't really mean it. I have to admit the card puts a small smile on my face since last year they either forgot or didn't care to celebrate.

Tucking the card in my messenger bag, I head down the hall to my room. When I open the door, I wish I would have gone to the library. Rob is sitting in my chair, relaxing with his ankle on the opposite knee and Jessa sits in hers with her legs crossed. They seem to be watching something on television. I don't want to be rude so I continue to enter.

"Hey, Sadie," Jessa says, looking at me over her shoulder.

"Hi, Jessa," I respond back. "Hi, Rob." I wave over at him.

"Hey," he states callously. That pretty much sums up my conversation with him.

I don't want to be here with them, so I decide I will change to go work-out. Placing my messenger bag on the floor by my bed, I swap it with my gym bag.

"Where you going, Sadie?" Jessa calls over when I get to the door.

"Over to the rec center," I tell her.

"See you, Gucci," Rob calls out, not taking his eyes off the television.

I open the door and roll my eyes. Jessa mouths sorry at me before I shut the door. I don't understand why she is with him and it hurts a little that she never says anything to him when he makes those comments.

I get to the rec center with only five minutes before the kickboxing class is going to start. Scrambling in the locker room, I switch my shoes and shove my bag into a locker. I jog out to the room the class is being held in and am happy to see it isn't as crowded as the night classes I usually attend. I sneak to the back row and recognize some of the girls from other classes, but am startled to see Brady's friend, Kara, two rows in front of me. She is wearing a tight tank top and short black shorts. A tattoo peeks out on her right shoulder blade but I can't tell what it says, just that it's written in italic print.

Sweat drips from my body and my shirt clings to me by the time the class finishes. I grab my towel and water bottle to head back to the women's locker room when I spot Brady leaning against the wall. Athletic shorts hang from his hips and a gray t-shirt with a ring of sweat around the collar covers his chest.

Being preoccupied with how stunning he looks, I didn't notice Kara standing in front of him. She touches his forearm while he smiles down to her. I automatically see red. *Friend, my ass.* I knew he was lying that night at Aces, but after last night, I wouldn't have thought he was playing me. I guess I was wrong.

I turn the opposite way. I need to work off some of this anger by running on the treadmill, but it's completely packed by the time I get to the room. Every treadmill and elliptical is taken. Change of plans. I'll do some weights but that room is full of guys that could bench press me and Jessa together. So I make my way down the hall, hoping to sneak into the girl's locker room without notice from Brady and Kara.

Thankfully, when I walk by the same spot, they are gone. I get my bag and switch my shoes out, rushing to get out and back to the dorm.

"I thought I saw you." Kara comes around the corner.

"Oh, hey," I say and give her a small wave of my hand.

"You were at Aces the other night, right?" she asks.

"Yes, I was. Sadie Miller," I introduce myself.

"Kara Billings," she shares and limply shakes my hand.

"It's nice to meet you." I smile.

"Just so you know, he's mine." Her lips go straight and her eyes bore into me.

"I'm sorry, what?" I ask, dumbfounded.

"You heard me. Stay away from Brady Carsen. He's mine," she repeats herself.

"Are you two dating? Are you in some sort of relationship?" I question her, praying she says no.

"No, but we will be. We would have already if it wasn't for you," she admits, her eyes narrowing, and she places her hands on her hips.

"I'm sorry, Kara, but Brady is a grown man and he will make the decision as to whom he dates." I walk by her.

She grabs my wrist and holds it tight. "Listen. Don't think you can come here and take something I have been working on for two years. He was ready to be mine this summer, but then you prance into town and he pushes me aside," she spews, her grip getting tighter with every word.

I yank my wrist free, holding it with my other hand. "Obviously, if it has taken two years, Brady isn't interested," I curtly respond and try to get out the door. She rushes by me and I can finally see that tattoo. On her left shoulder blade it reads The Invisibles in a calligraphy script with black hearts for dots on top of the I's. Oh, this girl has it bad, which makes me want to know exactly what her and Brady's relationship is.

I shake my head and walk out of the rec center, thankful I don't run into Kara a second time. Walking up the hill to my dorm, I notice the same homeless man asleep on the bench, wearing the same brown corduroys and plaid shirt. Someone has already left a bag of food next to him, so I reach into my wallet and tuck twenty dollars in his front shirt pocket. I wonder what he will do when winter comes. His clothes are not nearly warm enough to last through the cold and snow.

Continuing down my path, I pray that Rob has left my dorm room. I don't need or want his snide comments. Suddenly, goose bumps cover my body when I see Brady standing on the sidewalk directly in my path to the dorm. He looks inquiringly at me, but smiles when I get closer.

"Fancy meeting you here," I grin. I notice he still has those athletic shorts on, but sadly a sweatshirt covers up his chiseled chest.

"Don't do that, Sadie," he demands with a firm tone I have never heard from him before.

"Do what?" I tilt my head, confused.

"You shouldn't be leaving money for the bums. You shouldn't go up to them like that." He motions with his head to the homeless man on the bench.

"Oh Brady, he's harmless. I'm thinking about getting him a jacket for the winter." I start walking past him, ignoring his comments.

"Sadie, listen to me. They call that one Vodka Vince because he usually has a bottle of Vodka with him."

"Why do you think he would harm me, or anyone else for that matter? Just because they don't have a home and might have a drinking problem doesn't mean they are violent," I spit out. I turn around to him, surprised he can be so judgmental toward people less fortunate than himself.

"Please, just keep your distance. Alcohol can make people do things out of character." He gently touches my arm and heat rises through my veins.

"Alright," I shrug. I wonder if he is talking about himself.

"Thank you. It's nice of you to leave money, though." He smiles and I question his numerous mood swings.

"What are you doing out my way, anyway?" I try to change the subject.

"Well, I was on my way back from your dorm. Jessa told me you were working out. Sorry I missed that sight," he says, his eyes roaming over my legs and shorts, finally landing back on my face.

"Yeah, I finished my class about a half hour ago. I was going to do more but the place is packed." I decide not to inform him I saw him there as well.

"I was lucky, I got there just in time before class change. You should tell me next time you go." He starts to follow me back to the dorm.

"Do you want to come to my kickboxing class with me?" I laugh.

"I might surprise you some day, but I'm actually more of a runner." He puts his arm around me and I'm amazed at how comfortable it feels.

"Oh," I say and inch a little closer to him.

"So, when are you going to mention that you saw me there?" He grins down at me.

My face must be red from the flush that flowed through my body. "Um...you seemed preoccupied," I admit, biting my lower lip.

"Sadie, I'm never preoccupied when it comes to you." He squeezes my shoulder tighter, drawing me closer.

"What exactly is your relationship with her?" It's none of my business, but it's driving me crazy.

"Our parents worked together." He stops walking and looks down at me. "Sadie, I have no interest in her."

"Are you sure? She's cute," I reveal and meet his eyes.

"Cute is for puppies and kittens, Sadie. I prefer this stunningly sexy woman I have been seeing recently." He winks down to me and butterflies flutter in my stomach.

"Really?" I ask in disbelief.

"How many times do I have to tell you?" He holds my arms with his hands. "I'm a one-woman man, Sadie, and you are her." He bends down, letting his lips graze across mine while he moves his arms down to my waist, pulling me closer. Our chests rise and fall against one another and he sucks my bottom lip into his mouth before his tongue enters with purpose. His tongue finds mine and they engage one another while my hands move to his head. I twirl his hair with my fingers. Like every other time I'm with Brady, everything fades away and it's only us standing on the sidewalk in the middle of campus.

Chapter 9

Friday comes in the blink of an eye. The Invisibles have a show tonight, but I told Brady I'm not feeling well. I know I won't be much company tonight and I would never want to bring him down with me, especially on a night when he is performing.

I pull on my pajama pants and a t-shirt, curling up in my chair after I pop in a movie. Jessa is applying another coat of mascara when there is a knock at the door. I sigh heavily. I wish Rob would have just waited for her outside. Jessa opens the door and kisses him in greeting. He grabs her ass then gives it a little tap before he walks into our room. You could cut the tension with a knife. I decide to ignore him. If he wishes to address me he can, but I'm through with being polite.

"Hey, Gucci. You look like shit. What? Daddy didn't pay someone to develop a cure for the flu yet? I'm sure he doesn't want his little girl to suffer," Rob remarks snidely.

"No, Rob. I guess I'm not important enough to him," I sneer back.

"Surprise. Gucci has Daddy issues." He puts his hands up in the air.

"Go to hell." I turn back to my movie. I wish I could come back with some sort of smart-ass comment but Theo was always better at that than me. He would have known what to say to Rob to make him shut his mouth.

"Alright you two, stop it." Jessa playfully hits Rob in the chest and pushes him toward the door. "Call me if you need me, okay?" She glances back at me.

"Feel better, Gucci." Rob's voice travels in the room from the hallway.

I flip him off once the door shuts. I don't think I have loathed anyone as much as Rob in my entire life. Well...except for one.

I'm a half hour into the movie and my phone starts ringing. I pick it up without looking at the caller ID, assuming it's Brady.

"Hey, aren't you supposed to be on stage right about now," I answer.

"Excuse me. I'm looking for Sadie Miller, my daughter," my mom's soft voice comes across the line.

"It's me, Mom." I roll my eyes. How does she not recognize my voice after twenty-two years?

"Oh, Sadie. Your dad and I were just calling to wish you a happy birthday." She sounds like she is in a tunnel.

"Happy birthday, Sadie," my Dad's deep voice shouts in the background.

"Thanks, Mom. Thanks, Dad." I hate talking to one of them, let alone both at the same time.

"Are you doing anything special?" my mom asks.

"No, just staying in," I admit.

"You should go out and celebrate," she insists.

"Don't push her, Mags," my Dad chimes in.

"She can't hide out forever, Junior." My parents start having a conversation without me, another reason I hate speaker phone.

"Well...thanks for calling Mom and Dad. Have a good night," I say, attempting to end this conversation.

"Hey Sadie, your father and I are coming out at the end of the month for Parent's Weekend," she adds in at the last minute.

"Mom, Parent's Weekend is more for freshman. I'm a senior. I appreciate it, but there isn't really a reason."

"We are coming. You don't have to take us to a football game or anything. We want to come and make sure you are doing alright," my mom assures me. I don't know why they want to come; they didn't even come my freshman year at Drayton.

"I'm fine. You don't have to make that trip. I will be home at Thanksgiving." I try to change her mind, which is usually an easy task when it comes to me. Lately, she has done everything to ignore my existence.

"I told you, Mags. She's a tough cookie," my Dad gives me a backhanded compliment. He hates women with an opinion or any strength of character.

"Don't come, Mom. Really, I'll be home just a few weeks after that. You would be so bored. There is no shopping or nice restaurants around here." I pull out all the stops.

"Are you sure, Sadie? We will come." Either she has gotten better at faking her concern or she is actually worried about me.

"Yeah, Mom. Just wait until Thanksgiving."

"See. I told you she doesn't need us. She never has, right Sadie? You were born independent," my Dad shouts loudly in the background.

"Yeah, Dad," I agree, not mentioning they made me become independent. They made me not rely on others, except for Theo. I could always depend on Theo.

"Okay then. Well...happy birthday." She seems reluctant to hang up. "Bye, Sadie."

"Bye, Mom and Dad." I click the phone off.

Our relationship was never stellar, but the last couple years it had gone dramatically downhill. I think that conversation was more than I have said to my parents since I told them I was transferring out of Drayton last summer. It baffles me that my mom feels some motherly instinct to come and check up on me here.

I press play on the remote, starting the movie back up. Right as the girl is about to get the guy, two short knocks hit my door. I glance at the clock and see it's only eleven and since I'm not expecting anyone, I ignore it. The knocks get louder and more persistent. I shrug off my blanket and stomp over to the door, assuming it's some drunk ass that has the wrong room. But when I fling the door open, Brady stands there with a smile on his face.

"I thought maybe you were sleeping when you didn't answer at first." He walks right in without an invitation.

"Why aren't you at Aces?" My voice is harsher than I intended.

"Oh Sadie. I'm thrilled to see you, too," he sarcastically replies.

"No, I didn't mean it like that. It's just...you didn't leave on account of me, did you?" I shuffle my feet back and forth, trying to cover my chest since I'm not wearing a bra.

"Would it bother you if I did?" He raises his eyebrows at me.

"Of course not. I just would hate the rest of the band to be upset," I admit.

"Oh forget them." He throws his hand out toward me. "Let's go." He starts to walk to the door.

"I can't go anywhere. Not to mention, you don't want to get sick," I lie.

"Sadie, look at me." He places his finger under my chin, raising it so my eyes meet his caramel ones. "Are you really sick? And don't lie." His one eye brow raises in question.

"No," I confess.

"That's what I thought." He pulls me to the door again.

"Brady, I'm not even dressed." I pull back.

"It doesn't matter. We aren't going anywhere public."

"Where are we going?" I question.

"It's a surprise. Come on." His smile is so wide I wonder what he is up to. He couldn't have found out it was my birthday; I didn't even tell Jessa.

"What about your show?" I persistently ask.

"Did I sign up for twenty questions? What's my prize if I win?" His eyes move slowly up and down my body. "If you're the grand prize, I'll answer as many questions as you want."

"Brady," I sigh, struggling to hide my smile. "Why aren't you playing?" I ask him again.

"I cancelled the show. Well, not exactly. I played a couple songs and then told the guys I had to go. Rob sings, he took my spot." He shrugs.

"Why did you do that? I'm fine," I insist, upset with myself. People showed up to see him sing and he left because I'm feeling sorry for myself and didn't go.

"Let me get dressed. We will head up there now. You can finish the set." I walk over to my closet and sift through my clothes.

"Sadie," he calls over but I don't turn around. "It's over. Rob is finishing the set. Now get your little ass over here so I can take you somewhere." He stays where he is and waits for me to walk to him.

"Alright." I surprise myself by following his directions. Usually I'm not so submissive, but Brady has a way with me that no other male has had before.

"Finally." He wraps his arms around me and presses my face to his shoulder. "I swear girl, sometimes you make things more difficult."

Brady intertwines our fingers and leads me out to his car. I know autumn has officially hit when I feel the cool night breeze rising up under my shirt.

"As much as I don't want you to cover up, it's getting cold outside." He reaches behind me and pulls a sweatshirt from the backseat, tossing it over to me. I notice it's the one from earlier in the week. The smell of Brady fills my nostrils when I tug it over my head. I smile, knowing he won't be getting it back.

"Thank you," I say. I wait outside the car door for him to motion me in, but he shuts the door after grabbing another bag. He swings his guitar over his shoulder and takes my hand again, walking us away from the car. "Um..." I tilt my head, confused.

"We don't need the car." He looks back to his Camaro and then to me.

I already know where we are going by the time we are halfway there. This is his place, the spot he first saw me and his hide-out from the world. I remember now that there is so much I don't know about Brady. Why does he favor a spot where no one can see him? I have to find out soon because that spot in my heart for him grows bigger every day and I can't afford to get hurt again.

By the time we get there, I'm freezing. Brady grabs a blanket from his bag and spreads it across the lawn.

"Take a seat, Sadie." He points to the blanket and I sit down, wrapping my arms around my legs in an effort to keep me warm.

"So, what are we doing up here?" I ask.

"Alright, Sadie. We need to make a deal." He takes a seat across from me on the blanket.

"What kind of deal?" I hesitantly ask.

"If you stop asking me questions and answer one of mine, I will play you a song." He brings his guitar closer to him.

"How do you know I want you to play a song?" I hope my voice sounds casual, even though I would do anything for him to sing.

"Ugh...another question. Do you ever stop? Because you love my voice. Not to mention, you really need to hear this song." He leans in closer to me and my heart beats faster.

"Alright, shoot Carsen." I release my legs and cross them over each other.

He brings the guitar to his lap and starts to strum the strings a few times while he tunes the knobby things.

"Wait, I thought you had a question."

"I think I want to play the song for you first." He grins and starts to play. I recognize it from the first strum on the guitar but when Brady's voice tenderly begins to sing Happy Birthday, I know he just took a little more of my heart.

It is the most romantic act anyone has done for me. I don't know how he knew it was my birthday or when he found out, but I couldn't have asked for a better gift than him. After he finishes with the song, he places his guitar back in the case and instructs me to close my eyes, which is an easy task since I need to compose myself. I hear a flick of a lighter and know now he must have a candle.

"Open up your eyes," he whispers. I feel him closer to me than before. "Happy birthday, Sadie. Make a wish." When I open my eyes, there is a chocolate cupcake with cream cheese frosting topped with a mound of toasted coconut shavings and one lit candle.

"Brady..." I take a deep breath in. "You shouldn't have." Our eyes meet again and I hope he can see how grateful I am despite my words.

"Make your wish." He brings the cupcake closer to me.

I close my eyes, smelling the sweetness of the coconut and frosting. I feel the heat from the small flame on top and suck in a deep breath, secretly making my wish before releasing it to extinguish the flame.

"I hope I was part of that wish." Brady takes out the candle and places it inside the box. "So are you ready for my question?"

"Just so you know, I'm a true believer in not telling anyone what I wish for. It's bad karma and I really want this one to come true."

"Me too. I will never ask but...if you ever want to tell me, I wouldn't be upset," he laughs. "Sadie Miller?" he asks and I stare directly at him. "Did you have a good birthday?" He smiles up at me and my body can't be wrapped in his arms soon enough.

"The best, Brady. Thank you." I kiss him thoroughly with every fiber of my being. How I found this man is beyond me because I don't deserve him.

"Sadie, you are a mysterious girl." He places his hands on either side of my face, bringing it closer to his until our lips find one another again.

I'm happy he doesn't ask me any questions regarding my past. He hasn't asked me why I never told him it was my birthday or why I faked being sick. As much as I want to tell him about Theo and my life at Drayton, it scares me that he will run when he finds out and there is no way I can lose him now.

"Can I ask one question now?" I peek my head up from his, finishing our kiss.

"You aren't as sneaky as you think. Jessa found some confetti on the floor the other day and was curious. She may have checked out your driver's license to find out, but don't tell her I told you." He grins, pulling me tighter into him. "She didn't tell me until tonight when she and Rob got there, which is why this is so spur of the moment. If I would have had more time, it would have been better."

"It was perfect, Brady. I wouldn't have wanted to celebrate my birthday any other way," I confess and kiss his cheek.

"Happy birthday, Sadie," he whispers in my ear.

Chapter 10

We stayed up at the hill for a couple hours, wrapped in a blanket, talking about things we love. Brady told me how he ended up in The Invisibles with the guys and how he has always had a love of music. He said that when they asked him to sing, he decided he wanted a change of pace. What he didn't tell me was what he needed a change of pace from. The way he spoke was as though he was someone else before then. I didn't pry; I too have secrets I am not about to reveal yet.

He walked me home, kissing me goodnight at the door. Even though I desperately wanted to ask him to stay, I couldn't. I wasn't ready for this to end between us and I fear if I sleep with him, that is exactly what will happen.

He picked me up this morning, taking me to a Farmer's Market in town, where he buys us fresh vegetables and fruit. It surprises me that he knows almost all the vendors, introducing me to them by first name. When they ask him how he is holding up, he shrugs them off, saying he's great and interrupts any follow-up questions, telling them we have to go. I have never seen him this wound-up before. As the day continues and the questions from the vendors pry more, he barely smiles and eventually starts rushing us through the booths.

By the time we get to the last vendor, Brady is holding my hand, steadily moving us toward the street. The way he's pulling my arm, I feel as though there is some dangerous murderer following us.

"Brady Carsen? Is that you?" A sweet older lady with grey hair and a small frame calls out to him. Brady continues to walk, but I pull him back.

"Brady. That lady is calling your name." I tug my hand away from his. He turns around and his expression isn't casual and easy-going like usual. He appears cold and angry. I can tell he is mad that I stopped him. He looks at me and then at the elderly lady. Taking a deep breath and releasing it while his shoulders slump, he takes my hand again and leads me over to the table full of cookies, cakes and breads.

"I thought that was you. How are you, Brady?" Her voice is so soft and caring, and she reminds me of a grandmother.

"Hi, Mrs. Fletcher. I'm good. Thank you for asking," he replies, the same answer he gave to every other person who knows him here.

"I was sorry to hear about..." she starts but Brady quickly interrupts her.

"Thank you, Mrs. Fletcher. This is Sadie Miller. She's new to Western." He puts his hand on the small of my back and I offer my hand for her to shake.

"Nice to meet you, Sadie." She smiles, shaking my hand in return. "Very beautiful, Brady."

"I agree," Brady responds and grins back to her. The first real smile from his lips in the last hour.

"How did he get you, darling? I hope it isn't the bad boy band thing because my Brady isn't some rock star that loves 'em and leaves 'em." She peers directly in my eyes as though she can tell if I lie to her.

"You're ruining my image, Mrs. Fletcher," Brady laughs. God, I love that sound.

"He's a perfect gentleman." I look over at Brady; his lips turn up as he glances down at me.

"Glad to hear it. Now, pick something out. It's on me. You're too skinny," she adds, pinching my arm.

"Um…" I grab my arm, holding where she pinched. Obviously, I'm not too skinny since she got some skin. I pick up a package of Rice Krispie treats and dig in my purse for the money.

"Oh, Brady's favorites. I used to make these for him when he was little. Just a little brown mop-haired boy running around the streets."

Brady turns a nice shade of pink from embarrassment. "I promise to share," I tell her and hand her five dollars.

"No darling, it's fine. Any friend of Brady's is a friend of mine." She pushes my hand back.

"Are you sure?" She nods. "Well then...thank you, Mrs. Fletcher." I place them in our bag.

"Come give me some sugar, Brady. I never see you anymore." She holds her hands out for him to hug her. His large frame envelopes her small stature. I hear her whispering in his ear. Brady nods his head in agreement and then releases her, giving her a kiss on the cheek.

"You too, darling." She waits for me to walk to her. I gently wrap my arms around her, trying not to break her fragile body.

"Don't break his heart, Sadie. He can be stubborn and bull-headed, but your reward will be tenfold if you love him. He will try to keep you out but push your way in, okay?" she whispers in my ear, making sure Brady can't hear.

I return back to Brady's side and he takes my hand in his, as though it's natural.

"See you later, kids." She winks at both of us as we walk away.

"She's sweet," I say over to Brady as we walk over to his car.

"Yeah, she's like my grandmother," he responds.

"Did she used to babysit you or something?" I ask.

"Kind of." He shrugs, not divulging anything else.

Brady drives me to his house and informs me he is going to make me lunch. We pull up to an older green house with a porch in front. There are ivory shutters with red paint outlining the windows. The grass is neatly cut and trimmed along the sidewalk. Shrubs cover the front and sides of the house. It appears to be three stories, resembling a family home rather a college student's house. He parks in front of the detached garage and walks us through the back door.

I'm struck by how nice the house smells. After practically living in frat houses since I entered college, I have never smelled anything this nice in a place where a bunch of guys live. We enter through the kitchen where there is a small, round oak table with chairs around it. All the appliances are a little older and the cabinets are worn, but it's nice and presentable. There are no dishes in the sink or beer bottles strewn about.

"Take a seat, Sadie." He pulls a chair out for me, placing the bags from the Farmer's Market on the table.

"No, I'll help you," I insist.

"I got this. You want something to drink?" he asks.

"Sure. Water?"

He opens the fridge door filled with beer and I see my first sign that this is indeed a bachelor pad. Grabbing a bottle of water, he opens it before he hands it over to me.

When he puts it on the table, he leans over and kisses me. "I have been waiting to do that all day." He pulls away but I grab his shirt, bringing him back to me. I lick his lips and he opens with his tongue eager to meet mine. As he places his hand on the back of my neck, I loop my fingers through his hair and he groans into my mouth. He wants more so I slowly bring my tongue back into my mouth to end the kiss. The last thing I want to do is lead him on.

"Wow. Should have started that earlier," Brady jokes and walks back over to the fridge.

I take a sip of my water, the coolness calming me down a bit. I have never been with a man that kisses like Brady. He never rushes it or tries to stop, as though he has all the time in the world to kiss me.

"I hope you like egg salad." He takes a Tupperware container out of the fridge.

"I do. Did you make it?"

"This morning, before I came to get you."

"Brady Carsen, you are full of hidden talents." I bring my knees up and watch him move around the kitchen. It is sexy as hell seeing him go from the fridge to the counter, grabbing a knife and cutting the homemade bread we bought. His movements are smooth and decisive.

"Sadie?" He snaps me out of my trance.

"Sorry, yeah?" I shake my head back and forth.

"Something has been on my mind since that time at the Student Center." His back is still turned from me while he washes the lettuce in the sink.

"What?" I ask, curious.

"The deal breaker. What are yours?" he asks.

"Um…I don't know. I guess I just know them when I see them," I admit.

"Oh, come on. Tell me just one," he pleads.

"Alright..." I hesitate. I don't know him nearly enough for this. Theo and I would go back and forth all day with our deal breakers, but I knew he never judged me and I never judged him. "I don't like dirty shoes. The ones that are so worn and dirty, but I also don't like brand new blinding white ones either. I know it's stupid but..."

Brady interrupts me, "It's fine. Glad I don't have to worry about that." He makes me feel better.

"So, what are yours?"

"Well, I hate to admit this and it's probably some guys' opposite of deal breaker. I hate it when a girl bends over and you can see her thong," he confesses and turns around to face me. He casually crosses his ankles and leans against the counter.

"So if I bent over right now and you could see my thong, you would politely drive me back to the dorm and never see me again?" I raise an eyebrow at him.

"Like I told you that day, I don't think there are any deal breakers when it comes to you. Privately, feel free to bend over and show me your thong anytime but please don't do it in front of other people. I don't like guys seeing what's mine." He pushes himself off the counter to retrieve the two plates.

"I'm yours?" I question.

"Yep," he says, matter of fact. "I'm sorry, did you not want to be mine?" He smirks over at me, knowing my answer.

"I didn't say that." I bite my lip and stare down at the egg salad sandwich in front of me with a side of fresh fruit. I think I just agreed that Brady is my boyfriend. Too bad it will be short-lived.

After lunch Brady gives me a tour of the house. Like I assumed, there are three floors. The main floor is the kitchen, family room and dining room. The second floor has the bedrooms, each guy having their own room and they all share two bathrooms. Outside of Brady's room is a staircase up to the third floor, but he tells me it is all storage stuff so he doesn't take me up there.

I'm happy when he doesn't walk into his room but just shows it to me through the doorway. I definitely can't handle sitting on a bed with him. He does have a nice queen-size bed that looks appealing though.

We walk down to the basement. Brady seems giddy with excitement before opening the door. When he pushes it open, I'm speechless. He has a music studio. We are in the room with large oversized brown leather couches and chairs lining a wall. Switchboards face a glass window that overlooks a drum set, guitars, and microphones. It is incredible and I can see how happy Brady is just being down here.

"This is great, Brady," I say excitedly, brushing my finger along one of the couches.

"I know. I think I have slept down here more than in my own bed."

"So, this is where the magic happens with you guys?" I ask.

"I wouldn't say that." He wraps his arms around my waist, kissing my neck. "I could show you some magic if you prefer." He brushes my hair to the side, moving his lips down my shoulder and back up to my neck.

I close my eyes. His warm breath feels incredible. I can't let this lead to something more so I pull away, making my way over to the switchboard. "What does this do?" I fiddle with a button.

He comes up behind me and kisses my neck again. "Do you really want to know?" he whispers while his tongue flicks my earlobe. I close my eyes in pleasure again, willing my heart to calm down.

"Brady," I sigh.

"Come here." He grabs my hand and leads me to the couch. He positions me on his lap and rests his hands around my waist, bringing me closer to him. "I just want to kiss you, Sadie. I will never rush you," he promises.

Instinctively, I wrap my arms around his neck, letting him bring his lips to mine. As our tongues start to mingle together, he sucks my bottom lip and goose bumps travel up my spine. Brady's hands start moving up and down my ribcage. The anticipation of him touching my breasts is becoming unbearable. It's like a double-edged sword, me wanting him to go there but not wanting to lead him on. As soon as I think he is going to cup my breast, his hands move to my thighs, stroking the outside of my right leg. My fingers wrap around his hair while we continue to devour each other's mouths.

"God, Sadie. There is nothing better than kissing you," he murmurs to me, breaking our kiss before his lips crash into mine again. I don't think I have ever kissed a guy this long before. They are usually preoccupied with another part of my body.

I respond with a moan and wrap my leg over his waist, straddling him. He places his hands on my ass, drawing me into him and I can feel how hard he is. I don't want to tease him but I can't yank myself away. It feels so good, so right. His hands travel up my stomach and I know where their destination is and I'm unable to stop them. Just as both of Brady's hands cup my breasts and his thumbs rub against my peaked nipples, the door busts open and I fly off his lap, crossing my legs as though nothing is going on. Brady starts laughing and straightens out his pants, looking over at me.

"What's up guys?" Trey asks, making his way in the room, followed by Dex and Rob.

"Nothing now," Brady deadpans and brings me back onto his lap, caressing my hip bone back and forth with his thumb.

"Sorry to ruin your time with..." Rob leers my way, "Chanel."

"Rob, you need to shut the fuck up." Brady gently moves me off his lap to stand face to face with him, the tension in his shoulders so tight they could snap.

"Alright, alright. I'll be good." Rob backs away and moves into the glassed-off area, picking up his guitar.

"You staying to watch us rehearse, Sadie?" Trey asks and I notice he has a stud ring under his lip. It's oddly appealing on him.

I look at Brady and he raises his eyebrows, questioning if I want to stay.

"Sure," I agree.

Brady sits me down in the chair in front of the switchboards while he follows the guys into the room. They start testing their instruments, joking about something I didn't catch. Then Brady's voice fills the room and chills travel my body in excitement.

"This is for you, Sadie Miller." He strums his guitar a couple times before starting the song. The song is familiar, but I can't place it at first. Brady's soft brown irises are on me, patiently waiting for me to recognize it. Then the chorus comes and I figure out he is playing "Oh Sherrie" by Steve Perry, but he changes it to "Oh Sadie". I return his smile and Brady sings it, mimicking Steve Perry in the eighties video. He clutches his fist close to his heart and bends his knees close to the ground. My whole body melts with a warmth I have never felt. There goes a little more of my heart.

Chapter 11

I hate Mondays, but I especially hate this Monday. After spending the weekend with Brady the last thing I want to do is Algebra. I'm still too embarrassed to ask Brady for help so I resort to my usual victim in tutoring and head to the sixth floor of the library, praying I find Grant.

Luck must be on my side because when the elevator doors slide open, he is unpacking his backpack at one of the tables. He glances over to me and a smile comes across his lips, revealing his perfect white teeth.

"Hey, Sadie. It's been awhile." He takes a seat on the table, waiting for me to walk up to him.

"I know, I've been kind of busy," I admit. It suddenly dawns on me that this could be awkward since I'm about to ask him to help me in math even though I turned him down when he had asked me out.

"With Brady I assume?" The dislike in his tone is unmistakable.

"Um…"

"That's alright, it's none of my business." He gets off the table and moves to sit down in a chair.

"So, Grant. I need a favor?" I bite my lower lip and use my best puppy dog eyes.

"When is it?" He gives a look similar to a disapproving father.

"In two hours." I lift my shoulders and smile coyly.

"Sit down." He motions to the seat across from him.

An hour and a half later I think I finally have a grasp of the material so I stand up to say goodbye. "Thank you, Grant, you're a lifesaver." I start packing up my bag.

"No problem. I'll walk you to class." He stands up and flings his backpack over his shoulder. I can't help but notice how much Grant resembles Theo and every other guy I have ever known. The crisp polo and dark jeans with brown loafers. I could probably take any frat boy's face and insert it on Grant's body.

We make our way down and out of the library. Grant doesn't touch me or stand close. He doesn't ask me about Brady or tell me to watch out with him like he did prior. I'm starting to think a friendship between us could be possible.

Halfway to the Math building, we pass Vodka Vince and I have never seen him awake before. He still looks disheveled and unkempt but alert nonetheless. Brady's words of caution ring through my head. Grant grabs my elbow and leads me to the other side of the walkway so we don't pass directly by him. I glance over and give Grant a dirty look but follow his lead.

"Heya, Grant," Vodka Vince speaks low to him. I look over, confused.

"Hi," Grant responds, giving him a small wave of his hand and continues walking.

"You know him?" I ask.

"Doesn't everyone?" he questions in return.

"But he knew your name, Grant."

"Sometimes I leave him things." He shrugs his shoulders.

"That's nice," I admit. What a different perspective than Brady.

"I guess." He doesn't show a reaction, obviously assuming everyone else does it. "Here you go." Grant stops at the bottom steps, suddenly ready to get rid of me.

"Thanks again. I owe you one," I graciously thank him.

"Maybe next time, dinner?" he asks.

"Yeah, that's not going to happen." The chills hit my body before he places his hand on the small of my back and leans in to kiss me on the cheek. "Hey, baby." Brady tugs me closer to him.

"Hi, Brady." I allow him to be a little possessive of me before stepping away.

"So, you two are..." Grant says, annoyed.

"Together? Yes," Brady confirms, finishing his sentence. His smile is smug and big as he puts his hand on my hip, bringing me to him. This domineering behavior Brady portrays makes me upset and pleased at the same time.

Grant appears uncomfortable with the whole situation. He isn't taking a defensive stance back at Brady, instead he keeps his distance. It's odd behavior, almost sadness in Grant's eyes as he quickly glances between the two of us.

"Well, good luck, Sadie. See you around," Grant says quietly and puts his head down, walking down the path before I can thank him.

"I will have to keep a better eye on you. First Vodka Vince and then that douchebag." Brady puts his arm around me and walks me into the building.

"Brady, what was all that about?" I question, clearly irritated.

"He's a fucking frat boy. I don't trust him." He stops outside my door and I wonder how he knew I had a class, let alone the exact classroom.

"I think he's nice and I consider him a friend. Do you think you could be nice?" He has me leaned against the wall, enveloping me with his arms above my head.

"Sadie, let's get something straight. I'm not one of those domineering guys." I smirk, looking up at him and he grins down to me. "Well...not until I met you. I know what guys like him want and what he imagines in his head and I don't like it." His mouth is so close to mine, I can feel the warmth of his breath against my lips.

"He's just a friend," I argue.

"Maybe to you, but to him you are a conquest and believe me, he won't stop until he gets you." He lightly kisses the side of my mouth.

"Brady, this is way too much drama before an exam." I stay firmly against the wall and place my fingers under the waistband of his jeans, pulling him into me.

"Let me relax you," he whispers and comes willingly. He keeps his arms above my head, moving his head down to my mouth. Usually any form of affection in front of a group of people embarrasses me. A year ago this incident would have had me ducking under Brady's arm, running into the safety of my classroom. As he captures my upper lip between his, I find myself not caring who sees our display. He never lets his arms fall down, pinning me against the wall only with his lower body. I can barely keep my feet planted on the ground; they want to betray me and wrap around his taut stomach. I want him to grab my ass with both hands and carry me into some vacant room to have his way with me. But before my body deceives me, Brady pulls away.

"Good luck, baby!" He leans down one more time and gives me a kiss right next to my ear. "You look absolutely gorgeous today." He turns me around and gently nudges me toward the door and then walks the opposite direction down the hall.

I fumble into my room which is filled with mostly freshman. I see the stares and whispers around me. Oh shit, I don't think my body can hold off much longer. Thoughts of him in bed make me so aroused, I can feel the burn inside of me. I sit down at my desk and take a deep breath, willing myself to concentrate on Algebra but Brady continues to fill my imagination. His scent is so strong I would swear he is sitting next to me if I didn't know better.

Walking back to the dorm, I feel confident with my exam. I definitely didn't ace it, but I most likely achieved a B. Next time I see Grant, I will have to thank him. When I get to the hill, I stop in my tracks. Vodka Vince is sitting on a park bench with a middle-aged woman. She's dressed in a nice black pants suit and heels. They are eating sandwiches and I notice the woman is doing most of the talking while he eats. I can't explain why Vodka Vince piques my curiosity but I take a seat on a nearby bench and pull my phone out, pretending I'm checking my e-mails.

The woman is strikingly beautiful with short blonde hair styled so that every piece is in its specified place. Her long legs are crossed facing Vince, and I haven't seen her stop talking the whole time. She talks with her hands, constantly touching his arms, hands, or legs. I can't figure out if she is someone that is like that with everyone or if she has such a close relationship with him, it's just second nature to her. Vince doesn't acknowledge her except for a minute here or there. Otherwise, he stares over at her like he is trying to figure out why she is sitting with him.

After ten minutes, their sandwiches are finished. The blonde woman starts taking the sandwich wrappers, placing them in the bag. I see her dig in her purse and she hands Vince a couple of bills. He takes them from her and says thank you. With a small tap on his knee with her hand, she says goodbye and kisses his cheek. Vince stays sitting there staring out to the open field, appearing lost. It is getting colder outside and I hope he uses that money she gave him for a coat, but I realize it will most likely go to vodka.

I stand up to make my way to the dorm. My heart starts beating faster when I'm about to pass him. I could kill Brady for bringing these thoughts into my head. Willing myself to calm down and take a breath, I glance at a smiling Vince and nod my head.

"Heya," Vince's deep voice says as I walk by.

"Hi," I respond, my voice a couple octaves higher than normal. I give him a small wave and continue walking.

"Are you Grant's girl?" he asks, making me stop.

I turn around, shocked that I'm about to have a conversation with him. Brady would kill me right about now. "Oh...no, I have a boyfriend," I admit.

"That's good to hear." The smile that forms across his lips is wide and genuine. I smile back, unsure what to say as he continues to stare out to the open field, satisfied with the end of our conversation so I turn around and make my way back to the dorm.

When I reach my door, I can hear the music on the other side. This is a common occurrence when Jessa has a guy in the room, or if she's just happy. The last thing I want to see is Rob's ass in the air, grinding into her on top of her loft. The visual alone makes me nauseous. I slowly put my hand on the doorknob like I was taught if there was a fire on the other side. I know I should just turn away but I turn it gradually so if Rob is in there, I can shut the door quickly and flee to the common area. I peek through the small opening and then continue opening it all the way when I discover Jessa dancing all around the room, waving a scarf like one of those ballerinas with the ribbons. She turns around and finds me staring at her, and I quickly try to shut my mouth.

"Guess what, Sadie?" she screams over the music and runs over to me, grasping my arms with both her hands.

"What?" I ask in return, still shaking the image of Jessa dancing around the room out of my head. In the months I have known her, she has never been this chipper.

"Rob asked me to go home with him for Thanksgiving." I feel my mouth already turn down into a frown but swiftly attempt to lift it up. My hatred for Rob shouldn't interfere with my happiness for Jessa.

"That's nice," I say, closing the door behind me. I walk over to the stereo to turn it down a little.

"I can't believe it. I mean...I thought...well, you know what guys usually want. I thought for sure once I let him have the boom boom," she says, pointing down to her private area just so I understand what she is talking about, as though I wouldn't, "he would be on to the next girl." She flops herself into her chair.

"I'm happy for you. Won't your parents be upset that you aren't going home?" I ask, knowing there is no way I could get away with something like that.

"They understand that I don't want to go back there, plus it's such a short break. I'll see them at Christmas. Maybe Rob will want to come home with me." She quietly contemplates that thought and I envy the smile on her face.

"You really like him, huh?" I hope the disgust is concealed in my voice.

"I do, Sadie. He has completely kicked my ass, in a good way," she laughs. "When it's just me and him, he is so sweet and considerate. I've never had that, Sadie. I've never had a guy who puts my needs before his. You probably don't understand; the guys you usually date probably buy you diamonds and flowers." I forgot that under that hard exterior, Jessa is just a typical girl.

"Not really," I shrug. I don't tell her that the guys I date open the door for me when other people are around and always bring me flowers so people can see them, but when we are alone they have only been worried about one thing. I'm not ready to share with her that when Brady left the show last week and put something of his on hold to spend time with me, that was a first in my life.

"So, what's going on with you and Brady? I heard the guys walked in on you two getting hot and heavy in the studio." She beams over at me.

"Things are...good...great, actually. I really like him," I admit.

"So...have you hit it? Because an ass like that is made for grabbing."

"Jessa!" I scream. "No, we haven't. I'm not ready yet." It surprises me how easy it is talking to her.

"Sadie, can I ask you a question without you getting offended?" her voice lowers and I hope this isn't about my secret.

I nod over at her.

"Are you a virgin?" Her hazel eyes peer over at me through her eyelashes and I can't help but laugh.

"No. Is that what you think? Oh god, Brady probably thinks that, too." A heat wave hits me as guilt erupts in my stomach. That's what Brady meant when he said he wouldn't rush me. Oh Jesus, what am I supposed to do? How do I tell him I'm the furthest thing from that?

"Really? You can tell me, Sadie, I won't tell anyone." Jessa puts her hand on my knee.

"I promise you, Jessa, I'm not a virgin. Actually..." I want to tell her. I miss my girlfriends. The gossip sessions, girls' nights out. I need a friend right now, someone's advice on a boy who has me so wrapped around his finger, it makes it hard to breathe without him around. Pushing my worry aside, I finally tell her, "I have slept with a lot of guys, Jessa."

"You have?" From her reaction, you would have thought I just told her my dad is the president.

"Yeah. I'm afraid to tell Brady. It's killing me keeping him at arm's length. We've only kissed."

"He won't care." She waves it off.

"I'm afraid he will run, especially now that you asked if I'm a virgin. I think he probably assumes I never have as well, and here I'm going to tell him I slept with half the male population at Drayton."

"Sadie, you do know that boy is crazy about you, right? Even Rob told me he has never seen Brady like this over anyone. *Anyone,* Sadie." Oh, I've missed how girlfriends can make you feel so good.

"I'm sure Rob hates that."

"Who gives a shit what Rob says. I'm not sure what his problem with you is, but I'm going to find out."

"I worry he won't wait that long, but it scares me that even if he accepts it, it will only be to sleep with me and then he will be gone. I don't think I can handle that, Jessa. He came into my life so unexpectedly but honestly, I can't imagine it without him now."

"Oh, Sadie. Someone did a number on you, too," she says. Her eyes are so empathetic it makes me want to cry for myself. "Trust him, Sadie. I know it's hard to put yourself out there, but it might be just what you need to find happiness." She remains quiet for a few minutes as I mull over what she is saying. "Just think about it. Brady is one of the good ones, Sadie." She stands up. "Now let's go gorge ourselves on the desserts."

"Jessa?" I get up from the chair, waiting for her to turn around. "Thank you."

"Sadie, I consider you my best friend. I know it's unconventional and we appear to be complete opposites and we've only known each other for a couple months, but I can already see our similarities. Fate must have brought us both here to help each other heal." She actually reaches out and hugs me. Surprise doesn't even explain how stunned I am.

"Jessa, if I didn't know better..."

"Did you think I was a selfish bitch or something?" She laughs and opens our dorm door. I follow her, happy to have her as a friend. Years ago I would have made fun of her, snickering behind her back. Jessa was probably never a selfish bitch like I was.

Chapter 12

Fall is in full force by the time Halloween comes around. On my way to Brady's, I pass college kids in droves, dressed up in costumes. The Invisibles are playing at Ace's tonight, but Brady and I have opted out of wearing costumes. The last few weeks have been amazing. I talk to him at least ten times on any given day. He takes me on dates and we meet at the Student Center for lunch. I have even divulged to him my lack of math skills so he is my new tutor, making the reward system that much better when I get an answer right or score high on a test. Let's just say, I have extra incentives to study harder.

Hands have roamed while our lips are locked. Brady freely smacks my ass when I walk by and never hesitates to take me into his arms. The awkwardness that a new relationship brings has been replaced by the calm security of knowing that he is mine and vice-versa. But the butterflies still run rapid in my body when Brady even grazes my body.

We haven't slept together yet, literally or figuratively. Tonight might change all that. I packed an overnight bag, just in case I'm brave enough to face this. Brady has been patient, never rushing or pushing the limits, letting me take the lead. I'm trying to take Jessa's advice and put my trust in him. God knows he deserves it.

I ring the doorbell since the other three guys live here and I don't feel comfortable just walking in. I hear the big footsteps before Dex opens the door. "Hey Sadie, come on in." He moves aside and lets me through the door.

"I like it," I compliment his green painted body with purple ripped pants and no shirt. He definitely has the body to pull off The Hulk. My eyes rest on his stomach, trying to count the number of grooves. Is there such a thing as an eight pack?

"Thanks, the guys made it easy. Brady's upstairs." He sprints down the basement steps, I assume to get the instruments.

The house still amazes me. Do they hire a cleaning lady like the frat houses? Every time I come here, there isn't one speck of dust anywhere. Not even on all the oak railings going upstairs. Brady's door is closed when I get up there, so I knock softly.

He opens the door and I bust out laughing before walking in. He is dressed in a pair of khaki's with a crease down the middle of each leg and a polo shirt with a sweater tied around his neck. His brown hair resembles a pop star, parted to the side while long layers cover his right eye. He could model for Ralph Lauren on a yacht in the Hamptons the way he looks.

"Nice." I turn my head up to him, confused.

"First off…" He puts his arm around my waist and pulls me into him, shutting the door behind me. His lips find mine in two point two seconds, exploring my mouth. If this is the start of the night, I have no hope of making it back to my dorm later. As sudden as his lips find mine, they disappear. "You trust me right?" He smirks down at me and my stomach turns into knots with the possible intentions of that question. "I got you a costume." Relief washes over me until I see where he's pointing.

On the bed is a neatly folded pile of black clothes. A pair of red Doc Martens boots rest on the floor at the edge of the bed. I can't imagine what is in that pile. "I thought we weren't doing costumes?" I ask, picking up a black tank top from the stack.

"It's Halloween, we have to dress up, Sadie. Funny, right? It's like we are the opposites of who we are." He plops his body on the bed and rests his head in his hand, staring over at me.

"I guess so. I think my naughty witch and sexy nurse costumes had more fabric than this." I hold out the fishnet stockings he has bought me.

"You can't blame me, can you?" When he turns that right side of his lips up, I know I will be wearing it.

"Well…leave and I will change." I wave my hand to the door.

"Come on, baby! I will turn my back. I don't want to miss one second of you in that outfit."

"Fine, turn around," I reluctantly agree, twisting my finger in a circle and Brady turns his back to me, facing his headboard. Leaving my eyes locked on his back, I take off my black boots and skinny jeans. I'm thankful I wore a nice black panty and bra set tonight on the off chance Brady would be peeling them off me.

By the time I'm finished dressing, I have to admit Brady did a good job. Short black mini shirt with a black tank top and a red shirt that has a wide neckline exposing a bare shoulder. The black fishnets run down my legs ending in a bright red pair of boots. This might be the sexiest outfit I have ever worn. Definitely the most revealing.

Straightening out the skirt with both hands, I tell Brady he can turn around. I stare down at myself, taking deep breaths with the hope I can pull this outfit off. My eyes look up at him and in the whole time I have been with him, he has never possessed this look. So much heat radiates from his eyes as they roam up and down my body, I think he could ignite me into flames with the fire that fills his eyes. His desire is like nothing I have seen or felt in my life.

"Jesus, Sadie." I see his Adam's apple rise up and dip back down. "I'm speechless. You're gorgeous...you're sexy...you're so fucking perfect." In two steps he is in front of me. Without my heels, he towers at least a foot over me. "You have no idea how hard it is for me not to grab you and throw you down on my bed right now. It's taking every ounce of self-restraint I have to be this close to you and not be inside of you." He hasn't touched me but we are so close, our breaths rise and fall at the same rate. For the first time, I see small green specks in his brown eyes as they bore into mine.

"Would you want me to dress like this all the time?" I can't help but feel he would prefer me to be more his style.

"No. I would never want you to change, Sadie." His voice is steady. "I like my little preppy girl," he says, tucking a piece of my hair behind my ear.

"Promise?" I display my own insecurity with our differences.

"I promise." He rests his hands on either side of my face. "I hope I don't have to beat too many guys' asses tonight." He brings his lips close to mine but I slightly push him away and he looks at me, puzzled.

"Brady, no fights," I say sternly.

"Alright, no fights," he jokes.

"I'm serious, Brady. I hate fights." I start to pull away but he grabs me back.

"Okay, Sadie. I won't." His voice is serious now and I trust that he knows how serious I am. "Please let me kiss you now." He gradually brings my face to his.

After The Invisibles finish playing, they decide to go celebrate with all the other students down Main Street, where all the bars and clubs are. The streets are packed from building to building with drunken students dressed in some of the most absurd costumes. When we left Brady's, I thought I was dressed slutty but some of these girls take the cake. Trey cat-calls over to a group of four girls dressed as beer cans made out of duct tape, causing them to giggle and wave over to him as they stick their chests out a little more.

One guy passes us only wearing a pizza box around his downtown area. Brady jokingly covers my eyes, bringing me closer to him. I guess he hasn't figured out yet that he is the only one I want to look at. The image of him wearing just a pizza box makes my body tingle in all the right places.

Dex stops us at a small corner bar. Surprisingly, there aren't a ton of people in here. I guess everyone would rather party in the streets. Even with Brady keeping my body firming against his, we were pushed and knocked around just walking the three blocks to get here.

Trey walks over to the girl bartender behind the bar and embraces her in a hug. She appears thrilled to see him, as she wraps her arms around his neck and playfully smacks his back when he lifts her off the ground. Then he whispers something in her ear and she smiles and shoos him away.

Dex leads us to a long table in the back of the bar. When we take our seats, I'm happily situated between Brady and Trey. Rob is thankfully down by Dex with Jessa across from me. Crossing my legs, I pull my skirt down a little bit but it won't budge, resting higher than mid-thigh.

"Don't try to pull that down on the account of me," Trey jokes while staring at my legs.

"Back off my girl, Trey." Brady places his arm across my lap and positions his hand on the top of my right thigh.

"Don't get all paranoid, Carsen. I was just admiring." Trey grabs the pitcher and pours himself a beer.

"Go admire someone else's girl." Brady scoots his chair a little closer and pulls the table over our legs. His tone isn't the same as it was with Grant, which tells me he isn't threatened by Trey but he is with Grant. I can't shake the feeling that Grant and Brady had been close at one time and I'm curious what happened to that relationship.

"So, Gucci, you ready to drink like a real girl?" Rob screams over to me and my body automatically tenses. "Girls that dress like you tonight take down shots."

"Leave her alone, Rob," Jessa shouts over to him but he ignores her and walks up to the bar.

"You don't have to do anything you don't want to do, Sadie," Brady whispers in my ear while he massages my thigh, rubbing his thumb back and forth.

"I just want to shut him up, once and for all," I admit.

"Let me settle this. I will tell him to go to hell." Brady gets up to leave the table.

"No, I will fight my own battle, Brady. Sit down." My voice is sterner than I intend it to be.

"Yes, ma'am." He sits back down and resumes rubbing my thigh. "I like this feisty side of you." He leans in close.

Rob comes back with a round of Jack Daniels. Placing the tray down on the table, he passes them out, positioning one right in front of me.

"Let's go, princess." He knocks his glass against mine and the dark liquid spills over onto the table.

"You can call me Gucci, Chanel, or whatever the hell you want, except that." I tip the shot glass back, downing it like it's water. I don't cough or chase it down.

"You surprise me, Gucci. You want another?" Rob doesn't wait for my answer, he just walks back over to the bar where Trey is now flirting with the bartender.

"Sadie, what are you doing?" Jessa asks quietly across the table.

"Just wait, I can handle this," I reassure her.

Rob comes over again with only two more shots, one for me and one for him.

"Cheers, Gucci." He clinks my drink again and I down it just as fast as the first. This one goes down even easier.

Fifteen minutes later, the shots start to hit my body. My lips are tingling and I'm feeling more relaxed. Trey is with the bartender and Dex found a table of girls who seem to be counting his abs. It's just the four of us: me, Brady, Jessa and Rob. After the showdown of drinks and name callings, Rob has shut his mouth and is paying more attention to Jessa. They are wrapped tightly around each other, having their own private conversation. I still think Rob is an asshole, but the way he lights Jessa up forces me have the tiniest of soft spots for him.

Brady hasn't stopped caressing my leg all night and suddenly all I can concentrate on is his thumb making slow, gentle circles on my thigh, burning through me like the smoldering embers of a fire. His fingers inch further up to the hem of my skirt and they skim just under as his palm stays on top of my skirt. My breath hitches in my throat and I stretch my arm out, massaging the back of his neck, letting my fingers play in his soft brown hair.

He inches his chair closer so we are hip to hip and thigh to thigh. He bends down and kisses my neck. "I want you so bad right now," he whispers, sending chills up my back.

"And...I want you," I whisper in return. As though I just gave him permission, Brady's fingers make their way between my legs, inching closer to my panties. I can barely breathe as my heart starts racing with the anticipation of his fingers finding their destination.

My eyes close automatically with the slightest brush of his fingers on the outside of my silk panties. His fingers tease me for a few minutes before he pushes my lace thong to the side, allowing his fingers to slip between me, revealing how wet I already am.

His lips meet mine and absorb my moan as he plunges two fingers into me. I place my hand on his shoulder, begging him to keep his hand in place. Our tongues explore every part of the other's and Brady's lips become more aggressive as he forces his fingers in and out of me. Right when I can't take it anymore, his thumb finds my clit. He rubs it in small circles and I release the buildup that Brady instilled in me. Unfortunately, it does nothing to fully satisfy me. I know I need him in me, NOW.

Thankfully, the music has gotten louder and more people have found their way into the small bar, so people most likely assume we are just making out. To me, it is him and me and no one else is in this room, but when his fingers make their way out of me, emptiness consumes me.

Pulling his lips off mine, the smirk across Brady's face makes me grin back, turning a slight shade of pink. "That was the hottest thing I have ever experienced," he whispers so no one else hears him.

I slowly nod my head, agreeing with Brady when Rob's obnoxious voice fills my ears. I roll my eyes and Brady laughs.

"Hey, Frat Boy and Joan Jet. Break it up. Another round." He places two more shots in front of us. Brady pushes it back to him and Rob pushes it to me in return.

"Weak, Frat Boy. You take his shot, JJ." I look at the dark liquid in the two shots, taking one in hand and bringing it to my mouth. The smell is nauseating me now. All I want to do is go home with Brady and have him burn through me instead of this alcohol, but I'm not about to step away and lose my footing with Rob. I don't know if it's the alcohol giving me that liquid courage I would see Theo get, but I've had enough of Rob's mouth and I just want him to shut it.

"Alright, so if I down these two shots, I don't want to hear any more names. This will be our truce. I'm sick of it, Rob. I know you perceive me one way but that's not me...at least not anymore." I lean over the table and look right in his eyes.

"Okay...truce. I still think you are going to break my boy's heart when your daddy finds out, but if you down those two shots, I promise never to call you Princess, Gucci or any other goddamn names. On one condition though." He puts up his finger. "No throwing up. You throw up and the bet is off." He takes Jessa's shot from her. "We do them together," he finishes spouting his terms and raises his shot glass to me.

I glance over at Brady who is all smiles, probably hoping the drama will be over between me and Rob. I stare right at Brady as I tip the glass to my lips and down it with the hope he knows I'm doing this for him.

"One down Guc...Sadie," Rob says, stopping himself. That might be the first time I have heard my name cross his lips. Picking up his second shot, he holds it out for us to click glasses. Jessa smiles up at us as I clink Rob's glass. I let it run down my throat, happily not feeling the burn any longer.

"Done." I slam my glass down on the table. "We will see you all later." I grab Brady's hand and yank him up from the seat. His eyebrows scrunch together in confusion, but he slowly follows me away from the table.

"Remember my room is right next door. When I get home, I don't want to hear any 'Oh God, Sadie' or 'Fuck Me, Brady'," Rob's voice bellows throughout the bar, but I ignore him.

The night has turned cold by the time we make it outside. The streets have emptied slightly but now the fellow partiers are stumbling down sidewalks, throwing up on curbsides, and practically having sex on park benches.

"Where are we going?" Brady stops me just outside, cornering me against the building.

"Back to your place," I answer, attempting to give him my most flirtatious eyes.

"Sadie, you have no idea how bad I want to sleep with you. Especially after what just happened in there. I still haven't come down from that, but you have been drinking and when we have our first time, I don't want anything between us. I want to know every moan is pure ecstasy of you feeling me. When you scream my name, I want you to be completely sober." Brady leans in, kissing me briefly before backing away. "I still want you in my bed tonight. I want to wrap my arms around you, hold you close to my chest, and feel your heartbeat against mine." My knees go weak but Brady holds me firm, not allowing me to collapse onto the sidewalk. "Come on, let's go." Intertwining our fingers, he leads me down the road toward his car.

The walk is taking forever and I feel like a pinball between Brady and every object on my right, bouncing back and forth. I don't remember the walk taking this long and the farther we go, the more tired I'm becoming. My feet hurt and these boots are so heavy. I pull my hand out of Brady's and take a seat on the curb, leaning against a wrought iron trash can. My eyes droop and I can't fight it any longer, I just want to sleep.

Big arms pick me up and I nuzzle my head in his neck. That light scent of his cologne and the feel of his crisp linen shirt tell me I'm safe. My arm stretches across his broad shoulders while my hand rests on his neckline, touching his hair. He always takes care of me, he's forever my protector. "I love you, Theo," I mumble before everything goes black.

Chapter 13

The first thing I feel is the dryness of my mouth, as if I just walked a mile in the Sahara Desert without water. Peeking an eye open, I try to decipher my surroundings. Oh shit, I did it again. A guitar rests against the wall in the corner, some band posters fill the walls. It's oddly clean and thankfully no foul smell hits me, otherwise I'm pretty sure I would be running into the bathroom. Then I see the leather jacket hanging off the chair...Brady.

A breath releases from my mouth, realizing that I'm in Brady's room. I feel safe now. Then his words from last night hit me so I stare down at myself. I'm fully dressed although my skirt has risen a little higher, stopping just below my ass.

Brady isn't next me, or even in the room. In fact, it looks like I slept in this bed all by myself. Sadness automatically hits me. This is the way I always wake up, alone. I thought Brady was different, but he didn't even have to sleep with me to not want me the next morning. I sit up and see the water bottle next to my bed with two aspirin. At least he left me a goodbye gift. I put the two white pills in my mouth and unsnap the water bottle. I let the water fill my mouth, swallowing the pain relievers. The cold water tastes so good, I continue drinking it and before I realize, it's empty and I want about ten more bottles.

My clothes are neatly folded on his chair where I left them last night. I strip down from my rocker clothes and replace them on the chair, changing into my jeans and sweater. I pick up and smell Brady's leather jacket one last time before I make my secret retreat. I'm going to miss him.

I know this act well, carrying my shoes in my hand as I tiptoe down the stairs. The sound of every step bounces off the walls of the quiet house. When I get to the bottom, I make the turn down the hallway to go through the kitchen to go out the back door. The aroma of the coffee hits me when I'm about to walk into the large kitchen. Shit, Shit, Shit. I freeze in the doorway. Brady is standing in front of the counter, facing the stove in a pair of pajama pants and a t-shirt. The blue plaid pants rest low on his hips and the strands of his hair are going every which way. *God, he is sexy as hell.*

I turn around, making my way to the front door instead. I hope he won't see me out the kitchen window when I walk along the side of the house to my car.

"Sadie." His gravelly voice hits my ears and I close my eyes, willing the tears away as they threaten just below my eyelids.

I turn around to face him. "Good morning, Brady. Thank you for last night. I guess..." I have to swallow before saying my last words. "See you around," I quietly say, giving a wave of my hand.

"Come have breakfast with me before you go," he requests and I feel his body right against mine. If I turn around, my face will practically touch his chest. Those damn tears are prying to let loose. I can't have breakfast with him; he is different than the others.

"I need to get going, I have a paper to work on," I lie and keep my back to him. Then he rests his hands on my shoulders and one lone tear falls down my face.

"What's wrong, Sadie?" His voice is so quiet and empathetic, I would swear he knows already.

"Why do you want me to stay, Brady?" I hear my voice shake, praying he doesn't.

"Isn't it obvious? You're my girlfriend." With that, he swings me around and sees my face. "Baby, what's wrong?" he asks. He pulls me to him, wrapping me in his arms.

The tears come like rain. Actually, the sounds coming from the back of my throat probably sound like gasps of wind that flow through the air before a tornado hits its mark. I clutch onto the back of his shirt and his hand slowly brushes my hair.

"Shh, baby. Whatever it is, we will figure it out together." His soothing voice brings a feeling of safety. I step back a little, but stay entwined with him.

"You don't understand, Brady. I have to tell you something and I'm pretty sure after I do, you'll want me to leave," I confess, taking a deep breath while biting my lower lip.

"Come have coffee and we'll talk." Brady is silent while he heads to the kitchen. After he pours two cups of coffee, he turns back around. I follow him down the stairs to the studio. "I was afraid we would be interrupted if we stayed in the kitchen."

I take a seat in one of the brown leather chairs but Brady stands in front of me with his hand out. "What?" I ask.

"I want you by me. Whatever you have to tell me, I want to be able to touch and reassure you that nothing changes for me." I put my hand in his and he leads me to the couch. Stretching my legs over his thighs, he stares at me and I know this is the time. I can't hide from my past any longer.

"This morning when I woke up...I thought you were done with me, that you wanted me to leave." I keep my head down so he doesn't notice my tear-stricken face. If I let him see how badly he hurt me, it will just make it worse.

"Last night was," he starts to speak before he takes a deep breath, running his fingers through his hair, "complicated." He sips his coffee, then turns to me again. "It took all my willpower not to stay next to you last night, but that didn't mean I wanted you to sneak out of my house this morning."

"Brady, you don't know me." I shake my head back and forth, staring down at my coffee cup.

"Let's get something straight. There might be things in your past I don't know. Hell, there might even be things in the present I don't know about you, but I know you, Sadie." His brown eyes stare right at me as he slowly speaks.

"Well…" I take another deep breath. I feel like I'm in the middle of a yoga class with how many times I have sucked air in my lungs over the past fifteen minutes.

"You know you don't have to tell me, Sadie. One day, sure, when you want to, but it doesn't matter to me." He rubs circles over my shins.

"Brady, I need you to know. This morning I realized something, and as much as it will kill me if you decide you don't want this, I have to tell you," I say quietly, gaining my composure before starting. "I'm not a virgin."

Brady's laugh fills the room. "I never thought you were a virgin. Is that what this is about?"

"You have been so gentle, never pushing me further than I wanted to go." I bring my knees up to my chest, suddenly embarrassed.

"Sadie, I could tell there was something holding you back and I wanted you to be comfortable," he reassures me and scoots over to me, moving my legs back down across his lap.

"My past is bad, Brady. I have been with a lot of guys." I throw it out there fast with the hope that maybe he won't notice I just called myself a slut.

"Okay." His voice doesn't flinch. I hear or see no hint of disapproval and he isn't backing away from me.

"I mean *a lot,* Brady. I don't remember all their names or most of the experiences because I was usually so wasted. I woke up in guys' beds, not remembering. Most of the time they were gone long before I woke up." My eyes stare at the dark liquid in my hand, not able to see the disapproval in Brady's eyes while I tell him what I'm sure boyfriends fear hearing the most from their girlfriends.

"Okay," he says again, as though I just told him I prefer white bread over wheat.

"Don't you have anything else to say?" I finally let my eyes fall on him. He stares right back at me, continuing to massage my calves, seemingly unaffected.

"Not really. It doesn't bother me as long as I'm the only one you sleep with now." He raises his eyebrows, questioning me.

"You are. I haven't been with anyone for eight months," I admit.

"I assume you are worried if you sleep with me, I'm going to toss you out the next morning?" he asks the question in such a matter of fact manner, it scares me.

"Yeah," I respond quietly.

"You thought I left you this morning, hoping you would sneak out without having to see you?" He continues asking questions regarding my biggest fears, as though he knows my every thought.

"Yeah," I answer, softer.

"Sadie, when you are finally ready to sleep with me, I promise you I won't leave your side the whole night. I will hold you close to me and when you wake up in the morning, it will be my face you see smiling back at you. We will have breakfast and shower, hopefully together." He winks over at me. "Then we will spend the day together. I hope like hell it continues like that day after day. I dream of a time when you are in my bed every night and every morning." He sets his coffee cup on the table, bringing me completely on his lap. "I promise you, Sadie Miller, I will never leave your side, as long as you'll have me." He kisses me, firm and soothing.

"You are really okay with it? I know it's a lot to handle. I regret that part of my life every day, but I was in a dark time, held captive in self-inflicted pain." I rest my head on his shoulder.

"I have to admit, the thought of another guy's hands on you pisses me off, but that is just selfishness on my part. As long as I'm the only guy that makes you quiver when I touch you. The only guy who can kiss those soft red lips whenever I want." He brushes his thumb over my bottom lip. "The only guy allowed to climb on top of you or wrap those gorgeous legs around my waist and have my way with you time and time again. That's all that matters." Brady turns me so I'm straddling him.

"You are, Brady. You are the only guy in my life, present and future. Thank you for understanding." I wrap my arms around his neck while his hands are at my hips, smoothly moving up and down.

"I need an answer to one question though, Sadie." He stares at me with those caramel eyes.

"Of course, anything."

"Who is Theo?"

My stomach drops. I purposely left that part out. I'm not ready to relive the story of that awful night when I became half a person. When I was to blame for someone dying who had been with me my whole life, my other half, my confidant, leaving me alone and abandoned. I know I have to be honest so I say the only thing I can without tears pouring out of my pained eyes.

"Theo... was my twin brother."

Chapter 14

I was thankful that Brady didn't ask how Theo died that day. I assume he knows I'm not ready to tell him that story just yet. The sorrow in his eyes was evident, but he never pushed or asked any further questions. He told me that I mumbled Theo's name that night when he picked me up off the curb. To say I was surprised would be a lie. Theo had taken care of me my whole life. When we got to high school and the parties started with the drinking and drugs, he would always find me somewhere at the end of the night and make sure I made it home.

Theo was no saint; he drank like the rest of us, sometimes even more. He had worse vices, ones that I would try to keep him from. We were a pair, a pair of screwed-up siblings protecting each other from parents who didn't seem to care.

As hard as it is, I try to veer my thoughts away from Theo. Tonight is my time to be happy. Brady is picking me up in a couple minutes to take me away for the weekend. My overnight bag is packed with all of my clothes, toiletries, and a little something special for Brady. After our conversation last Sunday, we haven't had sex yet but I hope this weekend changes that.

I believe Brady whole-heartedly, that he won't leave me after we do. I have never had a guy who has been so affectionate and loving with me.

"Hey, is this it?" Jessa asks, peering down from her loft. "You finally giving up the boom boom?" I had divulged to Jessa that I had revealed my secret to Brady.

"Yeah, I don't think I could hold off anymore even if I wanted to," I confess.

"I don't know how you've gone this long," she replies and climbs down. "Have fun, you definitely deserve it."

"Thank you," I say, smiling over at her. Then there is a knock on our door so I make my way to answer it.

"Please tell me how you always manage to get in the dorm without calling me?" I jokingly smile at him.

"What can I say? I have a way with people," he laughs.

"You sure you don't mean a way with the girls?" I playfully respond.

"Maybe." He shrugs and pulls me into an embrace. "I don't notice who lets me in, my mind is solely set on getting to my beautiful girlfriend." He tightens his arms around me and kisses my neck.

"Sweet talker," I say, giving him a small nudge on his shoulder.

"Dangerous combination. Are you sure you want to go away with him, Sadie?" Jessa teases.

"She doesn't really have a choice. If she denies me, I will take her over my shoulder and drag her there," Brady retorts and picks up my bag.

"No worries...I like my hot, highly complimentary boyfriend." I kiss him on the cheek. "See you later, Jessa." I make my way to the door.

"Have fun you two," she says in a sing-song voice, revealing she knows what we will be doing.

"Don't worry, we will. Keep an eye on my place, will you?" Brady abruptly glances over at Jessa and then back at me. The look between them appears worried, as though they just got caught.

"Your place?" I question.

"You know what I mean." Brady hesitantly stares back at Jessa and she turns around as though nothing just happened. "Our place. I'm the one who keeps it up, the rest of those guys would live in filth if it wasn't for me," he tries to joke, but his laugh sounds forced.

"I always wondered who cleaned that house." I decide to let whatever just happened go. I don't want to ruin this weekend.

"Let's get going, we have a drive ahead of us." Brady places his hand on the small of back, leading me to the door.

"Well...see you Sunday," Jessa calls out to us and grabs her phone from the dresser.

Once we get out to his car, which is parked along the sidewalk again with his hazards on, I ask where we are going.

"You brought your passport, right?" he asks.

"Yes, but where are we going?" I inquire again.

"Canada...Niagara Falls to be exact," he says, smiling up at me as he opens the passenger door.

"Really? I've never been," I exclaim.

Three hours later, we pull up to the border and hand our passports over to the customs agent. She peers down at both of us, examining our pictures. After she asks us a series of questions, she signals Brady to drive ahead and we enter into Canada.

"So, what are we doing now?" I ask.

"Let's find our hotel and then we can do whatever you want." He brings my hand up to his mouth, kissing my fingers that are entwined with his.

"I would be happy staying in the hotel for the rest of the night," I admit.

"Sounds good to me," he says, glancing over at me. "Sadie, I would be immensely happy sightseeing with you during the day and holding you at night. Anything else...would just be a bonus."

"I know Brady but...thank you for saying that," I respond. We pull up to a high-rise hotel in the heart of the city. "This is too nice, Brady."

"Nothing is too nice when it comes to you." He parks the car and turns to me. "Listen, Sadie. This weekend is about us, as a couple. I have plans to pamper and spoil you, so just enjoy yourself. Your smiles and laughs are thanks enough," he says and leans forward, giving me a kiss. "Deal?"

"Alright," I agree, not wanting his lips off of mine. How is this boy still on the market?

We take the elevator up from the parking garage to the lobby. Brady carries both bags, placing them down by the front desk. The hotel is amazing. Giving Brady his distance as he checks in, I watch tourists venture in and out of the huge lobby. Observing the elaborate sculptures and water fountains, I wonder how a college student can afford this place. A twinge of guilt hits me, hoping he isn't going into debt for my benefit. As long as Brady is with me, we could stay in a cardboard box in a dark alley for all I care.

A few minutes later, Brady comes up alongside me, bags in hand. "Ready?" he asks and I nod, taking one more look at the elaborate water fountain.

We make our way to the elevators, travel up to our floor, and walk down the hallway. Brady inserts the keycard and I gasp from the doorway. The whole side of the room is lined with windows that overlook the Falls.

"Babe, can we move inside the room?" Brady asks.

"Oh sorry!" I reply, moving out of the way so he can put the bags down.

"I hope this is okay. If you want your own room, I can get you one. Not that I want you to." He misunderstood why I didn't walk in right away.

"Are you kidding?" I ask, walking over to him. "This is way more than okay and I don't want to stay anywhere you aren't," I finish, leaning up on my tippy toes to kiss him.

"Whew...glad to hear it," he says, releasing a big breath. "You scared me when you didn't want to come in."

"It's the view, how amazing...Brady?" I sigh. I know this must have cost way too much.

"Stop it, Sadie. Do you like it?" he asks.

"Of course."

"That's all that matters. Now come over here with me and appreciate the view." He grabs my hand and guides me to the window.

I stand there, leaning my back against Brady, wondering if the people below are as happy as I am. Brady Carsen is the most amazing guy I have ever known and the fact that he accepts my past makes me appreciate him even more. How I got this lucky I have no idea, but I'm not stupid enough to mess it up.

"Come on, let's get ready for dinner," he says, pulling me away from the view.

"Alright," I agree and walk over to my suitcase.

I shower while Brady stretches out on the bed, grabbing the remote. As the hot water streams down my body, I can't help but wish he was in here with me. Right now, it takes everything in me not to walk out of here and straddle him in bed. As I navigate the razor across my skin, I imagine Brady's hands there. Everything I know about him makes me believe his touch will be soft. That he will slowly relish my body when the time comes. Finishing in the shower, I step out, willing myself to cool down. I'm unsure how I will get through dinner, let alone anything else Brady has planned but I know he put a lot of thought into this so I would never ruin it.

After rubbing lotion across my whole body with the expectation of Brady's lips trailing kisses over it tonight, I put one of the robes on that the hotel supplies for their guests. I exit the bathroom and Brady seems ready to hop in after me but stops abruptly. "You are making this really hard, baby," he says, blatantly appraising my body. "You're naked under there, aren't you?"

"Uh-huh," I respond and bite my bottom lip, giving my best seductive look.

"You're killing me."

"You are the one with all the plans," I joke and turn around to my bag but Brady grabs my wrist and tugs me back to him.

"We will go to dinner, take a walk by the Falls, and then..." he kisses my neck and my hands instantly press against his bare chest. "I'm going to unzip your dress, slowly pulling it off each shoulder, trailing kisses down your body. I will unclasp your bra, letting it fall to the floor. Then I will guide your panties down and watch you step out of them one leg at a time, disposing them on the floor. I will splay your body on this bed and slowly make my way up to you, nibbling, licking, and kissing every area of your body until I capture your mouth. I promise you, I will devour your body, savoring every inch. It will be slow and gentle the first time but after that I won't be able to control myself anymore. I promise you, Sadie, I will fuck you until your voice is hoarse from screaming my name." He kisses my cheek and turns around to the bathroom and I almost pass out from the heat surging through my body.

Once I hear the shower turn on, I lay down on the bed, trying to control my rapid breaths. The anticipation of tonight just got knocked up about twenty notches. After what Brady just said to me, I have no doubt he will satisfy me. I just hope I'm enough for him.

Brady gets out of the shower a few minutes later, wearing only a towel wrapped around his waist. The room starts to feel small, as though it is closing in on me. His body is nothing short of incredible. Beads of water have fallen from his wet hair onto his chest and back and all I want to do is lick off each drop. I'm positioned in the chair in front of the vanity, applying my make-up while sneaking glances Brady's way. At one point, our eyes meet in the mirror and he smirks at me, catching me gawking. This dinner is starting to sound more like torture than enjoyment.

Thankfully, Brady grabs some clothes out of his bag and ventures back into the bathroom. When he emerges, my breath stops and I'm sure my eyes are bugged out of my head. He has on dark charcoal slacks and a crisp white button-down with the top two buttons undone. His dark hair is gelled forward a bit, replacing his rock look with a cover model for GQ magazine.

I stand up, never taking my eyes off of him. "I'm happy you kept these," I admit, pulling on one of his black leather bracelets.

"Really?" he asks, surprised.

"Yes, I love them. Don't get me wrong, this look makes naughty things come to mind," I say, slowly looking him up and down, "but I will always be partial to you in jeans and a t-shirt." I give him a brief kiss on his lips before I grab my dress and go in the bathroom.

"You surprise me, Sadie Miller," Brady calls out before I shut the door.

A half-hour later, I'm finally ready to leave the safe haven of the bathroom. My hair is curled in big ringlets that flow past my shoulders. I'm wearing a black cocktail dress, another request by Brady. The dress is tighter than the red one I wore on our first date, leaving one shoulder bare. It fits snug around each curve of my body, ending a few inches above my knee. I smile as I examine myself in the mirror because a few years ago I would have never been able to pull this look off.

Being away from Brady has calmed my desire a bit, but I know when I open that door and see the blaze in his eyes when he sees me in this dress, it will be back full force.

Exiting the bathroom, Brady stands up from the chair and walks to me. "God Sadie, you always surpass my imagination," he compliments.

"Thank you," I say shyly, looking down.

He kisses my lips and slowly enters his tongue in my mouth before pulling away. "This is going to be the hardest night of my life...at least until we come back here," he says with a wink.

"We don't have to go, you know," I suggest. I would rather stay in and see what luxurious things he has planned for my body.

"As much as this might kill me, we have to go out." He holds out his arm for me to take, escorting me out of the room.

Chapter 15

Luckily, we don't go far for dinner...only up ten floors. The restaurant is located on the top floor of the hotel overlooking the Falls. Since it is nighttime, an array of colored lights illuminate the water cascading over the edge.

"Good evening," a cute redhead greets us at the podium.

"Hello. Carsen," Brady informs her of our reservation.

"Party of two?" she asks and noticeably admires him.

"Yes," Brady confirms and draws me closer to him. I love the way he lets others know I'm with him.

"Follow me," she says. Her voice suddenly becomes curt.

Brady and I follow her to a table along the windows. He pulls my chair back and pushes it to the table before folding himself in his own chair. He sits, leaning back in his chair while he peruses the menu.

Our waiter comes over and I'm thankful it's a man. I don't want to share Brady with any other women tonight. His name is Jonathan, and he's an attractive older man with gray in his hairline. Brady orders a bottle of wine and I'm surprised he not only orders alcohol, but picks a specific wine without ever looking at the list.

"Brady Carsen, who are you?" I ask, smiling over my menu.

"Your white knight, with an edge," he jokes.

"I can't help but think there is a lot more I need to find out about you," I admit.

"You know the true me...that's all that matters." He suddenly becomes distant and stares out the window.

"Did I say something wrong?" I feel as though I hit a nerve with him. His eyes now veer anywhere but me.

"No, of course not, Sadie." His incredible smile comes alive again like nothing just happened. I have a decision to make, whether to put my foot down and demand answers or let it go and enjoy the evening. I decide on the latter.

"This is way too nice, Brady. We could have gone anywhere and I would have been happy." I honestly mean it.

"Then I wouldn't have been able to see you in that dress," he confesses, peering down at my chest and then back up to my eyes.

"And I wouldn't have been able to see you pull off the GQ look," I say and grin back. "In all seriousness though, this is all...too much," I declare.

"Do you think I did this because I think you *expect* this treatment?"

He stares into my eyes.

"Uh-huh." I peek through my eyelashes, embarrassed.

"Sadie, I did this because you *deserve* this, that's all. I booked the suite and dinner reservations because I want you to always remember our first time together. The reason for this trip was because the thought of having you all to myself for the whole weekend was too tempting to pass up. So, truth be told, I'm a selfish bastard," he laughs.

"Thank you, Brady," I say with genuine appreciation.

"You are welcome. Now...end of conversation."

The rest of the dinner we admire the view, eat our dinner, and drink our wine, although I think I drank more than Brady. He maybe had a half a glass. It seems like a waste of money, since the bottle is practically full.

After dinner, Brady steers me by the small of my back to the elevator and presses the lobby button. We stroll by the Falls hand in hand until we finally rest along the railing. Brady wraps his arms around my stomach and pulls me closer as we watch the water descend over the edge of the enormous oval.

Feeling Brady's breath on my neck brings goose bumps across my body. His tight hold of my body pressed against his hard one takes everything I have not to take him right here. As though he can hear my thoughts, he kisses my neck and moves his lips behind my ear before he whispers, "I can't hold off any longer baby, let's go."

His hand moves down and entwines our fingers, guiding me away from the massive waterfall. Our steps seem almost frantic, the hotel so far away. Brady glances over at me a few times, his eyes overflowing with pure lust. I wonder if it will even be possible for us to go slow at this point. I get my answer when the elevator doors close and we are alone in the small space.

Brady pushes me against the wall while his lips dive to my neck and his hands roam my body. He slowly places them on the back of my thighs and I instinctively wrap my legs around him. His body is warm but the tips of his fingers and nose are a little chilled from the cold Canadian temperature. When his cold nose hit my neck, shivers shoot through my body but I don't want him to pull away.

"I don't know if I can keep my promise, baby. It's incredibly hard not to press that stop button and take you right here," Brady says breathlessly as his lips envelop my earlobe, biting slightly.

"Do it, Brady...take me here...now," I beg. I want nothing more than him inside of me.

"No...I will at least get you to our room because once I get you naked, I don't plan on seeing you covered up for a while." Like magic, the doors open to our floor and Brady carries me to our room, never letting me down. With my legs wrapped around him, I lick and bite softly across his neck. With every nibble, he groans and grasps me harder. I know I'm making it harder on him and I'm not sure which one of us wants this more.

We reach the door and I have no idea if anyone saw us, not that I care. Brady opens the door and kicks it shut with his foot. The door bangs hard when it slams shut. "Whoops," Brady says and we both laugh before he tosses me on the bed.

Then our eyes meet and the room is silent. He slowly takes off his jacket and places it on the chair behind him. Brady stares down at me and the way his eyes take me in almost undoes me. He crawls his way up to me and takes my hand, bringing me back up. "Sorry, I got a little out of hand there," he apologizes.

"No need to apologize," I say and swing my leg over his lap, straddling him. I take his earlobe in my mouth and twirl it around with my tongue. His hands mindlessly squeeze and rub my ass. The bulge in his pants is evident as he pulls me closer and small moans escape my mouth.

His hands roam up my back and carefully unzip my dress. Taking the strap down, he kisses my collarbone and down to my shoulder as I pull my arm out. Brady is bound and determined to take his time and I want nothing more than to relax and enjoy this ride with him.

My dress is now scrunched up into a round piece of fabric around my stomach. I realize Brady has entirely too many clothes on. I unbutton his shirt while I stare into his gorgeous brown irises. If my eyes have as much fire in them as his, I know this night will be one I will remember for the rest of my life. He's going to ruin me for all others.

I place both my hands on Brady's toned shoulders and push his shirt off, exposing his bare chest. He leans back, resting on his arms to let me admire him. I bend down and give him small kisses across his stomach and chest and he whimpers when I pull away. Scooting up, he brings me with him and slides his fingers behind my back to relieve me of my bra. Before it hits the bed, Brady's mouth devours my left breast while he massages my right nipple between his fingers, pinching slightly. My body arches to him, desperate for more.

He rolls me over so my back rests on the bed, him on top, making his way down my body. Pulling my dress down over my legs, he tosses it onto the chair with his coat, his eyes never leaving my body. I lie there with my head on the pillow, torn between closing my eyes to enjoy his touch or watching Brady consume my body. He starts to explore me by kissing hip bone to hip bone and pulling my panties down little by little. He cherishes me as though I'm his last present at Christmas.

After he disposes my wet panties, his lips travel up my inner thighs and an electric current travels up to my stomach when his tongue swipes along my inner folds. My reflexes kick in instantly and I place my hands on his head to keep him there, but he takes my hands and holds them out to my sides. "Lose all control, baby. Just relax and enjoy." I stare down at his eyes between my legs and I have no choice but to listen. I lean my head back, closing my eyes. Hearing the little groans coming out of Brady's mouth makes it unbearable for me to hold off. The pressure inside of me intensifies and builds higher and higher. Right when all I need is his fingers in me, he raises his mouth and makes his way to me.

"Sorry, baby. I want us to come together." He positions himself right at my entrance and I can't think of anything but having him inside of me. When I place my hands on his ass, I feel his pants. I tuck my hands between us and push the sides down, first with my hands, finishing with my feet. "I want nothing between us," I whisper.

"Me either, Sadie. Nothing...Between...Us," he says back, staring with such intensity into my eyes, I can't help but feel he is talking about more than just this moment.

He slowly moves into me, taking his time, like he said he would. As he moves in small circles and kisses me gently, the build-up happens so fast I clench harder, willing myself to hold on. Brady's hips start to move more frantically and his tongue more urgently. "God, baby...you are killing me." Brady tips his head back and closes his eyes.

"Please, Brady...I won't be able to hold off much longer," I breathlessly plead for him to tell me it's okay to release the pressure.

"Look at me," he says. He thrusts deeper in me and I oblige. "Go ahead, baby...but I want you to look into my eyes and say my name."

Instantly, I say, "Brady." Staring into his eyes, I watch him come unglued as well.

"Sadie...," he whispers and collapses on top of me.

I wrap my arms around his chest, not wanting him to leave my body just yet. He seems more than willing to stay. He rests on his forearms and gives me small kisses. "You okay?" he asks.

"Better than okay," I respond.

"Me too," he says before he slowly pulls out of me. Rolling me on top of him, he curls me into his body. His hands lazily slide across my arms with his breath tickling my neck. Keeping his promise, I've never felt more cherished and loved.

Brady keeps me naked for the rest of the night. We stay in bed, entwined in the sheets while fingers graze across each other. Our talks have started to bring up more questions regarding our pasts, so I don't know why I'm surprised when he asks me about Theo. I should have expected it.

"Sadie, you don't have to tell me if you don't want to, but what happened to Theo?" Brady asks while his fingers flow through my hair with my head on his stomach. The way he refers to Theo by his first name and not as my brother or my twin, makes me realize how much Brady cares for me.

I sit up and Brady follows, leaning against the headboard. Releasing a couple breaths, I finally start to tell him the story of that fateful night.

"Let me start by saying that Theo was the charismatic one. Where I was shy, he was outgoing. He was funny, smart, and good-looking. A combination for disaster," I say, glancing up at Brady. He holds all three of those characteristics as well but holds himself together much better than Theo. "Anyway, Theo was the younger twin but anyone who knew us would think differently. He protected me in every facet of our lives. In high school, when we started going to parties, all the guys knew not to touch me because of Theo. He was Mr. Popularity and the spineless guys wouldn't dare cross him. So I spent most of my high school holed up in an artist studio with a couple of true friends." Brady pulls me closer and kisses the top of my head.

"I wanted to go to a different college than him. Don't get me wrong, I loved Theo, but I wanted to spread my wings without him near. My parents wouldn't hear of it, demanding we both go to Drayton, their alma mater. Of course, I agreed and Theo and I attended there. I told him before we went that I wanted my space and he reluctantly agreed, but warned if anyone hurt me that it would be the end of him. Luck was on my side when we got placed in dorms on the opposite sides of campus. Other than a few run- ins, Theo and I co-existed in college amicably. But when we both pledged our parents' fraternity and sorority, things got tricky." I pause for a moment. I know I have to tell him my whole story. I would want the same from him.

"There's something I haven't told you yet." I pause, trying to get the courage to tell him. I take a deep breath and continue, "I was kind of overweight in high school and college. Probably about thirty pounds heavier than I am now. So, it's not like the guys were in line waiting for me." I peek my eyes up to him. I want to see his expression. His eyes are filled with sympathy. "So after pledging, we started running into each other more in social settings instead of the planned dinners we would schedule on our own. I don't want to give you the impression we never saw each other. Theo and I were close; we talked about everything, except dating. Well...my dating. We talked about his girl issues plenty." I smile, remembering Theo's revolving door of girlfriends.

"Siblings...I get that," Brady says, making me believe he must have at least one. I smile up at him and bring his hand in my lap to play with his fingers.

"There was this guy, Craig McKnight, who was in Theo's fraternity but he was older than us by two years. He was the first guy to show interest in me, which I thought was the best thing ever. He asked me to a formal and I accepted, which pissed Theo off and he came over to my sorority house, asking me to decline. He told me that I could date anyone, but not someone in his fraternity and definitely not Craig McKnight. I can still recall our conversation," I whisper and a tear falls from my eye.

"Please, Sadie, he's a jackass," Theo begged.

"No, Theo. I told you, you have to let me date."

"I will set you up with anyone else, Sadie. He is only looking for one thing," he argued.

"Am I not attractive enough for a guy to want me, Theo? Am I not hot enough that Craig might actually want to take me on a date?" I spat back, angry that he didn't think a guy would want me for anything other than sex.

"God, Sade, that's not it. There are tons of guys who think you're hot and would love to go out with you. I just get to them first," he joked. I walked over to him and placed my palm on his cheek, "Let me handle it, Theo. If he gets handsy, I will call you...like always."

"Promise me, Sadie," Theo demanded.

"I promise."

"It was a promise I would come to regret making," I say to Brady and wrap my arm around his neck, burying my head.

"Don't tell me anymore, Sadie. It's okay...it can wait." Brady runs his hand over my hair, rocking me back and forth.

"No, I want to tell you. I just need you to hold me, is that okay?" I ask, wiping tears from my eyes. He remains silent, but pulls me closer and firmer against him.

"We went to the formal, which was in some fancy hotel in the city. I drove up with Craig and another couple, who were both older than me. I knew I wasn't going to sleep with him, but I wanted this date more than anything. Craig was the perfect gentleman all evening until the end, when he dangled some room keys in front of my face. I knew what he expected, but I honestly didn't think he would be mad when I denied his advances. I don't know if I was being naïve or just plain stupid, but I agreed to go up to his room. I didn't tell anyone where I was going, except another sorority sister, Lexi. She just winked and told me to have a good time. Once we got in the room, Craig took off his jacket and cornered me. He was probably six foot three inches and two hundred and fifty pounds. I didn't stand a chance against him." Brady's body tenses against mine and I instantly massage his fingers to relax him.

"So, I kept trying to get out, while he kept coming at me. At one point, my dress got ripped from him grabbing it and me pulling away. I don't know what his true intentions were or if he would have gone ahead with it. Just as I thought I had nowhere else to go, I ran into the bathroom and locked the door. Craig pounded on the door, but I pulled my phone out and called the one person I trusted with my life, Theo. He didn't answer the first time but after a text and another call, he picked up, panicked, thinking the worst. Little did he know, he was right."

T - "Where are you Sadie?" he asked, frantic.

Me - "Room 458," I revealed, thankful I noticed it when we walked in.

T - "Just stay locked in the bathroom. You hear me, Sadie?" he asked sternly.

Me - "Yes, please, Theo...hurry." Craig pounded again on the door.

"The door started to bow a little and I worried Craig would get in before Theo could get there. I don't remember how long it was before I heard fighting and yelling, and I knew that Theo had arrived. From what I could hear, there were more guys than just him. I unlocked the door to see Theo hit Craig in the jaw. Craig had Theo in weight but Theo was comparable in height. The two went at it, while some other fraternity brothers tried to get in the middle. It was a combination of Craig's friends and Theo's friends, but they were all fraternity brothers so many of them seemed confused on who to help. The two of them kept going at each other. Theo kept saying to stay the hell away from his sister and Craig kept yelling back that he should stay out of it. I just wanted to curl up and cry. Then Craig said, 'I just wanted to see what screwing a fat chick was like.' And Theo came unglued. He wouldn't stop hitting him. It was a rage I had never seen in him before. He threw himself on top of Craig, throwing punch after punch, until a couple of the guys pulled him off. He eventually shrugged it off, watching Craig for any movement before coming to me." Brady's body is now a ball of knots.

"Theo wrapped his arms around me, pulling me to my feet and took me out of the room. He put me in the backseat of his car and drove me and his date home. He tucked me into my bed and whispered 'Never listen to them, Sadie. You are beautiful and one day you will find the perfect guy, I promise.' I look up at Brady, seeing now that Theo was right. He smiles down at me and wipes a tear from my eye with his thumb.

"The next week, Theo was jumped by Craig and a couple of his friends. They beat him so badly, they put him in a coma. My parents had to sign the papers to turn off the life support machine. The doctors said there was so much damage to his brain, he would most likely never wake up and if he did, the damage was so severe..." I trail off, not able to give all the horrific details.

"Oh Sadie, I'm sorry baby," Brady says, kissing the top of my head.

"That was a year and a half ago." I continue, not wanting to accept his apologies for something that was my fault. "After he died, I stayed home that summer. I tried to release my anger, guilt, and sadness by working out at the gym. That and rarely eating, I ended up losing weight. My parents forced me to go back to Drayton that fall. I wish I would have had a spine and told them it was too painful, but they are firm believers that you jump back on that horse. Craig and two of his friends had gotten arrested and sentenced for manslaughter, but I was still a part of the sorority and it was across the street from the fraternity. Eventually, all I did was get drunk to help me forget. Then guys started showing interest in me since I lost the weight. More wanted to sleep with me, so I let them. Sleeping with them made me feel comforted and safe like I did with Theo. It is hard to understand, but losing him was like half of me disappeared and I was desperately searching to fill the void with every guy who showed interest. Theo and I shared everything. We co-existed through life together, each living the same thing at the same time. He was my brother, my twin, and my best friend." I finish, suddenly feeling sleepy.

Brady must have noticed because he scoots us down on the bed and spoons me from behind. "I'm so sorry you had to go through that, Sadie. I honestly don't know what to say, other than that," he whispers in my ear.

"I know," I yawn.

"Just sleep, beautiful, you are protected now...and always."

I pull his arms closer to me, knotting our fingers before I succumb to sleep.

Chapter 16

The next morning, I wake up to the bright sun of Niagara Falls filtering into the room. I guess we forgot to shut the blinds before falling asleep. I get up to use the bathroom when strong arms tug me back.

"Good morning, gorgeous," Brady sleepily says, resting his arms around my shoulders.

"Good morning, handsome," I mimic back. Oh, how different it feels to have someone there for you in the morning.

"I was going to go get us some coffee and breakfast, but I didn't want you to wake up alone." He stayed in bed this whole time for me. I know at this moment that Brady isn't still carving his way into my heart, he holds the whole thing in his hands.

"Thank you," I say genuinely.

"No need, baby, I'm your boyfriend. Your needs come first," he tells me. I thought my feelings couldn't get any stronger for this 'knight with an edge' as Brady refers to himself. "Now, let's take a shower," he winks. "Then we will go sightseeing. I'm taking you on that boat ride under the falls, maybe play at the casino…" He lists what he has already planned out for our day.

"Sounds great…let's just start with the shower." I'm more than ready to take it easy today and just enjoy being with Brady, especially now that we have made it past this hurdle.

"I'll go warm the water," he says and pushes the sheet off himself. A wide smile crosses my face as I watch his mighty fine naked ass walk into the bathroom.

I throw the sheet off me and check my phone for any messages. I don't know who they would be from, maybe Jessa, I say to make myself feel better. As I walk across the room, I pick up our clothes from last night. I put them on the chair when Brady's cell phone falls out of his pants onto the floor. I contemplate in my mind for all of two seconds if I should go through it, but shake my head no. I know I can trust Brady. I will not diminish what we have by snooping. Just as I set it on the table, a text message comes across from someone named Maura.

M - Hey B, please call me…urgent!

I freeze, not knowing what I should do but decide to place the phone on the table. I walk into the bathroom and Brady is happily humming some song I have never heard while he brushes his teeth. As I walk by the mirror, I catch a glimpse of my naked body. I hurriedly go over to grab the robe from last night and secure it around me tightly. Him seeing me at night by the moonlight is one thing, during the day in florescent lighting is completely another.

Brady frowns. "Hey, why so shy?" he laughs and pulls on the belt around my waist. He undoes the knot and the robe falls open. He lets the toothbrush rest in his mouth, while he places his hands on either side of my stomach to draw me near. Keeping one hand around my waist, he turns around and spits out the toothpaste in order to get rid of the toothbrush.

"I'm going to shower," I say. "You had a text message come through," I admit and his face goes blank.

"Oh," he says and I can tell by his voice that he is wondering if I read it. "Let's get you washed." He spins me around, taking the robe off my shoulders. He opens the shower door and leads me in. I'm taken aback when he follows.

"Brady...I can wash myself," I tell him.

"Remember my promise, Sadie?" he questions and I nod. "We would shower together in the morning and spend the whole day together," he says, reminding me of his promise from that morning after Halloween.

"Okay, well then, I have been dying to get my hands through that hair. Bend down a little," I instruct him.

I place a dollop of shampoo in my palm, rubbing back and forth to get a lather. I scrub it through his dark wavy hair and then rinse it.

"Now my turn," he says and I happily allow him access. "Man, you have a lot of hair," he comments.

"I know, I can do it," I admit, moving my hands up to my scalp.

"Um…no," he places my hands down to rest on his thighs and I try not to move. His excitement is evident from behind me.

After my hair is finally rinsed through, I turn to Brady. I soap his body, appreciating every inch. He in turn washes mine, concentrating on some parts more than others. Just as we are about to finish, I drop the soap and it falls to the shower floor.

"Uh oh…you dropped the soap," Brady jokes and I start to laugh, bending over to pick it up. When I get up, Brady's hands are on my hips and I feel his erection pressed up behind me. "Sadie, you are so beautiful, remember that always. Don't ever think you are anything less than exceptional because in my eyes, you are everything," he whispers in my ear and I can do nothing else but fall back into his arms.

"Now I know why you are such a talented musician; you know how to write lyrics," I giggle.

"You're my inspiration," he admits, his hands grazing my breasts and tweaking each nipple while his mouth descends on my neck. "I love your neck," he says, nibbling it.

I can't control myself any longer so I turn around to him and crash into his lips as he pulls me up against the shower wall. I wrap my arms around his neck and he enters me in one swoop, making me gasp for air.

"Fuck, Sadie…I don't think I will ever have enough of you." His breathing is rapid as he drives into me harder and harder.

"You feel so good, Brady." I grip his neck, trying to meet his every thrust.

"Don't come baby, wait for me, okay," he says. Knowing this is his second time making this request, it must be important to him.

"Yes," I scream and dig my nails into his back.

"Shit babe, I'm going to lose it soon. Show me how bad you want me," he pants.

I pull my body closer to him, wrapping my arms fully around his neck so my breasts are practically in his face and he starts picking me up and down off of him, each time going deeper inside of me.

"I can't....hold...it, please," I plead to Brady.

"Let go, baby...let go," Brady says softly and comes inside of me. He rests my body against the shower wall, trying to catch his breath.

I slowly release my legs and Brady steps back and gets a towel from the rack, holding it open for me. "Thanks." I'm desperate to get covered up. I briefly wonder if I will ever be comfortable being naked in front of him.

I stay in the bathroom to do my hair and make-up while Brady goes to get dressed. The text message comes back to my mind but I quickly disregard it. If this is ever going to work, I need to trust him. He has given me no reason not to. There are secrets in his past, but I will have to give him time like he gave me.

By the time we get to the Maid of the Mist ride, my feet are killing me. Brady has had us traipse all around town to see every nook and cranny of Niagara Falls. It's a beautiful city though and I'm happy to experience it with him. We go up to buy our tickets and Brady looks at me, disappointed.

"What's wrong?"

"You're not wearing white," he deadpans.

"I'm sorry." I look around at the other patrons and see that everyone is in an array of colors. "Am I missing something?" I ask.

"I was just hoping for a little tease," he laughs and stares down at my breasts before meeting my eyes again.

"Brady," I say, playfully slapping him on the shoulder. "I believe you just had your hands on them not six hours ago."

"You should be happy...you have marvelous tits," he whispers in my ear, pulling me into him and kissing my cheek.

"I'm happy, deliriously happy, Brady Carsen," I admit. This is the first time in my whole life that everything seems right. Except for Theo not being here, but for some reason, I can still feel him with me.

"Me too." He winks and walks up to buy our tickets.

That night, I'm able to convince Brady to pick up some sandwiches and junk food and stay in. We sit at the small table and eat the dinner that somehow I still was unable to purchase. I thought I had it; my money was concealed in my hand. Since I ordered before him, I was first to the cash register. Just as I was ready to pass it to the cashier, Brady came up and held his card out. The girl cashier was so enamored with him, she took his card while staring at him the whole time, never even realizing I was there.

"Nice try, baby," he whispered to me.

"One of these days, Brady, I will buy you a meal," I joked and the girl finally looked my way. Now she notices me.

The Falls look amazing all lit up at night. Brady rests back in his chair, looking totally relaxed. His phone hasn't gone off all day and I suddenly wonder if he ever answered that text message.

"What are you thinking about?" he asks me.

"Nothing," I lie. He raises an eyebrow but lets it go.

"Do you want to play strip poker?" he casually questions and tilts back on the two legs of the chair, gulping down his water.

"Um...no," I respond.

"Why not?" he asks.

"Because."

"Because why?"

"Who has the twenty questions now?"

"Payback," he teases and holds his arms out for me. He places me on his lap so that my legs hang over his. "You have an amazing body, Sadie. Please don't hide it from me," he tells me.

"Brady...it's hard. I'm not one of those girls," I stare into my lap, unable to look into his eyes.

He places his finger and thumb around my chin and brings my face up to him. "I'm not sure I understand what you are talking about, but to me, Sadie, you're perfection," he says and a tear slips down my face. "Why are you crying?"

"Because…I love you." I gasp and cover my mouth, shocked I let it slip.

"Finally," Brady starts to laugh. "I've wanted to say it for weeks, but I didn't want to scare you." He places his hands on either side of my face and stares into my emerald eyes. "I.love.you.Sadie.Miller," he says, pausing after every word and then kisses me deeply.

Later that night, we are making love and Brady is exploring my body. I have come to realize he loves to slowly relish every inch. I'm not complaining; I thoroughly enjoy it as well. When he gets to my outer thigh, I tense. There are small light lines of stretch marks from when I lost the weight. Although they are barely visible, I know they're there and I hate it that Brady sees them. He doesn't skip a beat and kisses that area multiple times before coming back up to me. When he kisses me, he says nothing about them, as though they don't exist. I'm in awe of him again. Where did this man come from?

We are naked, wrapped up in a blanket and stretched out on the chaise lounge in front of the windows while firecrackers go off above the Falls. Out of this whole weekend, this is by far the most romantic moment. Brady nuzzles his head close to my ear and I hear his small oohs and ahhs when the bursts of colored flames light up the sky. I know now that I'm completely his.

The room is dark when I open my eyes, the lights of the Falls long gone. I notice first that I'm alone on the chaise. Where is Brady? I see the bathroom light on so I get up to move over to the bed when I hear him talking.

"Maura, I told you. I'm out of town. You will have to do it this time. I'm sorry," he says, his voice angry but compassionate at the same time. "I deal with it all the time."

"I know you have obligations," his voice starts to sound drained.

"Okay...I'll try to call someone, but I can't make any promises."

"Kara? No, I'm not calling her. She has some kind of stalker thing going on with me recently."

"Yeah, I'm with her."

"She's asleep."

"Listen Maura, I'll figure it out but I can't keep doing this. I'll stop by when I get home tomorrow."

I fumble back to the chaise and pretend to be asleep, but Brady doesn't come back out yet. I hear his muffled voice talking to someone else. All I can catch is thank you and that he owes them one. He turns off the light in the bathroom before he opens the door. I close my eyes and try to slow my heartbeat. Brady picks me up off the chaise and places me on the bed before curling up behind me. "God...I hope you love me half as much as I love you. You'll have to in order to deal with this bullshit," he says softly before I eventually feel his body relax into mine.

174

Chapter 17

Brady drops me off at my dorm and walks me to my room. I'm reluctant to leave him; I don't want us to separate. He tells me he will call me tonight, but he appears distracted now. I wish he would let me in, maybe I could help him. He gives me no reason to worry, kissing me before he leaves and telling me how much he loves me. If he is cheating on me, he would win the Oscar for best actor.

I open the door to my room and Jessa isn't there; she must still be at the boys' house. Everything starts to float in my head now that I'm alone. Where is Brady going now? I can't help but feel a little upset that he hasn't shared his problems with me when I have revealed everything to him. I decide if I'm going to be naked around Brady all the time, I better keep my body halfway decent. I look up the schedule for fitness classes and decide to go to a spin class.

On my way there, I notice that Vodka Vince's bench is vacant and I wonder if he ever got a coat or has somewhere to stay during the winter. I get to the class in plenty of time, so I adjust my bike and hop on. Slowly, I let my legs warm up for the work-out they will soon endure. The class starts to fill up and I'm relieved when Kara isn't in attendance. The instructor comes in. A god-like male creature, but way too drill sergeant for me. He hops on his bike and his legs move a mile a minute, while he spouts out facts about the bike and what route we will take. The door opens and a lady in her thirties hurries over to the bike next to me.

"Sorry everyone," she says and puts her water bottle down, climbing on the bike. "It's been one of those days." It takes me a couple seconds before I figure out she's talking to me. "Kids have been crazy, family drama. You don't know about that yet, but you will someday." She smiles over at me. Her hair is up in a sloppy ponytail on the top of her head. Her shorts and shirt are mismatched, as though it took every ounce of energy for her just to get here. I wonder how she will complete the work-out since she already appears exhausted.

"Oh, yeah...I'm sure I will," I respond and smile her way.

"Let's go, you two in the back...stop talking and start pedaling," Mr. Drill Sergeant yells from the front of the class.

"Sorry, Chad," the lady screams out to him over the music. "He only cares about our physical well-being. What about our emotional well-being? Sometimes you just need to vent, ya know?" she continues to talk and I'm torn what to do.

"Anytime now, Professor O'Brien," Chad jokes and winks her way. Apparently they know each other.

"I'll remember this in class on Tuesday," she laughs.

For the rest of the class, this lady to my left entertains us with her quick wit and funny outbursts. She is a spitfire and I instantly want to befriend her. The class ends and she says her goodbye to me, making some joke about how one day I will have to work my ass off to keep up that body. If she only knew.

I don't bother with the locker room today. Instead, I throw Brady's sweatshirt on and head home. A surprise greets me when I walk up the hill. I spot the professor who was just spinning next to me, towering over Vodka Vince. They appear to be in a heated, one-sided argument. Vince seems unfazed by her words and instead of responding, he just stares my way. She looks back and sees me, giving me a tight smile and a small wave of her hand before she shakes her head and storms off.

Brady's words ring in my ear to stay away. Our relationship is going so well; the last thing I want to do is make him angry, but Vince looks almost hopeful that I come over. As I pass him by, I see Professor O'Brien speed off in her black SUV.

"Hey ya, Sadie," he says and I glance up, confused.

"How do you know my name?" I hesitantly ask.

"Grant. That's a good boy, you know?"

"Yes, I know."

"Have a seat, let's chat," he states and pats the seat next to him.

"Thank you," I accept, wondering what on earth we are going to talk about.

"So, Grant says you don't see him much anymore. That you got yourself a possessive boyfriend?" he questions.

"Unfortunately, I haven't seen Grant. I do have a boyfriend, but I wouldn't say he's possessive...just protective." I shrug my shoulders, curious why I'm even having this conversation.

"Protective is good, possessive is not," he deadpans.

"Is Grant your good friend?" I ask.

"I've known him his whole life," he answers.

"Oh," I say, surprised.

"Well, it was nice chatting with you, Sadie." Vince ends the conversation, stands up, and walks down the hill.

"You too, Vince," I call out to him. He turns around, as though shocked I knew his name.

When I get back to my dorm, Jessa is back.

"So, tell me." She is eager to find out the details.

"Absolutely amazing," I sigh, falling into my chair.

"Oh, I'm so happy for you, Sadie. See what happens when you let it all out," she explains.

"I do. I've told Brady everything about Drayton. He knows about the guys, about Craig the loser, and Theo and the fight. You were right, it feels good to have it off my chest," I respond, hoping Brady will feel the same one day and share his secrets with me.

"Yeah, Brady looked completely relaxed when he came home," she discloses. "Then he left right away. I thought maybe he was coming over here."

"Nope, I worked out," I state, knowing he was doing something secretive.

"Oh," she sighs and gives me curious eyes.

"I trust him, Jessa, it's alright. We don't have to be together every minute," I say and place my hand on her knee.

"Oh God, I know. I don't think Brady is the cheating type," she rapidly answers, making sure I don't get the wrong impression. She still looks sad, and for the first time I think she might know something I don't.

I'm studying Algebra when my phone chimes. "Hey baby," I answer.

"Sadie? It's your mother," a woman's voice comes over the phone instead of my boyfriend's.

"Sorry. Hi, Mom," I state. I'm still on the fence about going home for Thanksgiving. I want to stick around here with Brady.

"So, your flight is booked. You get in Thursday morning at ten. Dad will meet you outside after you get your baggage," she gives me my instructions. As much as I wish I could stay here, they would never understand if I don't come home.

"Alright, see you then," I agree, ready to hang up.

"Sweetheart, how is everything going? We haven't talked to you much."

"Fine, everything is fine. I will see you Thursday," I say.

"Okay, well it's just the four of us this year. Me, you, dad, and grandma," she informs me.

"Sounds good…see you then," I say, attempting to end the conversation again.

"I love you, Sadie," she says.

"You too, Mom," I say back and hang up the phone.

I lie in my bed and fiddle with my phone, waiting for it to ring. It never does. Jessa crawls up to her bed and we face each other. She sees it on my face, the disappointment of Brady not calling.

"I'm sure he just got tied up, Sadie. Maybe he has an exam or paper due," she says, trying to make me feel better.

"Thanks, Jessa. I told him I loved him this weekend," I confess.

"You did?" she exclaims, her voice rising a couple octaves. "What did he say back?"

"He said he has wanted to say it for weeks but didn't want to scare me."

"Yeah, I kind of figured," she says.

"You really think he loves me, Jessa?" My insecurity is coming back full force because he hasn't called.

"Not a doubt in my mind, Sadie. That boy is head over heels in love with you...he just...needs to get his shit together." I don't say anything, unsure of what Jessa means. Brady always seems like the most put-together person I know.

My eyes start to droop before my phone dings.

B – Sorry baby, had some last minute stuff. If you're awake, call me. If not, I hope you are dreaming of me. Love you.

I decide not to call him. Instead, I put my phone down and fall asleep.

Chapter 18

I'm awakened by my phone dinging.

B – Good morning, beautiful. It's not the same waking up without you. I have been spoiled beyond repair. Meet me at Student Center at ten? Love you.

Me – See you there! Love you.

After my restless night's sleep, I agree with Brady. Sleeping is hard without him next to me. I sit up to get ready for class. I have an eight a.m. and then I will meet Brady before he walks me to Algebra.

When I get to the Student Center, I'm surprised to find Brady talking with Kara and a pang of jealousy hits me. When he spots me, he stands up and waves good-bye to her. He already has two coffees in his hand as he walks over at me. He rests them at the nearest table before he embraces me and lifts my feet off the ground.

"What a nice hello," I say.

"God...I missed you. How the hell am I supposed to go this whole weekend without you?" he asks. Thanksgiving weekend is going to suck.

"I'm sure you'll manage," I say and glance Kara's way. I wish I could take the words back. I have to remember, I trust him.

"She's starting to freak me out a little. You might have to start a cat fight, baby," he jokes. I see Kara, blatantly staring at us with dislike written all over her face.

"I don't know babe, she might be able to take me. She seems kind of scrappy," I admit and giggle.

"Spend the night tonight," he says, trying to change the topic.

"Okay," I agree. How could I not?

"Great...here's your coffee." He picks it up and hands it to me.

"Thanks," I exclaim, kissing his cheek.

"You can thank me later," he teases.

"Brady, what are doing for Thanksgiving?" I ask.

"Um...I haven't really decided yet. I have some family in town and I've been invited for dinner." His mood comes down a little.

"Are all the guys going home?" I question.

"Yeah, they've all asked me to come but I would never impose."

"What about your parents?" I can't help but dig for information; he has given nothing so far.

"My mom is in Florida with her new husband. I'm not very close with her. My dad isn't going to be around so I don't know. Mrs. Fletcher invited me over to her house, so maybe I'll just swing by there. When do you leave?" he asks, changes the subject. I can't help but feel bad that his parents don't care to spend the holiday with him.

"Thursday morning. Do you want to come home with me?" I ask the question before I can think of the repercussions.

"Really?" he asks disbelievingly.

"Yes, why do you look so surprised?"

"I'm pretty sure your parents won't be happy when they see me come off that plane with you." He smiles at me and a twinge of guilt hits. He's right. But I love him and my parents are going to have to face us at some point.

"Who cares? Come home with me," I beg.

"Are you sure you're ready to deal with this, Sadie?" he asks, and I can't help but feel he has no faith in us.

"Yes, I love you. Either they accept you or lose me," I state and he quirks an eyebrow my way.

He releases a deep breath before saying, "I love you. I would be happy to escort you home for Thanksgiving."

"Thank you, Mr. Carsen," I joke.

That evening, we book the same flight for Brady as I have. He demands to pay, even though I offer. We were lucky there is a seat left since my flight is on Thanksgiving Day. I guess people prefer to get to their destination earlier.

I call my mom to inform her that Brady is coming home with me. She seems hesitant but says okay. She keeps me on the phone, asking me questions about him. What fraternity is he in? What do his parents do? Where does he live? I finally tell her that he is in a band, not a fraternity. I don't know what his parents do, but they seem like jackasses since they don't try to see him on holidays. He has lived here his whole life. She is silent for a minute before happily saying she can't wait to meet him. *Yeah right!*

On Wednesday, we have the house to ourselves, since all the boys and Jessa left to go home. We are downstairs in the recording studio, relaxing on the couch while listening to music. I'm dreading going home but not because of Brady; he will only make it better. I just hope my parents don't scare him away. Like always, Brady can sense when I'm deep in thought.

"It will be fine, baby. I will be on my best behavior. I'll hide my tattoos," he jokes.

"You don't have any tattoos," I laugh. "Why not?" I ask.

He shrugs his shoulders, "Honestly, I've been a zillion times with Trey and Robbie and I have no idea why I haven't gotten one yet."

"Do you think you will ever get one?"

"Maybe," he responds, completely indifferent to the whole conversation. "Enough of this, I only have you to myself for a few more hours." He picks me up and throws me down on my back, climbing on top of me.

"Brady," I sigh.

"Say it babe," he smirks down at me. He started this Monday night.

"Take me," I laugh.

"Is that all you have?" He kisses his favorite spot on my neck, licking up to my earlobe.

"Fuck me?" I giggle. I'm lost on this whole dirty talk thing that he enjoys.

"Love the words, hate the conviction," he says, and I can hear the humor in his voice as his hands roam up my shirt. "Where do you want my hands?"

"Keep going..." I imagine my face is beet red at this point but Brady stares, waiting for me to continue. "Cup my breasts," I finish.

"Or another word?" he asks and I hesitate, clearly embarrassed. "Alright, progress baby. Great progress," he chuckles and continues his way up, bringing my breast out from my lace bra. He pulls up my sweater to expose me. "I love your *tits*," he says, enunciating the word I couldn't say. I giggle in response.

I love the fact that we can go at each other with enormous intensity or playfully joke around while making love.

He engulfs his mouth around my nipple and sucks it into his mouth,

186

while his hand fiddles with my pants. The anticipation of his fingers on me makes my skin burn. I grasp his shirt and he pulls it off himself, grabbing the back collar. My hands make their way to his pants, unbuttoning and unzipping his jeans. With his lips on mine, he tries to shrug them off. Then I push him up so he's sitting on the couch. I slowly get up and take off my sweater and bra, bending down between his legs.

"Take it all off, Sadie. If you are going to suck my cock, I want to see you naked while doing it." His face is serious, and although I can't talk dirty back, when he speaks to me like that, I unravel and turn into a hot, wet mess.

I stand up, slowly pulling my jeans down and revealing my purple cotton panties. When I turn around to let Brady have a slow look, he grabs my ass and bites it hard.

"Ouch," I holler and he laughs.

"Just following directions, babe," he says, rubbing the part of my ass he just bit.

I totally forgot my underwear says 'take a bite' on the back.

"They might be my new favorite panties of yours." He hooks his fingers on the sides and pulls them down my legs. "Just a little love bite, don't worry." He continues to rub it, chuckling to himself.

I bend down between his legs, naked as he requested. This is my first time doing this, and I worry I won't be good at it. That I'll embarrass myself.

"Take it in your hands like this." Brady's hands wrap around mine, showing me exactly how to do it. "Now lick up and down before you wrap your mouth around the top." I follow his directions and hear a moan escape his lips. "Keep doing what you're doing, it feels amazing. But keep moving your hand on my shaft while sucking me. Yeah...just like...that." His head falls back onto the couch and his eyes roll back in pleasure. Hearing the noises coming from his mouth brings a build-up within me. I continue doing what Brady instructed. I feel him get harder and tenser, making me go faster. His moans rise in volume. This is the most erotic thing I have ever experienced. "I'm going to come, baby," he warns me but I stay put, continuing. "Baby..." he warns again. Unable to stop it, he thrusts and I continue to stroke him while he comes in my mouth. I swallow and stare up at him.

"Do you have any idea how fucking fantastic you are? Jesus, Sadie...I almost came the second your warm mouth descended on me," he says, bringing me up. "Now, it's your turn."

He stands up and grabs our clothes, pulling me with him. He walks me up the two flights of stairs to his bedroom, disposing me on his bed. His lips and hands travel my body up and down before resting between my legs. He gets me to where I was last weekend in no time at all, but this time he continues until I come undone from his mouth. Then he wraps himself behind me and we fall asleep.

The next morning, Brady kisses my shoulder up to my neck. "Wake up beautiful, time to see Daddy," he chuckles and pushes the sheets off me.

"Brady…" I sigh. "Ten more minutes," I whine.

"No can do, we have to get to the airport." I hear the zipping of bags.

"Why don't you come to bed with me?" I use my best seductive voice.

"I want to more than anything, but if you are going to take a shower, you have to get up," he says. Sitting up, I see Brady is already dressed and ready. He has on a pair of khakis and a fresh, button-down shirt with a pair of black dress shoes. His hair is gelled like the other night and his wrists bare of the bracelets I love. This is Brady trying to impress my family.

"Oh, no you don't," I say and wag my finger at him.

"What?" he asks sheepishly. "Let's not scare them off the first day," he counters.

"Brady, I want them to meet *you*, the 100% authentic Brady Carsen. Please put your bracelets back on, style your hair the way you want, and for heaven's sake, put your jeans and t-shirt on," I beg.

"Sadie, I feel like you're asking for trouble," he argues.

"Please, Brady. I meant what I said. If they don't like you, it's their problem," I say with finality and walk into the bathroom to take my shower.

When I emerge, Brady is resting against the headboard in his now made bed, strumming on his guitar. I crawl up and kiss him on the nose.

"Happy Thanksgiving," I say.

"Happy Thanksgiving, gorgeous," he responds back. "You better get moving," he instructs.

"I'm happy to see you listened to me." I twist his bracelets around his wrist.

"Well, what can I say? You made a good point but...are you sure, Sadie? I have no problem changing my appearance for the first time I meet them." He brings me onto his lap.

"Never, Brady. I love *you*." I point to his chest.

"Alright, end of discussion. Now get that hot ass up and get ready. I refuse to miss our flight and have your parents think I'm some lazy slacker who didn't have the decency to get their daughter there on time." He slaps my ass when I stand up.

An hour later, we run through the airport, trying to get through security. We might have gotten a little carried away before we left the house. Finally, we get to our gate and are the last two to be seated. I take the middle seat, leaving Brady the aisle.

It's a short flight so we only get a drink. We both order orange juice. I lean against Brady's shoulder and he smiles down to me. I notice his leg is going a mile a minute and he keeps tapping his fingers on his knee.

"Are you okay?" I ask.

"Maybe...a little nervous," he confesses. "I've never met parents... at least not ones I cared if they thought I was good enough for their daughter."

"Relax, Brady, it will be fine," I say, praying to God I'm right. I have no doubt my parents will be nice and cordial to his face. "Their opinion doesn't matter."

"It does to me, Sadie," he admits. When he turns his face to me, I can't help but see the anguish in his eyes.

"Whatever happens...please just be yourself," I request and he nods his head slightly.

We land and file out of the plane. Brady remains quiet and I can't help but feel bad for him; this situation sucks. I squeeze his hand on the way to baggage claim and he turns toward me. "Thank you, Brady," I say.

"For what?" he asks.

"For doing this. I know this is hard for you."

"It's worth it, Sadie. Anything is worth it for you," he says and bends down to kiss me.

"I love you," I whisper.

"I love you," he whispers back.

Chapter 19

Brady and I leave the safety of the airport to wait for my dad outside. I text him to let him know we're here. He pulls up along the curb in his sleek, silver BMW and pops the trunk. As I walk to the back, Brady puts our bags in the car, giving me a sideways glance, confused as to why my dad never got out of the car. I tell Brady to take the front and I sit in the back.

"Hi Dad, this is Brady. Brady, this is my Dad," I make the introductions. My dad looks the same with dirty blond hair brushed to one side and too tanned skin this close to winter.

"Nice to meet you, Brady," my dad says cordially, but I see the disapproving look in his emerald eyes that match mine.

"Nice to meet you, Mr. Miller," Brady politely says and shakes my dad's hand.

"Please, call me Junior," he tells him.

"Okay, thank you for picking us up, Junior," Brady responds back.

"No problem." My dad pulls the car out, making his way to the freeway.

The ride is quiet. My dad asks a few standard questions to Brady. What's your major? Engineering, Brady answers. I'm sure my dad isn't impressed. Business would have made him happy and pre-law would have made him happier, but he doesn't say anything.

I still remember Theo wanting to major in Archeology, but my dad told him he was better suited for political science. He told Theo he wasn't raising a bum of a son who was going to gallivant around the world digging up fossils no one gave a shit about. That with his charismatic personality, he would do better in political science and joking that he might become the president.

We pull up to my house and my dad parks in the garage next to my mom's white Range Rover. I see they still haven't removed Theo's car. It's hidden under a cover a few stalls down. How they pull in and out every day with it there amazes me.

My dad turns to walk into the house while Brady and I get our bags. Brady appears more relaxed now after meeting my dad. My dad's always been a good bull-shitter. He can make anyone feel like they matter. That's why he's in sales.

I give Brady a chaste kiss before we shut the trunk and thank him again for coming here, facing my parents. He takes our bags and my mom opens the door leading to the house. She still has short, blonde hair and an average, thin figure. Her look is typical to a mom who golfs and plays tennis at our country club, attending a few social charity events at my dad's request.

"I thought I heard you," she's exclaims, drying her hands on her apron and walking toward us.

"Hi, Mom," I say, embracing her. She holds me tight against her and I hear her sniffle. *Is she crying?*

"It's so good to have you home." She backs away from me, then sets her attention to Brady. "You must be Brady; it's a pleasure to meet you," she says, placing her hand out for him.

"The pleasure's mine, Mrs. Miller. Thank you for having me," Brady states.

"The honor is all ours. Please, call me Maggie," she remarks. I look at her and see genuine happiness to have me home and meet Brady. I don't notice any judgmental looks his way and I think he notices too. When I glance back at him, he gives me the first authentic smile I've seen since we landed. "Let's get you guys settled." She hurriedly gestures for us to go inside.

The house is still elaborately decorated with statues and paintings worth more than my college tuition. I walk Brady upstairs and show him his room. I'm thankful he has the guest room instead of Theo's old room. The door is shut and I don't plan on going in there this trip either. We lay Brady's bags on the queen-size bed.

"How are you doing?" I ask.

"Fine. Sadie, stop worrying about me. I can handle this," he says, reaching down to cup my face.

"You aren't going to leave me if my parents are jackasses?" I ask.

"No," he laughs. "That's not a deal breaker."

"Okay. Hey, have you found any new ones yet?" I question and grab his hand, leading him out of the room.

"I think I'm in too deep to start thinking about deal breakers." He smirks at me, kissing my forehead.

We enter the hallway and I hear my grandma's voice in the foyer. "Come on," I say, yanking on Brady's arm. "Meet my Grandma Ida. She's the only sane one in the family."

My grandma is a petite, redhead who speaks her mind. "Sadie darling, you look so beautiful," she says, hugging me.

"Hi Grandma Ida, it's good to see you," I reply and take Brady's hand so he is in front of her as well. "Grandma, this is Brady, my boyfriend," I inform her, holding his hand firmly in my own.

"Let go darling, let the boy hug me," she insists, extending her arms.

Brady doesn't flinch, wrapping his arms around my small grandma. "It's nice to meet you, Mrs..."

"Ida, just Ida," she informs him. "Strong and gentle, good mixture." She lets Brady go and winks my way.

"Mom, do you want to rest before dinner?" my dad questions her, trying to get her eyes off of Brady, who smiles back to my grandma, unfazed of her admiring eyes.

"No, I sat on my ass the whole ride here." Brady and I chuckle and my dad rolls his eyes.

"Come on Ida, take a seat in the entertainment room," my mom instructs her.

"Theo, be a dear and get my bag. I have something for Sadie and I brought my sweet potato and apple pies," she turns to my dad and Brady looks my way, confused.

"Sure, Mom," my dad takes her keys and walks out the front door.

"I told you I was going to make the pies, Ida. You didn't need to bring anything." My mom takes my grandma's arm, guiding her into the other room.

"Darling, you can cook a gourmet meal that will melt in your mouth, but I'm not about to eat some store bought pie on Thanksgiving, no matter what high-end bakery you bought it from." Brady and I chuckle, following them.

"My dad is Theo as well. He's Theodore Benjamin Miller, Jr., my brother was the third," I whisper in Brady's ear to clarify the situation. He nods his head to me in understanding.

I'm surprised how much Brady appears to be into football. I guess I never asked but he is sitting in the living room, cheering for the Detroit Lions along with my dad and grandma. My dad was born in Detroit but only lived there until he was three. My biological grandpa died and

Grandma Ida met and married my Grandpa Pat, who brought her and my dad to live here in the east. Every Thanksgiving, they cheer on the Lions because they think of them as their hometown team.

After I peel the potatoes, I sit next to Brady and cozy up to him but he moves over, only holding my hand. I give him a quizzical look and he shifts his eyes to my dad and then back to me. I smile, realizing he wants to be respectful. I guess I should as well.

We all go into the dining room to have dinner. I instruct Brady to sit next to me; my parents are at each end and my grandma across from us. My grandma is right, my mom is a magnificent cook. The golden brown turkey looks juicy and delectable. The potatoes are whipped to perfection with homemade gravy, accompanied by fresh baked rolls and butter shaped into leaves. My mom knows how to entertain, even if it is just us.

"Great job, Mags," my dad compliments her and she gives him a tight smile back. *What was that about?*

"Yes Maggie, it all looks so tasty," my grandma joins in.

"Thank you all, please dig in," she says and motions with her hands out to the table.

We all start to pass the dishes, making small talk about school and my grandma's senior condo building. My dad talks about his clients and my mom fills me in on some former classmates of mine. When dessert arrives, the game of twenty questions starts, all of which are directed toward Brady.

"So Brady, where is your family this holiday?" my dad asks.

"I told Mom, his dad and mom were busy," I answer for him and Brady squeezes my leg under the table.

"Sadie is correct. My mom lives in Florida and my dad wasn't available."

"Where does your mom live in Florida?" my grandma asks.

"Um…Miami," Brady stutters as though he had to think about it.

"I go down to Melbourne Beach during the winter," my grandma adds. "You and Sadie should come down during your holiday break." She smiles up at us. "You could visit your mom while you're down there."

"I'm sure Sadie and I would love to visit you," Brady says, leaving his mother out. I'm afraid there are more issues than I know.

"Come on down. Hell, I'll pay for your ticket if you wear a speedo," she laughs.

"Grandma!" I shriek.

"Mom!" my dad screams while my mom laughs along with my grandma.

"Oh Sadie, you can't keep that all to yourself," she says and winks at Brady, who laughs.

"Brady, what do your parents do?" my dad asks. "My mom is a realtor and my dad is a retired professor," he says. I try not to look surprised; these are things I should have already known.

"Oh, so was your father a professor at Western?" my mom asks.

"Yes, he retired last year." Brady never looks up, moving his pie around on the plate.

"Wait." My dad sets his fork down. "Is your dad Dean Carsen of Contemporary Music?"

"Yes sir, he was," Brady says, his voice is quiet and shaky and I wonder what I'm missing.

"I have a friend whose son went there. He gives your dad credit for his son's success. His name is Jack London, the producer for Heavensky Records."

"Yes, I know him. He used to come by the house sometimes when I was younger," Brady says. "He also attended my dad's retirement ceremony last year."

"Isn't your dad young to already be retired?" my mom inquires.

"He had been teaching there since he got his doctorate so he retired early in order to work on some other projects," he says, void of any emotion.

"Why didn't you follow in his footsteps and pursue music?" my dad asks.

"I wanted something different." Brady shrugs his shoulders.

"But you are in a band, correct?" my dad clarifies.

"Yes, but that is more of a hobby," he answers. I notice Brady is getting exhausted from all of the questions. He isn't an open book when it comes to his family.

"So, I think I'm going to take a year off next year," I blurt out to change the subject for Brady's sake. Let the firing squad direct my way.

"What?" my dad's upset voice asks.

"Dad, it's way too late for me to apply for my Master's. Not to mention, I don't know where I even want to go to school," I answer truthfully.

"You can go back to Drayton. I can pull some strings and get them to accept you." He continues to eat his pie as though he just solved the problem.

"I'm not going back there," I spat.

"Junior, I don't think that's a good idea," my mom chimes in. "Maybe you could go to Western. I'm sure they will understand why you haven't applied yet." She directs her comment to me.

"I don't want to. I want to take a year off," I say, standing firm.

"Is this your doing, Brady?" my dad asks him and I gasp. "What? Are you going to follow him and his band around the country, living in some van and getting drunk?"

"Stop it, Dad," I respond through clenched teeth.

"Ohh...you're in a band. You just keep getting better and better," my grandma adds, smiling at Brady. His eyes are on my dad only.

"I promise you, sir, I have nothing to do with this." Brady removes his hand from my lap.

"What are your plans after graduation?" My dad narrows his eyes at Brady.

"I haven't decided just yet, but I promise you, my band has nothing to do with it." Brady's eyes still haven't left my dad's, as though this is a showdown and Brady doesn't want to show weakness.

"We can discuss these issues later. Can we please just enjoy our Thanksgiving dinner?" my mom requests and everyone quiets down.

After dinner, Brady and I help my mom clean up the dishes and then go for a drive. My mom offers me Theo's keys but I decline, taking her car. It's nice to finally be alone with Brady. I drive him around my hometown, seeing Theo everywhere. We stop at an ice cream place and walk over to a pond, cuddling up on a park bench.

"Sorry for my dad today," I apologize.

"It's okay, baby. I knew he expected the worst." He pulls his arms around my shoulder tighter, kissing the top of my head.

"It isn't right that he said that," I say.

"He is your dad, Sadie. He just wants what's best for you. I want that, too."

We walk back to the car, and Brady drives us back to my parents' house. I'm happy the lights are off when we pull up. We tiptoe up the stairs and Brady kisses me goodnight at my bedroom door. I'm half afraid he will sneak out in the middle of the night so he doesn't have to deal with my parents.

Chapter 20

I walk downstairs, rubbing my eyes. I stop at the bottom when I hear voices in my dad's office. Hovering by the door for a moment, I hear my mom talking with a man who is not my dad. They are discussing Theo's death. My mom informs him that she wants to change all of the paperwork to my name only, instructing him to combine the two accounts. They start saying their good-byes so I scramble into the kitchen where my grandma is sipping her tea at the table.

"Good morning, Sadie dear," she says.

"Good morning, Grandma," I respond.

"Where is that hunk of a boyfriend?" she asks, winking my way.

"I assume he's still sleeping." I go to the cabinet to get a mug for my coffee.

"What are you doing down here then?" she jokes.

"Grandma!" I scold her, laughing.

"We have to be respectful, Ida," Brady's deep voice declares as he enters, and I grab another mug for him.

"Good morning, beautiful. I missed you last night," he whispers in my ear before kissing me on my cheek and then sitting down at the table.

"You didn't have to get dressed on my account," my grandma jokes.

Brady laughs and joins her at the table, "Good morning, Ida."

"Good morning, Brady. I'm glad I caught you both before Theo and Maggie come down." She pushes her tea to the side, waiting for me to join them.

I set Brady's coffee in front of him and take the seat next to him. "What's up, Grandma?" I ask.

"Brady, don't take it personally what Theo did last night. He just wants to protect his family. Hell, if I had a daughter and she came home with you, I would have been scared, too." She shakes her head, imagining it.

"Grandma, it's just outward appearances. I know we seem different but..."

"God Sadie, get over that. I could give a shit about that. Who cares about the clothes or hair, but I do think I would like you better with tattoos," she says and winks at him. "It's the two of you. There is something there that doesn't come around often. God knows Theo and Maggie don't have it. You two have it though. I can't explain it except to say that when you look at each other, everyone else instantly feels like an outsider, as if you two hold some secret they don't know about." She finishes her tea and stands up.

"Don't let Theo bully you, Brady. I raised him to be a prissy bastard; should have kept him in Detroit," she says and ventures out of the room.

"Wise Grandma," Brady says and leans forward.

"Kiss me," I say and he happily obliges.

My mom comes in a few minutes later, after I hear the front door shut. She makes us all breakfast and my dad joins us a little later. We spend the day lounging around the house until my parents tell me that they want us to join them at the country club for dinner. I insist we will not be going but Brady contradicts me, saying we will. I wish he would stop trying to please them.

We enter the dining room and there are way too many familiar faces here. Brady entwines our hands and I smile up at him. He is always so in tune with my feelings. I was upset he took off his bracelets and combed his hair down tonight while sporting a pair of slacks and a button-down shirt. You would think he was born in this crowd if you didn't know better but I hate it. I love him the way he is and I don't want him changing for anyone, especially these people.

My parents work the room, while Brady and I follow behind on the way to our table. I have been coming here for years so I know where we are sitting, but I'm trying to be respectful to my parents. To my amazement, they introduce Brady to every person we come across, but

I'm sure it's because of his new appearance tonight. My grandma talks with a couple of older gentlemen at a table by the front of the room. She already told me she was going to eat there instead of at our table. Her exact words were, 'Sadie, I'm going to try to get lucky, so I'm sitting here rather than with your boring father.' I just laughed and walked away. She loves men, even though I know she misses my Grandpa Pat every day.

Relief washes over me when we finally reach the table. Brady scoots my chair out for me before he sits in his own. My dad follows suit with my mom but she doesn't give him her usual smile, just a curt thank you instead. Something is wrong, but I can't put my finger on it. My mom has always appeared to be enamored with my dad.

Dinner is filled with long streams of silence. I'm still mad at my dad for last night so I refuse to talk, and therefore barely any conversation is spoken. I feel bad for Brady; he looks uncomfortable while glancing over to me every once in a while. Then the unthinkable happens.

"Brady Carsen, is that you?" a gentleman from two tables over calls out.

Brady turns around and an instant frown appears across his face before he quickly replaces it with a fake smile. "Jack, how are you?" He stands up and holds out his hand.

"I'm great. I thought I recognized you. What on earth are you doing here?" His enthusiasm is refreshing to our table.

"I'm here with my girlfriend and her family," Brady answers quietly and turns toward our table. "This is my girlfriend, Sadie Miller." I stand up and shake Jack's hand. "These are her parents. This is Maggie and I think you know her father, Theo."

"Yes, nice to see you again, Theo. Pleasure to meet you, Maggie." Jack shakes everyone's hands.

A couple of heads turn in our direction, wondering how my boyfriend knows the famous Jack London. Everything is who you know and what you have around here.

"Will you accompany me tonight? I play in about an hour. Nothing spectacular, just some ballroom dancing pieces." Jack's appears hopeful.

"I don't think so," Brady answers.

"You should play, Brady. I would love to hear you perform," my mom tries to change his mind.

Brady's eyes veer my way and I smile, encouraging him to do it.

"Alright, maybe a couple," he grudgingly agrees.

"Great. Finish your dinner and I can meet you in forty-five minutes. Sound good?" Jack doesn't wait for the answer. Brady sits back down at the table and I grab his hand under the table. It's clammy and cold and I look at him with confused eyes, but he shakes his head.

"I can't wait to hear you, Brady," my dad says with way too much sarcasm in his voice.

I'm eager to hear Brady play, so I take a seat next to my grandma at her table where I can be right up front. My mom grabs the chair on the other side of me. I have no idea where my dad is, but I really don't care at this point.

Brady and Jack are on stage, fiddling with instruments and talking about what pieces they will play.

"He really is attractive, Sadie," my mom whispers in my ear.

"I know," I exclaim.

"He seems to love you. Do you love him?" she asks.

I stare at my mom, stunned by her question. There is something different about her since I have been home and the change is nice.

"Yes," I nod my head. "I'm sure it's not what you expected from me, but I do love him, Mom."

"I thought so, honey. If you love each other, that's all that matters." Her comment makes me skeptical, like I'm waiting for the other shoe to drop. This is the same woman who told me I should stay away from Kayla Jacobs because her parents couldn't afford to belong to the country club when I was eleven. Shallow and vain have always been qualities my mom possessed.

Brady's voice brings my eyes back to the stage. He is gorgeous in his black slacks and button down. "Good evening, everyone. I'm Brady Carsen," he starts talking and my grandma whistles, making him chuckle into the microphone. The nice shade of pink is refreshing on him.

"I know that none of you know me, but I have known Jack here for quite a number of years. He has asked that I accompany him tonight and I hope you don't mind." He strums his guitar a few times.

"You know when someone comes into your life and you wonder where you were headed before you met them. Your whole life takes on a different meaning and you start living for them, instead of yourself? Well, that happened to me two months ago when Sadie Miller fell into my arms. This is for you, beautiful." His sultry voice fills the room, accompanied by his guitar with "When you Say Nothing at All" by Ronan Keating.

I notice the stares from the corner of my eyes. I want to run up on stage and jump into his arms, showing all of these people that he's mine. For the first time in all of the occasions I have seen Brady sing, his eyes stay open the whole time, staring directly at me. He never looks down at his guitar while he strums along with Jack. It is only the two of us in the room. I imagine if this were a movie, everyone else would fade into a black abyss, leaving a spotlight just on us. As the song draws to a close, Brady puts his guitar down, allowing Jack to fully take over. He walks over and bends down in front of me while taking my hands in my lap and sings solely to me. A tear falls down my cheek and he cups my face to catch the next one with his thumb. When the song is over, he leans forward and kisses me.

"I love you, baby," he whispers in my ear.

Before I can say it back, he is already on stage, grabbing his guitar again. When he turns around again, he gives me his signature wink.

"Sadie...you need to marry that boy before he gets away," my grandma says loudly.

"Thanks, Grandma," I giggle in return, my eyes only on Brady.

The rest of the night, Brady plays a variety of songs with Jack. Numerous songs are popular hits that they turn into an acoustic mix for this stuffy crowd. I happily agree to dance with an older gentleman from our table. He spins me around the dance floor, making it hard to keep up. Brady laughs every time his eyes land on us and I look at him, worried at what I got myself into.

Brady and Jack announce that they are playing their last song, making me grateful. I'm done sharing him, especially with these self-absorbed people that most likely don't appreciate his talent. A familiar, deep voice taps me on the shoulder and asks if I want to dance. I reluctantly stand up and take my father's hand.

He leads me to the dance floor while Brady switches over to the keyboard. He starts playing "Hard to Say I'm Sorry" by Chicago, but for the first time, his song choice is off. The last thing my dad will do is apologize.

"Sadie, I'm not sorry for last night. I see how much you care for him, but he won't be able to give you the life you deserve," he says softly so no one else hears him.

"What kind of life? A happy one?" I sneer at him.

"How will he support you? Eventually those looks will fade."

I roll my eyes. "Dad, Brady is talented and he doesn't rely on his looks. Did you ever think that I don't want someone to support me? I don't want this life," I say, looking around.

"Why the hell not? Was your life so bad, Sadie? Was your closet too full of high- end clothes or your new Mercedes at sixteen that terrible? I can imagine having your college tuition plus spending money must be a nightmare. Did I give you such a horrible life that you want to spit in my face now?" His sarcastic voice escalates but for the first time, I don't care if we make a scene.

"I want someone who loves me and Brady does. He accepts me...fully," I confess.

"Really? Does he know you were a slut in college? How about Theo and why he died? Does he know that you got your brother killed?" he asks me between clenched teeth, tightening his grip. I may have always felt the guilt, but hearing it hurts that much more.

I pull out of his arms and run out of the room. In the hallway, I hear the music stop abruptly. When I get outside, Brady is right behind me, already wrapping his arms around me. "Take me home," I whisper through tears.

"Okay." He whistles for a cab and when we get in, I give the driver my parents' address. Brady holds me the entire ride, not asking any questions.

When we pull up into the drive, I open the door and inform the cab driver to stay and tell Brady to pack his bags.

"No Sadie, I will not let you run from your family on account of me," he says, grabbing both my arms.

"I asked you to take me home," I say.

"You are home Sadie," he answers, confused.

"No, take me back to Western. This is no longer home to me." I run up the stairs to get my bag. I hear Brady's footsteps behind me before entering the room across the hall to get his belongings.

Just as I shut the front door to leave, my mom, dad, and grandma pull up.

"Sadie Marie Miller, you better think twice before leaving here," he screams.

"What are you going to do?" I yell back.

"This life that you hate so much. Let's see you live without the privileges it provides. You walk away and it's gone...all of it," he hisses.

"Relax, Junior," my mom pleads. "Sadie...stay, we can talk about this," she begs.

"What's it going to be, Sadie?" he asks, the ultimatum clear.

"Stop this, Theo," my grandma tries to step in. "Brady, talk to her," she instructs him.

"Sadie...let's go inside and talk," Brady tries to reason with me.

"Listen to him, Sadie. I don't think you realize what you are deciding here," my dad responds.

"Do you really blame me?" I ask. "You think I killed Theo," I state, my voice shaking. My mom and grandma gasp between us.

"Of course he doesn't, darling," my grandma speaks up.

"Do you?" I demand and my dad remains silent, standing in the headlights of the cab. "Take it, take everything. I don't care," I yell and get in the waiting car.

"Sadie...just so we are clear. Your car, your credit cards, your tuition. All of it, gone." My dad stands outside the cab door now as Brady stands in limbo between us.

"I don't want anything from you," I tell him, looking straight ahead.

"No, Sadie please, don't do this." My mom comes around the other side of the car, begging me through the window.

"We can deal with this darling, come in the house," my grandma begs.

"I'm sorry, Mom...Grandma. I love you. Good-bye," I say and Brady enters the cab in silence.

Brady tells the cab driver to pull away and I curl into his chest, not looking back. I sob into his shirt, hearing my mom's screams get fainter with every minute.

Chapter 21

My dad kept his word. My car was towed this morning and my credit cards were cut off. I know my tuition is paid up through the semester, and hopefully I will be able to get a loan or assistance to pay for my last semester. As I look up financial aid information on my laptop, Brady comes into his room. I see the guilt in his eyes; he blames himself.

"Baby, don't worry about this now. I will help you figure it out," he says and closes the laptop, which technically belongs to my dad.

"Okay," I agree and curl back up in a ball on the bed.

"Stay with me, Sadie?" he requests.

"I am staying with you," I respond.

"No, move in here with me. I'll take care of you," he kindly offers.

"No, Brady, but thank you. You and the guys have your place. I still have the dorm until Christmas break."

"I want you here...with me. I want to wake up to you every morning and kiss you goodnight before I fall asleep," he says, kissing my neck.

"I can't ask you to do that, Brady." I move my hands to the back of his head, holding his lips to the back of my neck.

"Please, Sadie. Just think about it?" he asks and moves his lips behind my ear.

"Okay...I'll think about it," I finally concede. It takes everything inside of me not to agree to move in with him.

Brady is lightly snoring next to me, while all of the things I will have to do consume my mind. Get a job, get a loan, and find a place to live. The list is unending and suddenly I feel very overwhelmed and unable to sleep. I get up out of bed, tiptoe out of the room, and begin making my way downstairs. The door to my right catches my eye and I walk over, slowly turning the knob. It's locked. Was Brady telling me the truth about it just being storage stuff? Before we can continue moving forward, he has to trust me with his secrets. I recall the exchange he had with Jessa before we left for Niagara Falls, when he told her to take care of his house.

Curiosity overcomes me and I travel down the hall to the other bedrooms. With the boys out of town, I peruse their rooms. Rob's is a disaster with clothes strewn on top of a chair and guitar picks in every nook and cranny. Dex is fairly neat, although his bed isn't made and there is an inch of dust on every piece of furniture. Trey's seems to be in the best shape. His bed is made, but there are numerous water and beer bottles on his dresser and nightstand. I walk down the hallway, and after checking to see that Brady is still snoring, I decide to make my way downstairs.

I never noticed all of the nice, older furniture before. The house isn't filled with mismatched items from thrift stores or garage sales. Even the carpet is void of stains. Deciding to get a bottle of water, I dig my phone out of my purse and take a seat on one of the nice couches in the living room.

Scrolling through my phone, I see the missed calls from my mom and grandma. My mom sent me a few texts. She tells me not to worry about my dad, that it will work out and I won't be cut off. I guess this was before he took my car this morning. I don't bother to listen to the voicemails; nothing will change my mind.

They fail to understand that after Theo's death, those things aren't important to me anymore. I don't want a slew of houses with large walk-in closets. I want to love my children and know their likes and dislikes. I want to be the one who tucks them in at night and wishes them good morning with kisses and hugs. The day I buried Theo, I promised myself I would live for happiness and love, not money and prestige.

I flip through the pictures on my phone. The urge today is greater than previous days. I need to see his face. My lips curl up as soon as I see that smirk of a smile. I snapped the picture a few days before the incident, when he was sprawled out on my bed complaining about some course. I wish I could remember the conversation, but I was too preoccupied with what I was going to wear to that formal. The feeling of failing him overpowers me and one tear drops down, resting on the edge of my nose. Then another one. Soon my face is drenched with wetness as I stare at those emerald eyes staring back at me, not unlike my own. I almost feel his arms around my shoulders, telling me he's with me. That he will always be there for me. Even now I feel him watching over me, protecting me.

I wake up in Brady's bed. I assume he found me downstairs and brought me up to his room. I grab one of his sweatshirts and make my way to the kitchen, where I hear music. Brady sits at the kitchen table, reading the newspaper and tapping his fingers on the table to the beat of the music.

"Good morning, beautiful," he says, smiling when his eyes find me in the doorway.

"Thanks for bringing me upstairs," I reply, sitting across from him.

"I prefer you in bed with me," he grins. "Coffee?"

"I can get it." I stand up and walk toward the counter but Brady cuts me off, chuckling to himself. "Really, babe, let me get it."

"Here you go," he turns around, holding my cup.

"Thank you," I say and rise to my tip toes to give him a kiss.

"Always," he responds and walks back over to his seat. "So, we have about four hours before the roommates start coming back. What do you want to do?"

"Hmm..." I put my finger up to my lips, jokingly contemplating.

"Me too. Come on over here," he instructs. I walk over and straddle him on the kitchen chair. We haven't had sex since before we left for my parents. I appreciate Brady giving me the space after we got back, but there is nothing I want more than to be with him.

"Lose the shirt," I command.

Brady's eyes sparkle as he hurriedly takes his shirt off and tosses it to the floor.

"What next?" he asks eagerly, clearly enjoying my assertiveness.

"Take my shirt off." He happily takes the hem of my shirt and tears it over my head.

"No bra." He smiles widely. "Could this morning get any better?" he comments. "Next, baby?"

"Please touch me," I beg and lean down to kiss him. His hands go right to my breasts, kneading and pushing them as I moan into his mouth.

"Do you want me to suck them?" he asks. I nod my head and he ducks his head down, wrapping his mouth around one of my nipples, sucking it into his mouth.

"God, Brady, more. I need more," I pant.

"Like?" he questions, taking a break from my breasts. He peeks up at me through his eyelashes.

"I need you...inside of me," I confess.

"What do you need inside of you, baby?" he asks, with his hands already on their way up my thighs, venturing to the inside of my boxers.

"Your..." I trail off, too embarrassed to finish.

"Say it, baby, and it's yours." Brady's fingers peek through my shorts and now graze over my clit before he inserts one finger in. When I still don't answer, he inserts a second one, making me buck into his hand.

"Your cock...I need your cock in me," I answer him breathlessly and a smile consumes his face.

"It's ready, come and get it," he instructs, leaning back in the chair. I pull down his pajama pants and expose his erect hardness while he slides my boxers to the side. When I climb entirely on top of him, letting him fill me, I gasp from the pleasure. "Shit, you feel good."

Brady pushes me back a little, while I move up and down over him. He plays with my breasts, thumbing my already taut nipples. Moving his hands to my face, he inserts a finger in my mouth and I automatically suck it in response.

"Fuck me, Brady!" I scream and he brings his hips up to meet mine. As I go down, he comes up. We are in perfect harmony with each other. I can't hold the ecstasy back anymore; it is right on the edge, teeter-tottering back and forth.

"I love fucking you, baby," he shouts through erratic breathing. With that, I fall into rapture and grip his shoulders while he slows his movements into gentle circles, enabling me to enjoy the thrilling waves of pleasure.

"Now, it's your turn. I want to see you come," I whisper to him and he starts going faster again, guiding my hips up and down, harder and harder, before he stills inside of me and his head falls on my shoulder.

"Shit that was hot, baby." Brady hugs me to him, kissing my neck.

"I'd say it was," a deep voice calls out in the doorway and I freeze while Brady pulls me closer to him, trying to shield me from Rob.

"Get the fuck out, Robbie," Brady yells and throws a spoon at him.

"I'm going," he says, backing away from the door. "I think I have to get Jessa or solve this problem on my own," he mumbles to himself, walking upstairs.

I anxiously get up and throw my shirt over my head, tossing Brady his. I imagine my face is beet red from the heat I feel across my cheeks.

"Just think. If you move in, I could always kick him out." Brady pulls me into his chest.

"How could you kick him out?" I ask. I believe I already know the answer, but I want Brady to tell me.

"Shit...," he says, shaking his head, obviously upset with himself. "Sit down, Sadie," he requests.

I take the chair across from him and Brady brings my coffee to me. He tells me that it's his house, the house he grew up in. His dad left to live somewhere else and gave him the house, free and clear, no mortgage. He only charges the guys the bare minimum to pay for utilities and a cleaning lady…mystery solved. When I ask him why he kept it from me, he admits he was worried I wouldn't like him for him but rather what he owned. Jessa knows because Rob told her and he wishes it wouldn't have been like that, but he didn't know what to do. As much as it hurts thinking that Brady thought I could have been a materialistic bitch, at the same time, I understand why he was scared. A few years ago, that's exactly what I was.

After he reveals the truth regarding the house, Brady appears happier, as though a burden is lifted off his shoulders. Unfortunately, it brings about a whole new set of questions. I need to know more about Brady's parents. Brady says his dad is around, but I never see him and he never talks about him. From what I understood from the conversation with my dad, he retired last year after being the dean of contemporary music. I desperately want to google him, but I'm torn between waiting for Brady to tell me and finding out on my own.

Chapter 22

My mom has called a couple dozen times today. I still haven't picked up; I don't even want to mend this fight. After Brady dropped me off last night, I told Jessa the whole sordid story. All she said was 'Fuck him. I know he's your dad, Sadie, but what a jackass.' I couldn't agree with her more. Then she took me to the cafeteria and we gorged on junk food.

I have already been to the financial aid office this morning, where I was informed that I don't qualify because of my parents' income. They told me that a student loan would be the best way, handing me a pamphlet with some names and numbers. After calling a few numbers, I found out that it will be virtually impossible to have the paperwork done since I only have less than two months before second semester starts. I'm probably going to have to take my final semester off, and maybe everything will be handled by the summer. Then I can graduate next winter.

I look at my watch and notice I'm running late to meet Brady. He wants to go with me to spin class. I think he's just worried about me. When he dropped me off last night, he begged me for ten minutes to pack my bags and come home with him. I insisted that I have to do this on my own. I refuse to go from my dad to Brady.

Swinging my bag over my shoulder, I leave the dorm, practically running to the rec center. When I reach the hill, Vodka Vince is sitting on his usual bench.

"Hiya, Sadie," he says.

"Hi Vince, how are you today?" I ask, trying to sound unrushed.

"Seen Grant lately?" he questions. Now that he mentions it, I haven't. Ever since Brady and I got serious, I haven't gone up to the sixth floor or seen him anywhere else.

"No, I haven't," I admit.

"Because of your boyfriend?" For the first time, Vince stares right at me. Something seems different about him today.

"I guess. I spend a lot of time with him," I say, shrugging.

"Do you love your boyfriend?" Why is he asking me such personal questions?

"Yes," I honestly answer.

"That's good." He smiles. "Well, I see you're on your way somewhere, get to it." He motions with his hand to continue down the sidewalk.

"It was nice talking with you, Vince. Take care," I say, breaking out into a full sprint to get to the rec center on time.

I get to the doors of the building and run right into Brady's chest. "I was getting worried," he says, catching me by both arms.

"Sorry...I got held up," I respond, trying to catch my breath.

"It's almost starting, let's go." I'm happy he doesn't ask me for more details about my tardiness. I know how he feels about Vince.

We enter the room and the instructor is already there. I'm thankful it isn't Chad again, but am disappointed that it's some girl in tight, spandex biker shorts and a small sports bra. She has a spectacular body, all tanned and toned. I notice her eyes following Brady from the door to our bikes. It isn't the first time I have seen that look from the female population when it comes to my boyfriend. Can I really be offended? They have good taste.

I help Brady set up his bike and he admires me as I'm bent over by making sly comments about my ass. I playfully push him back and he exaggerates losing his footing. We get on our bikes and he starts to change the gears, and I have a feeling this is not his first spin class.

"Brady Carsen!" I quietly chastise him.

"What?" He looks at me sheepishly, knowing he just got caught. "It was too enjoyable, watching you bend over and press your ass against me," he jokes.

"I thought I heard your annoying laugh," a female says, stopping beside his bike.

"Maura!" Brady announces, obviously surprised to see her.

"Why on earth are you taking this class? Shouldn't you be running on the hamster wheel or something?" she teases him and when she finally comes into view, I'm surprised to see who it is.

"I'm here with my girlfriend," he tells her and leans back on his bike, revealing me.

"Sadie?" she asks, and I have never been so happy to hear my name.

"Well obviously, Maura," he says, sounding annoyed.

"Sadie." He looks over at me. "This is my sister, Maura," he introduces. "Maura, this is Sadie, my girlfriend," he finishes the introductions.

"Shut up! You're his girlfriend?" she screeches.

"Yes," I answer, just as shocked.

"Maura, what the f...?" Brady questions her tone.

"Oh, stop worrying so much. I met her last week at a class. Well, I technically didn't meet her but we chatted.

"I can only imagine what about," Brady says, rolling his eyes.

"It would have been a lot more if I would have known she was the infamous Sadie," Maura answers and takes the bike on the other side of me.

"Just keep the stories to yourself," Brady tells her seriously, giving Maura a look.

"So, Sadie. Tell me about yourself." She turns my way, ignoring Brady.

"Um…" I stutter. Then the instructor interrupts us, starting the class. I can't help the feeling of relief that flows through me. How do you tell your boyfriend's sister you just got disowned by your parents?

"Pst…Brady," she loudly whispers.

"What?" Brady answers with annoyance in his voice.

"I need to talk to you after class, something about…" Brady nods his head before she finishes, and then she looks over at me and gives me a small smile before facing forward to concentrate on the class.

I have to admit, watching my amazing boyfriend do a spin class leaves me breathless in more than one way. I want to grab him and run into the locker room to have my way with him in the shower. His silence throughout the class surprises me. Night and day to him in the bedroom. He makes no grunts or noises, just steadily completing the work out. If it wasn't for his drenched shirt and body, you would have thought the spin class was nothing to him.

After the class, I grab my towel and rub the sweat off me. Sipping out of my water bottle, I notice the playful Brady is gone, replaced by a very serious one. He makes no jokes about my shirt clinging to me, outlining my body. Quietly, he sips his water and stares at Maura. They seem to be having a conversation with no words. Theo and I could do that; I had always thought it was a twin thing but I guess it's a sibling thing. Before I can ask any questions, Maura says, "It was nice meeting you, Sadie. Brady should bring you over to the house so you can meet the kids and hubby." She embraces me into a sweaty hug and turns to Brady, doing the same before leaving.

"Sorry about that," Brady apologizes.

"Why would you be sorry? What a coincidence that I met your sister last week," I remark, following Brady out the doors.

"She's a little...excitable." He stands to the side of the door, allowing me to go first. When we get out to the hallway, I see Kara talking with Maura and I know my shoulders slump and I let out an exasperated breath.

"Oh, look who it is." I roll my eyes in annoyance. "She knows your sister?"

"Yeah, well...remember I told you, she's a family friend," Brady answers and walks us over to the last place I want to go.

"Brady!" she exclaims, swiftly making her way over to us, embracing him. "I feel like I haven't seen you in forever."

He slowly removes her arms from his neck and says, "You remember Sadie, my girlfriend?" He reaches his arm around my waist. One of the things I love about Brady is that he's always forthcoming to people that we are a couple.

"Hi, Sadie," she leers my way and gives me a once-over before her eyes land back on him.

"So I hear you are playing Grant's frat party this weekend?" she asks and my head shoots up to him as he glances down at me.

"Oh, how is Grant?" Maura questions Brady.

"I'm only playing it because of the money. Rob booked it. If it was up to me, I wouldn't play for those fucking douches." Brady's voice is full of hostility.

"You really need to let it go, Brady," Maura says sympathetically and Brady gives her the same shut-your-mouth look that he did earlier.

"Anyway," she says, clearly irritated. "I need to get back to the kiddos. I swear girls, when you become a mother you will wonder what you did with all that time before them," she jokes, waving good-bye.

"Bye, Maura," all three of us say in unison.

"So, can I come to the party?" Kara eagerly asks, and I wonder why she's asking Brady's permission.

"Call Grant, I'm sure he'll let you in," Brady says with no emotion.

"But I could just come with you and the band," she whines and it dawns on me that she is asking Brady to bring her to the party. *Um…no.*

"Kara, you can ask one of the guys if you want. Sadie and I will only be there to play and then we are leaving right after," he reveals and I look up at him, surprised for the second time in this short conversation. Not only did I just find out I'm going to a frat party, but Brady has already decided how long I'll be staying as well.

"You used to always take me. Remember, Brady? It was always you and me." She glares at me.

"Well, now it's me and Brady. I'm sorry Kara, but we have to get going." I loop my arm through Brady's, walking us forward. "See you later."

We get down the hall and Brady leans into my ear, "I like this jealous side of you."

"There's something about her Brady I don't like," I admit.

"She's just a young girl, trying to be something she's not," he says. He is blind to her infatuation. "Come home with me and show me how much I'm yours," he requests.

"Gladly," I say and stop outside the doors to kiss him.

Chapter 23

I finally pick up my phone when my mom calls me for the millionth time. It's Wednesday and I have punished her unfairly for too long. She's not the one I have a problem with.

"Hi, Mom," I answer.

"Sadie," she sighs and releases a breath. "Finally."

"I'm sorry, Mom, I should have called you," I apologize.

"You should have or at least answered your phone. But now that I have you, I don't care. How are you?" she asks.

"Okay." I respond, letting her have her say so I can get off the phone.

"I put money into your account today," she reveals.

"You didn't have to. I will manage but... thank you," I quietly express my appreciation.

"Yes, I did. Listen sweetie, I'm coming out this weekend. Don't try to talk me out of it. I have some things to talk to you about. I won't be there until Saturday afternoon. I'm only staying one night and then coming back. Your dad thinks I'm going with Audrey to the city for the night."

"Mom, really, it isn't necessary. I'm going to get a job..."

"Sadie, I'm coming. You will not talk me out of this. Please be at your dorm around two o'clock," she interrupts me.

"Okay, Mom," I grudgingly agree.

"Great, see you then. Love you, Sadie," she says.

"Bye, Mom," I reply.

The whole conversation is short and weird, and I can't imagine what she possibly has to talk to me about. My whole life has been her fulfilling my dad's wishes. He is the alpha male and head of our household. You don't dare cross him and I did just that. He holds the checkbook and doles out the money to what and whom he sees fit. My mom has always been given an allowance every month and nothing more. I remember Theo and I sitting at the top of the stairs when we were little, hearing my parents fight over what she spent.

My mom had grown up with money. She was the heir to a multi-million dollar real estate company. But when her father got sick, he had to assign the responsibilities to someone and ultimately signed the company over. Since her mother had died during childbirth and my mom was an only child, there was no one else to leave it to. My grandpa chose my dad, assuming he would be a better fit than his own daughter. That was ten years ago and my dad has reaped the rewards ever since. Obviously, my dad was an educated, wealthy man but after grandpa left him the already established company, he turned filthy rich and instantly changed into someone I didn't recognize.

Regardless of my dad's personality shift, my mom has remained on his arm, always smiling and laughing at his jokes while following his directives as though she was his employee. They would go on vacations, leaving Theo and me with our grandma on holidays, always buying us anything we wanted to make up for abandoning us. So I'm curious to why now she is so concerned about me.

I try to push that aside; I can deal with it this weekend. I have an errand to run. Jessa and I went to the thrift store today and I bought Vince a gift. It's gotten cold and I honestly can't stand the thought of him sleeping outside without a jacket. Walking up the hill, I spot him on his usual bench overlooking the field. When I get closer, I see Grant next to him, talking.

Going back and forth in my head if I should stay or go, I decide to stop. Grant gave me no reason to feel uncomfortable talking to him. "Hi, Vince. Hi, Grant," I say, giving a wave of my hand.

"Hiya, Sadie," Vince says in return.

"Oh...hey, Sadie," Grant states.

"I just wanted to drop this off for you, Vince." I hand him the parka I bought, along with gloves, a scarf, and a hat.

"Thank you, Sadie." Vince voice sounds grateful, making me relieved. I didn't want to offend him.

"That was nice of you," Grant adds, not looking straight at me.

"Take a seat." Vince shrugs the jacket on and pats the seat next to him.

"I didn't know you knew one another?" Grant questions and I nod my head.

"This is on my way to and from the dorm so..." I trail off.

"Oh. Brady's okay with it?" he whispers in my ear so Vince doesn't hear and I briefly wonder why he cares.

"Probably not, but that isn't going to stop me," I reply.

"Brady's really private, Sadie. I think you should tell him," he says and I quirk an eyebrow in confusion.

"So, Vince. I should probably get going, but I'll be on my way back in a couple hours. Can I bring you a coffee or anything?" I ask, ignoring Grant. Since when does he care about what Brady thinks? The whole dynamic between him, Brady, and Kara is increasingly getting on my nerves.

"I'm fine, Sadie. This jacket is more than enough." He pats my knee in a fatherly manner and I get up to walk away.

I make it a few steps away when I hear Grant's voice, "Hold up a second, Sadie."

I turn around, finding Grant lightly jogging my way. "What's up,

Grant?"

"I didn't mean anything back there. It's just...I know you and Brady are a couple, and I know the way he feels about Vince."

"How do you know that, Grant? I thought you didn't like each other. Remember telling me to stay away from him?" I hammer question after question, mostly because I'm baffled by the whole situation.

"Like I said, Brady's private. It's his thing to tell you. I don't want to interfere but believe it or not, even with our differences, I do care about him," he admits with concern in his voice.

"Okay," I draw out, clearly annoyed.

"Sadie, I wish I could tell you more, but," he looks back at Vince, who takes a sip of alcohol from a small flask, "I can't." His face looks truly pained and for the first time since I met Brady, I'm mad at him. I have been letting all the secrets go, believing that when he is ready he will tell me. Now, I feel like I'm the only one in the dark, and the fact that Kara knows more about him than me makes this unbearable.

"Thanks, Grant. I will talk with Brady," I respond and start to walk away.

"I should have never told you to stay away from him. He really is a good guy, just needs to be reassured of it occasionally" he calls out to my back.

I go to my class and instead of meeting Brady at the Student Center, I text him, telling him I have a meeting at the bank for a loan. I can't see him right now, afraid of what would come out of my mouth. I walk to a coffee house off campus. I just need to get away from everything. I have been shunned by my family, my boyfriend is keeping something from me, and I have no idea how I'm going to pay for next semester. I came to Western for a trouble-free life and now I have anything but that.

I order a passion tea and take a seat next to the window. Watching all the college students stroll by, I wonder if they have as many problems as I do. Then I shake my head, knowing they do. These problems aren't new or different than anyone else's; the problem is, I miss Theo. He would have sat with me, brainstorming on what to do. He would have told me to stop wallowing in self-pity and do something about it. He would have told me to confront Brady and make him tell me what is going on. The longer I sit here thinking of Theo, the more emotional I become and the madder I get at Brady.

Just as I'm about to get up from my seat, I spot Brady walking on the other side of the street with a woman. I squint my eyes to get a better look and realize it's the same middle-aged woman I saw having lunch with Vince that day. She laughs at something he says and gently touches his arm and he turns back to her, smiling.

Rage starts to flow through my whole body and I can't help but follow them. I try to remain calm but the more I see them laugh, the worse the feeling gets in my stomach. Is this what Grant was talking about? They end up outside Shubert Hall, the music building. They embrace in a hug and she kisses him on the cheek before they part. It's all I can do not to run over there, screaming like some crazed psycho to stay away from my man.

I turn around, starting to make my way back to the dorm. Then I change my mind. I'm sick of being pushed around; Brady will answer my questions now. Turning back the way I just came, I stomp around the building and stop abruptly, speechless to see who Brady's with.

Sitting on the same bench I just occupied a few hours prior, Brady talks with Vince. Not wanting to make a scene in front of Vince, I sit down on the bench behind them across the parking lot. Their mannerisms toward one another appear comfortable, yet standoffish at the same time. Brady sits on the far opposite side of the bench, with his forearms resting on his legs. Even from this distance, you can feel the tension between them. Suddenly, I figure out something I should have a long time ago. I may not have all the answers but I know one for sure. How did I never notice those same deep-set caramel eyes or long eyelashes? Vince is Brady's father.

Almost as soon I come to the realization, Brady stands up and turns around in my direction. I stand still, as though if I move it will give me away. His eyes find mine and he instantly realizes that I know his secret. He closes his eyes slowly, no doubt wishing I would have found out differently and I wish I would have, too. I'm not sure if he mumbles something or not, but Vince turns around and smiles my way. He touches Vince's shoulder before he heads in my direction. My heart races and my breathing is erratic until he touches me. The minute Brady's hand touches my arm, I instantly calm. How does he have this effect on me?

"I'm sorry I haven't told you, Sadie," he whispers.

"Why didn't you?" I ask, unsure of the question coming out.

"I was embarrassed. I don't want you to think I will end up like that." He glances back over to Vince.

"I shared everything with you, Brady. Why didn't you give me the same courtesy?"

"I was going to tell you. I just didn't know how."

"You just say it, Brady. You just spit it out," I say, my voice escalating.

"Are you going to break up with me?" he asks and my heart breaks.

"Of course not," I assure him, placing my hands on either side of his face. "But you need to start explaining some things."

Chapter 24

Brady grabs my hand and leads me away from Vince, who surprisingly has turned around to resume staring out at the field. The apprehension rolls off of Brady and I can tell he's worried. I remember my own insecurities when I told him about my past. I know I need to reassure him like he did me. That no matter what he tells me, it won't change my feelings for him.

"Brady, let's go somewhere private, just us," I request, remembering how he held me the whole time I told him my secrets.

He stares down at me for what seems like minutes and then says, "I want to show you something first." Then he turns us in another direction and goes right into Shubert Hall.

I tense when we walk through the doors that I just saw the mystery woman walk through. He walks me down the hallway, passing auditoriums filled with different instruments and classes being conducted. He stops us in front of a wall, filled with pictures of professors and deans, current and past. A picture of a cleaner, more well-kept version of Vince is positioned high on the wall with the label 'Dean Vince Carsen' under it.

"Obviously, you already figured it out. Vodka Vince is my dad," he says and I see him wince, referring to his father by that name. "He chooses to live on the streets instead of staying with me or Maura. He worked here until last year, but when the drinking got too bad, they forced him to retire. They tried to work with him, but he left them no choice." His voice is quiet. Staring at the wall, I notice the picture of the woman that just walked in. She looks a couple years younger in her picture, which identifies her as Professor Jeanine Billings.

"Who's that?" I point to her picture on the wall. I pray he tells me the truth.

"It's Kara's mom," he informs me.

"Oh." I don't know what else to say. I hope the mother doesn't feel the same way about Brady as her daughter.

"Yeah, I'll get to all that in a second," he assures me. "So, my dad has always enjoyed his cocktails but became a full-fledged alcoholic after my mom left us. I was sixteen when it happened and Maura was completing her doctorate. Although she lived at the house, she was rarely home. She and Brandan, her husband, had just met so she spent most of her time with him, leaving me with my dad. I kept his secret the best I could, taking care of him and getting him to bed. At first he could function during the day, only getting smashed at night. Like the movie "Groundhog Day", he would wake up and do the same thing the next day. But then it got out of control. He stopped coming home at night and then a year and a half ago, he left all together, living in shelters and on the streets. The only time I see him now is when I come to visit him here or get a call from the police. Maura and I run interference the best we can, but he refuses our help in any way and won't go to rehab." He walks me out of the building and I see his car parked in the lot. "Will you come with me?" he asks.

"Always," I try to reassure him, squeezing his hand in mine.

We get in his car, unsure of where we're going. "I'm sorry, Brady, for what you have to go through." I don't want to try to solve his problems, I just want to listen.

"Thank you. I handle it better now. When I saw you leave money for him that day, I wanted to run over there and rip the money from him. I knew what he would use it for. That's why I told you to stay away. I didn't want you wasting your money or your time on him." Anger fills his voice. We sit in uncomfortable silence for a few minutes until Brady starts talking again. "He told me about you," he says, his voice a little calmer.

"He did?" I ask, shocked.

"Yeah, I guess after he saw you with Grant, he asked him and Grant told him we were together. He really likes you." He looks my way, giving me a half smile.

"I like him, too," I say.

"Thanks for getting him the coat and stuff. I try to get him to stay in shelters during the winter, but he's stubborn and you have to be sober and usually...he isn't."

"Can I ask you a question?"

"Sure."

"Where does Grant come into this?" I ask.

"Oh...well, that brings up a whole other problem." He turns his face to me and then starts. "Grant and I were friends since childhood. Up until my mom left, we were inseparable," he confesses, and I notice we're pulling up to his house.

"What happened then?"

"His dad was a professor of music as well. Long story short, my mom left with his dad. They were having an affair. Grant's mom died a few years before, so my mom and dad would go over and help Grant and his dad out. I guess somewhere during that time, they fell in love or some shit." The anger in his voice appears again. "They decided to move to Florida and Grant didn't want to go down there so he stayed up here. My dad let him live with us, but I was so pissed at him for what his dad did that he eventually moved in with Kara's parents. That's where she comes in. All of our parents were professors of music and we've known each other our whole lives." Finally, I have some answers.

"I saw you earlier, with Kara's mom," I admit.

"Why didn't you say something?" He looks curious but then understanding dawns on him.

"Oh shit, Sadie. I was just telling her about Kara calling me all the time. She said she would talk to her. I swear to you, nothing is going on there." He shakes his head, exiting the car and walking to my side to escort me out.

"I have one more thing to show you," he says and takes my hand, leading me into the house.

"What is it?" I ask.

"You'll see." I'm happy that none of the guys' cars are in the driveway. "Good, I think we are alone," he says, as though he read my mind.

He pulls me up the stairs until we are outside of the door that leads to the third floor. "I lied to you about this." He stares down at me, but I nod my head in understanding. Then he puts the key in the lock and turns the knob. He moves so slow and hesitant, I'm not quite sure he's ready to show me this. Walking up the stairs, a musty smell fills my nostrils. Once we get to the top, I find a master suite that covers the whole top level of the house.

There is a king size bed, dressers, and an armchair and ottoman. There are built-in bookcases in a small corner, filled with books from top to bottom. It's an amazing room and I automatically envision what it would be like to live in this house with Brady.

"This was my parents' room. I locked it up after my dad left because I didn't want anyone else going in there. I don't want any more lies or secrets between us, so I wanted to show you so you knew the whole truth."

"It's beautiful, Brady." I walk around the room, admiring the space.

"Think about it, Sadie. This could be our room."

I turn around quickly and wonder how the change of topic happened so fast. "Brady, I told you. I have to stand on my own," I say, hating to turn him down again.

"You can stand on your own while being by my side. Just keep thinking about it." His head is down now, staring at the floor.

"I promise, I won't." I walk slowly toward him.

"I want you with me," he says quietly.

"Brady, I'm with you. But I don't want you to wake up one day thinking 'Why did I let this crazy girl move in here?'" I say, placing my hand on his cheek.

"You just don't get it, Sadie. In my whole life, I have never felt like this. Since that moment I saw you, I felt like there was a purpose in my life. I no longer feel alone and I never want that feeling to leave." He places both his hands on either side of my cheeks. "I knew I was no good for you, but I was too selfish to stay away," he whispers and bends down to kiss me.

His confession reminds me of the lyrics to one of the songs that he put on my iPod: 'I now walk alone...'

"Brady?" I ask while he rests his forehead on mine.

"Yeah."

"When you told me you have never written a love song, what did you mean?"

"Exactly that. I never wrote a love song…at least at that point, I hadn't," he answers, smirking down at me.

"Those songs you put on my iPod, they were slow love songs," I softly argue.

"No, they were slow songs but there was no love in them. I wrote those songs out of pain, not love." He starts to kiss my neck.

"Oh, and here I thought some girl had completely destroyed you," I say.

"You're the only girl that could destroy me," he admits and I capture his lips.

"I love you," I murmur against his mouth.

"Say it again," he requests as his lips make their way down my neck.

"I love you, Brady Carsen," I whisper again.

"I don't think I will ever stop wanting to hear you say those words." He picks me up and I wrap my legs around him.

"You don't have to worry about that," I confess and lick his neck up to his earlobe. "Now…fuck me, Brady." I try to say it straight-faced and with a sexy voice.

"Yes, ma'am." He walks us over to the bed and places me down before climbing on top. "Just think, baby. I could do this to you every night." He grabs the hem of my shirt, raising it up to expose my blue lace bra. "I could make you come every morning." He starts to unbutton my jeans and then scoots them down my legs. "Staring at you with only your panties and bra on makes me want to kidnap you and lock you up here until you agree," he jokes and I giggle in response.

"Why don't you show me what I get if I decide to move in?" I smile up at him.

"Do you want me to do a strip tease?" he asks, slowly pulling the hem of his shirt back and forth. I scoot to the top of the bed and rest my body against the headboard to enjoy the show.

"I would never deny myself seeing your body," I answer.

"Well then, baby. I believe you asked me what you would get if you moved in." He slowly moves his hips side to side, a playful smile spreading across his lips. "You see this flat, amazingly defined stomach?" he teases and I nod in response. "You could touch, rub, kiss, or lick it whenever you want." He throws his shirt to the floor while kicking his shoes off. "If you move in with me, these smooth, large feet can warm your small ones on cold winter nights," he continues to talk, slowly taking off his socks and I giggle, enjoying this immensely.

"Hmm...as appealing as it is to see you shirtless with those jeans hanging low, I think I need more convincing," I say, leaning forward.

"I've been waiting to pull out the big guns, baby." He unbuckles his jeans and undoes his zipper, his eyes never leaving mine. The mood is starting to get more intense and less playful. When his jeans hit the floor, my eyes fixate on him. The tight, grey boxer briefs show me how excited he already is, making the ache grow inside of me. "Ready?" He smirks at me and my eyes jerk up to his.

"Come here, Brady," I say quietly, motioning with my finger.

"Did I convince you?" he asks and climbs toward me on the bed.

"It's not just looks, babe. I need to see how you use your body," I state, surprising myself how easy this feels.

"Sit back my darling and enjoy. After I finish, you will be begging me to move in," he softly says and starts to take my bra strap down, kissing my shoulder. "Let's see, do you want me to show you with my tongue or cock?" he questions, and I think I just became wet from his words. When I don't answer, he asks, "Sadie?"

"Tongue...please," I desperately request and he licks down my body, unclasping my bra and throwing it off the bed. His tongue moves in circles around my nipple before his mouth closes over it, twirling my nipple around.

I moan when he moves over to the other breast, doing the same thing. Then his tongue licks down the center of my stomach and over my belly button, moving slowly under the top of my panties. When I feel his tongue graze over my clit, I realize I never felt him take off my panties. Placing his hands against my thighs, he pushes my legs farther apart against the mattress, displaying me in front of him.

"Is this what you want, baby?" he asks and I groan an inaudible yes.

He slowly licks all the way up and back down, inserting his tongue inside of me before moving to my clit. He sucks and twirls it around his mouth, making it hard for me to keep control. My body rapidly approaches an edge I won't be able to hang on to. "Please, Brady." I squirm underneath him, desperate to find my release.

"You asked for tongue…," he teases me, peeking up at me through his eyelashes.

Taking his fingers, he widens me more, giving himself better access inside of me. His tongue feels incredible as he moves it teasingly from my clit and then back again inside of me. I grip his head and twirl his hair around my fingers, trying to keep him in place. He starts working faster, urgently thrusting his tongue into me while moving his hands to my ass, holding me in place. As soon as I hear him moan, I shudder, feeling the tingly sensation flow through my body.

"Do you want me to ask the question now?" he asks, moving over me and I can feel him at my now slick opening.

"Not yet…you still need to prove one thing," I taunt, already feeling relaxed.

"Thank God," he says, and thrusts into me deep as I grab his biceps to hold myself steady. "I love fucking you, Sadie."

"I want to see you, Brady," I say and he picks his head up, staring into my eyes. He moves back and forth inside of me and I raise my hips to join in. "I love you," I exclaim.

"I love you…so, so much," he responds and stills inside of me before collapsing. I think that was the fastest and quietest Brady has ever come. He runs his fingers through my hair, resting on his forearms above me. "So, Sadie. Did I convince you?" he asks and, although he still seems to be playing around, I see that he desperately wants me to move in.

Right before I'm about to answer, loud footsteps hit the stairs and I suddenly remember that we never shut or locked the door.

"Why the hell is this door open?" Dex's voice asks.

"I don't know, do you think Brady…" Trey's voice trails off when he reaches the top.

In those two seconds, Brady was able to turn to the side and shield me from their view. "Fuck, sorry guys," Trey says laughingly, turning around while pushing Dex down the stairs. "Nice ass, Carsen," he calls out before we hear the door slam shut.

"You might as well move in; all three of the roommates have already walked in on us having sex." Brady laughs and stands up to hand me my clothes.

I quickly get dressed before someone else walks in, thankful that Brady hasn't asked me again. I was about to say 'yes', but I don't know if it is from looking in his eyes while he pleasured me or if I truly am ready to take this next step. The last thing I want is to disappoint him, so when I say yes, I want to make sure it's for the long haul.

Chapter 25

It's Friday and The Invisibles are playing Grant's frat party tonight. To say I'm less than thrilled would be an understatement. After all this time, the last place I want to be is a frat house. Not only because of my past experiences in them, but also because of Theo. He loved his frat. It was the brotherly bond he always wanted when we were younger. He begged my parents to have another child after us, praying they would have a boy but that never happened. When we were young, he would bribe me to play baseball, basketball, and football. He had turned me into a tomboy of sorts, but I secretly loved it. Not to mention, I never told anyone all the times he played house or Barbies with me.

Brady could feel my apprehension so he already told the guys the set would be short and we would be leaving right after. I said it would be okay and Jessa jokingly told Brady that she would protect me, not letting any frat douchebag touch me. He insisted on driving me, even though Jessa said she would bring me right before the show started. 'I want all those fuckers to know she's mine when we walk in,' was his response to her.

When I open my dorm door to Brady, he looks me up and down while I wait for his signature smirk. Instead, the first words out of his mouth are, "You aren't wearing that".

I look down at myself, confused. I'm wearing a pair of black skinny jeans and a looser fitting pink blouse that falls off one shoulder. My hair is pinned up into a messy bun style with fallen strands down the sides of my face. "How about, you look beautiful baby?" I tease, smiling up to him but his face is serious and his lips are tight.

"Sadie, I will be up on stage. If I was going to be by your side tonight, I would say okay. But do you know how many guys are going to look at your shoulder and neck, imagining what it would be like to kiss it?" He walks into my room, clearly thinking I will change my outfit.

"You only think that because it's your favorite spot to kiss," I inform him, and turn around to my dresser, putting my earrings in.

"I wouldn't say my favorite spot." He comes up behind me, starting to kiss my shoulder. "Definitely the top five though," he agrees and I catch his eyes smiling at me through the mirror.

"It's yours, Brady...all yours," I answer, and place my hand on the back of his head while he continues to trail kisses up my neck.

"Don't forget it, baby. When you see all those frat guys tonight, don't forget who you belong to." I see the insecurity in his eyes. He's suddenly afraid that I'm going to change my mind about him. How could he ever think that?

"Hey," I say, turning around. I place my hands on either side of his face and bring it down to me. "I'm yours...always. You never have to question that." I get up on my tiptoes and kiss him. "Okay?"

"Okay, it's just...we are going to a place that holds good and bad memories for you. Maybe you will think I'm not enough," he admits and my heart breaks.

"For once, it's you who doesn't get it," I laugh.

"What?" he asks with no trace of humor.

"You are it for me. Game over. I'm yours...and you're mine." I wrap my arms around his neck and rest his forehead against mine.

"Well, those guys wouldn't have gotten you disowned by your family," he sadly says, revealing where this sudden insecurity comes from.

"Brady, it's not your fault my dad disowned me. I don't care about the money or the car. All that matters to me is you. If I can only have one in my life, I prefer it to be you. It's my dad's problem, Brady, not ours." I give him a chaste kiss.

"But your degree, Sadie. I wish I had the money to pay for your last semester. I feel guilty because I get mine for free."

"It will all work out. If I have to take a semester off, it will only give me more time to spend with you," I joke, holding him firmly against my body.

"Sadie..." he sighs.

"No, Brady, let's just enjoy tonight. I will have enough heavy conversation with my mom tomorrow. Take me to your gig," I say and Brady chuckles at the wording I use. "Then take me back to your place and make love to me all night," I request.

"With pleasure, babe," he says and holds out his arm for me to take. I grab my purse and position my arm through his, letting him escort me out of the room.

Cars align the street and co-eds mingle in the front yard. The shadows of people fill the windows of the house and a sudden pain fills my stomach. Brady entwines his fingers with mine, looking down at me. "You sure?" he questions and I nod my head in agreement. "Let's get this over with," he says and guides us up the walkway.

The stares are automatic but for the first time, I realize it's mostly girls, admiring my boyfriend. I remind myself this isn't Drayton. Just because we are at frat party doesn't mean it will be the same. This is just a college party, nothing more. What happened at Drayton was because of the people, not because it was a fraternity.

Walking through the doorway, I'm taken aback by how crowded the room is. Wall to wall college students fill every inch of the house. Brady squeezes my hand harder, leading me to the makeshift stage. From the way he knows his way around, I assume he has been here before. The rest of the guys are already setting up and Jessa sits on the stage, observing them.

"Hey, guys," she says, sitting up straighter. With one more squeeze of my hand, Brady bends down and kisses me before hopping up on the stage. I walk over to Jessa and ask, "Hey, how long have you guys been here?"

"Not long. Don't take this wrong, but how on earth did you hang out with all these people," she comments and glares across the room.

"I didn't know any better," I joke and knock her shoulder with mine.

"Now that you do, let's keep it that way," she laughs, knocking me back.

I look up when I hear a familiar deep voice. It's Grant talking to the guys and I'm surprised to see Brady speaking back politely. After he finishes telling them some stuff, Grant makes his way to me and I notice Brady's eyes follow.

"Hey, Sadie," he says, looking at me, then Jessa, and back to me.

"Hi, Grant. This is my roommate, Jessa," I inform him, motioning back and forth. "Jessa, this is Grant."

"Hi, nice to meet you," Grant says, putting his hand out.

"You too." She shakes his hand back and I see her eyes peruse his body before a smirk appears. Huh, I wonder if Rob noticed that.

"Can I talk to you for a second?" he asks and I bite my lip, glancing over to Brady, who is watching us while setting up a microphone.

"Sure," I agree, but not moving away since there's no way Brady won't follow.

"I'll leave you guys to it," Jessa says and stands up to help the guys.

"Everything work out? Vince told me you found him and Brady together," he divulges.

"Um...yeah. Brady filled me in. Thank you. Whether you want to recognize it or not, you are a good friend to Brady. He might not say it but I know he appreciates it," I tell him.

"I'm glad you know the truth," he states, looking down at his shoes. "You went to Drayton, right?" he asks and I wonder why the change of topic.

"Yes, why?" I answer.

"Well...I guess some of the guys met a couple guys from our frat in Drayton at a party during Thanksgiving. Anyway, there are two guys here and I wanted to give you a heads up."

"Oh," I mumble. Why does Grant think I need a heads up? What does he know?

"Sadie, I don't know if it even matters," he says, as if reading my mind. "I just thought there must be a reason you transferred senior year and thought you deserved to know. I just told Brady before coming over to you." He looks toward Brady and my eyes follow. He is setting up the drums with Trey and not even looking our way, showing me he trusts me with Grant now.

"What did he say?" I ask.

"He wanted to cancel the show and leave, but the guys convinced him to stay. Now I guess you have me as your bodyguard for the night, at least until the show is over." He smirks up at me. "I don't know what happened and you don't have to tell me. But you are right. Brady is a friend, no matter what has happened between us. You're his girlfriend so I will help him out." For the first time, it dawns on me how close they must have been to put all of their issues aside for tonight. I vaguely wonder if it was Grant who Brady called when we were at Niagara Falls.

"Thank you, but I don't need protection. I think Brady is just feeling a little overprotective right now." I glance up at him on stage. He still makes my heart skip a beat and my breathing erratic. Tonight his hair is gelled into a faux Mohawk and the black bands wrap around his wrist. The jeans hang low with his Converse and his black hoodie.

"Please, just let me stand by you while Brady's performing?" he asks and I nod, agreeing.

Grant goes off to get us some drinks before The Invisibles start to play. Jessa bounces back to me, asking a million questions about who Grant is, how I know him, and any information about him. I look at her questioningly and she laughs at me, stating she's just curious and to stop reading into it. Brady jumps off the stage and walks toward me.

"You okay, baby?" he whispers in my ear. "We can leave right now," he says.

"No...I probably don't even know them. I'm surprised though you are allowing Grant to be my bodyguard," I remark, wrapping my arms around his waist.

"He's the only one I would trust you with...besides me," he admits, pulling me closer.

"You didn't feel that way a few weeks ago," I remind him.

"It was a grudge I needed to let go. He came and warned us ahead of time. He has always had my back, I've just been a jackass these past few years," he informs me.

"Well, go finish your show so *you* can be my bodyguard," I say, kissing his chin.

"Stay close to Grant and if you need me just give me a signal, okay?" The worried look on his face makes me uneasy.

"It will be fine, just go," I tell him, giving him a nudge toward the stage.

"Hold up, one good luck kiss." He brings my face to his before thrusting his tongue possessively into my mouth, making my whole body heat up. "Love you."

"Love you," I whisper to him before he jumps on stage.

Grant is at my side as soon as Brady pulls the microphone off the stand. Jessa stands on the other side of me.

"Okay, everyone ready?" Brady's voice fills the room and it quiets down a bit. "We are going to start this off fast and aggressive, any problems with that?" he questions and everyone screams. Does he know what a great stage presence he has? "Alright then...I'm going to get a little sappy first. When I first saw my girl, this song came into my head and I haven't been able to shake it. Sorry, babe, I haven't told you this but here it goes...I want to see a lot of jumping and singing along, got that?"

Trey starts beating the sticks together and I know the song from the drum beat. When the guitar and bass fill in, I'm astonished by the song choice. Brady's voice comes over the microphone and he finds me in the audience, giving me a wink before he starts singing, "I Want You to Want Me" by Cheap Trick. I'm oddly flattered and surprised that, out of all of the songs in the world, this song came into his head when he first saw me.

The crowd goes crazy. Drunk people thrash their bodies around, enjoying the band. Grant holds me by my arm to keep me steady and I grab Jessa in response. Everyone sings along including Jessa, who I jokingly question her with my eyes but she playfully slaps my shoulder. Brady's eyes find mine periodically throughout and I blow him a kiss up to the stage. I glance at Grant. He doesn't seem to be having fun at all so I take his hand and then put his other hand in Jessa's, making us all dance together. His eyes divert to Jessa, appearing embarrassed. It only lasts a second before they are both dancing around. The three of us are in our own world, and even Grant sings along to the songs as The Invisibles continue playing their own after the Cheap Trick tribute. As the night goes on, I suddenly start to feel like the third wheel between Jessa and Grant. Brady smirks over at me with raised eyebrows, obviously noticing it too. My eyes find Rob, who seems more interested in flirting with some girls standing in front of the stage. I watch him for a while and he never even glances Jessa's way. I start to think my first instinct about Rob was accurate.

"Okay everyone, we are going to take a break," Brady announces. "Continue partying and drinking. The more you drink, the better we sound," he jokes. I wonder if it bothers him being around alcohol like this because of his dad.

"Hey baby, are you enjoying yourself?" He wraps his hands around my waist, pulling me into his sweaty body.

"I am," I confirm, kissing him.

"You want anything?" he asks, taking a gulp of his water bottle.

"No, I'm good now," I answer. Jessa and Grant have moved over to the side of the stage and are talking to each other. Dex and Trey sit on the stage with their feet dangling while swarms of girls circle around them. I don't see Rob anywhere, but Jessa doesn't appear to be looking very hard for him.

"What's up with that?" Brady motions his head in Jessa and Grant's direction.

"I don't know," I respond and smile curiously up to him. "I have to admit, I felt like I was imposing after a while."

"I noticed," he agrees while his eyes search the crowd.

We stand together, him holding me from behind, slowly kissing my shoulder and neck like always. He is whispering things he will be doing to me later while my body heats in anticipation. "Sadie Miller, is that you?" a voice calls over and when my eyes meet his, my stomach drops. Before the guy can even approach, Brady is on one side of me and Grant is on the other.

"Hi, Jeff," I say. It's Jeff Soren, the last guy I slept with at Drayton.

"I thought I heard you transferred here," he remarks, glancing first at Brady and then at Grant. He leans in as though he wants to give me a hug, but Brady steps up to him.

"Jeff, this is my boyfriend, Brady." I signal my finger at him. "And this is my friend, Grant." I signal to him and he steps up next to Brady. I'm practically hidden behind their two large bodies.

"Uh...hey guys," Jeff says nervously, waving his hand at them.

"Hi," Brady says, straight-faced.

"Hi Jeff, this is my fraternity house," Grant informs him.

"Sorry," I say and step through the two of them. "Grant told me there were some people here from Drayton. I'm surprised it's you." I let Brady and Grant stand beside me.

"Yeah, it's just me and Jacobs." He stands there, appearing uneasy while my two pseudo-bodyguards keep watch.

"Oh... Miles is here too?" I question, not really knowing what else to say. This situation is entirely too uncomfortable for all of us.

"I should probably go find him. We miss you at Drayton, Sadie. The girls said they never hear from you. Do you like it here?" he asks sheepishly. Even though he slept with me when I was drunk out of my mind and right after a crying fit over Theo, Jeff Soren has always been a nice guy.

I look at Brady and a smile lifts my lips automatically, "I do, thank you, Jeff." He smiles in return.

"I'm glad, Sadie." He stands there for a minute and I step forward, hugging him before Brady can say anything. "You look really happy. You deserve it," he whispers in my ear before I step back and Brady puts his arm around my waist possessively.

"Bye, Jeff." I give him a small wave, watching him as he's swallowed up by the crowd.

When we turn around, Brady gives me a brief kiss and a wink, noticeably calmer than earlier. Dex and Trey are up on stage getting their instruments ready, while Rob and Jessa are making out in the corner. I look at Grant out of the corner of my eye and notice his tense stance watching them, but when I put my hand on his arm, he smiles my way, trying to appear unfazed.

The Invisibles start to play again, and the guys and girls pick up where they left off. After the show, the guys pack up the equipment and then go enjoy the party. Grant leaves us, giving one last look in Jessa's direction. She seems to be enthralled in Rob's world again. Once Grant turns around, I see Jessa open her eyes, peering over to Grant while Rob's tongue invades her mouth. I knew she felt something with Grant but wonder if she will admit it to herself. Brady tells him to hold up for a second and the two of them shake hands as Brady says something to him. I can't explain their friendship, but I'm glad it is starting to head in the right direction.

Brady tells the band we are leaving and we make our way out the door. His arm is around my waist as he leads me down the sidewalk and that's when I hear my name again.

"Sadie…Sadie Miller?" A drunk voice questions and we turn around. "Man, are you a welcome sight. These girls are all a bunch of teases." He walks toward us and Brady steps in front of me.

"Whoa, Miles, let's go." Jeff runs down the sidewalk, trying to stop him but Miles continues my way.

"Listen to Jeff, Miles. Go back inside." I put my hand on Brady's arm to back up a little and he surprises me by doing it.

"Come on Sadie, just like old times," he continues to slur his words and Brady is tensing next to me. I feel it coming.

"Jacobs, stop talking. I'm really sorry," Jeff apologizes while looking at Brady, who I'm sure at this point is ready to pounce on Miles.

"Just get him the hell out of here," Brady's low voice speaks with his fists clenched at his sides.

"Get the fuck off, Soren. You always had a soft spot for Sadie. Even when she was fat, you loved her." Miles turns toward Jeff and he looks at him in disgust.

"I suggest you listen to your buddy and leave," Brady coolly directs Miles, stepping right in front of me.

"Who the hell are you?" Miles slurs.

"Her boyfriend." People have started making their way outside. Grant comes up next to Brady, along with Dex, Trey, and Rob.

"Man, Sadie, you really had to dig into the bottom of the barrel to find a guy who wouldn't use you for the good fuck you are." The minute his words fall out of his mouth, I see the fist already rising.

Brady lands a punch across Miles' cheek. "Don't you ever talk to her like that again. Actually, don't ever fucking talk to her at all." Brady steps forward as Miles steps back.

"Fight, Fight," shouts ring around me and suddenly I'm in the middle of a circle of people chanting and yelling.

"Listen, man. Believe me, I know she's good but come on. I was just going to have her for a little while and you can have her back in twenty minutes," Miles' cocky voice slurs and Brady hits him again. I notice Dex and Trey are holding Miles from behind now.

"I really hope Daddy has good medical coverage because he's going to have one hell of a bill after I'm done with you," Brady yells and throws another fist into his gut. "Let him go, guys," he says to Dex and Trey. "I want him to realize what a little piss rich kid he is when he can't land a punch." They let Miles go and he lamely tries to punch Brady, who sidesteps away from it.

Jeff seems to have stepped away after Miles' comment to him, and the rest of the guys have made their way to me, watching Brady and Miles.

"Man Sadie, you get your brother killed and you go right out and find someone new that likes to fight. Are you going to get him killed, too?" The whole crowd silences with this revelation and Brady starts throwing punch after punch, screaming at him.

I watch Brady beat the shit out of Miles and I'm back in the hotel room, watching Theo fight Craig. Jessa wraps her arms around me while sobs explode out of me. Guys like Craig and Miles don't take embarrassment well. Miles will find Brady and kill him, just like Craig did to Theo.

"Stop it, someone stop it!" I scream, rocking back and forth on the ground. "Brady!" I yell. Jessa whispers in my ear, telling me it will be okay, but everything in me tells me it won't. Brady ignores my screams, continuing to punish Miles. I don't know how it ended, if someone pulled Brady off or if he left on his own, but his arms have replaced Jessa's and he positions one arm under my shoulders and his other arm under my knees, picking me up.

"Take her, Brady, we'll take care of this," I hear Grant's voice tell him.

"Thanks, Grant. I owe you...like a million," Brady says sincerely and carries me to the car.

"I'm sorry, Sadie. I should have taken him away sooner." Jeff comes to our side, but I keep my face buried into Brady's chest.

"Just go get your friend and get the fuck out of Western," Brady spats at him. "It's alright baby, I have you," he whispers before kissing my head.

Chapter 26

My body is warm and at peace. If it weren't for my itchy eyes and my dry, raw nose, I wouldn't remember that I'd cried most of the night in Brady's arms. Sitting up, I notice I'm not in Brady's bed but in the king-size one on the third floor. Brady's blood- stained t-shirt is draped over the chair and a bag of thawed frozen vegetables now rests on the nightstand next to Brady. His hands are raw, red, and swollen. As he lies there peacefully, I recall last night. It hurt so much watching someone I love fight again. I understand why Brady did what he did because Miles' words hurt, and the fact that they were said in front of Brady kills me even more.

He had to stand next to me while another man told him what a great fuck I am. Another guy who I had been intimate with, who had kissed the body that Brady now desires. Just as I was forgetting who I was at Drayton, Miles Jacobs comes and throws it in my face again, reminding me of my past. I worry this won't be the last run-in with someone and I can't do it to Brady again. He shouldn't have to hear the words that were so carelessly conveyed last night. His hands shouldn't be swollen and red from fighting a battle to defend the weak person I had been. God, I wish I would have met Brady two years ago; then all these issues would be non-existent.

I get up and look over at him sleeping. A tear falls down my cheek, but I know this is for the best. He deserves much better than me. I take one last look around the room that should have been ours. Last night, I was ready to tell Brady that I would move in with him. It seems so sudden, but I feel like I've known him forever. My decision made, I quietly walk down the stairs, out the front door, and out of Brady Carsen's life.

Walking the two miles to my dorm sucks, especially with the cold front coming in, but I had to get out fast. I know that when Brady wakes up, he will be calling me, wondering where I went. My mom's visit couldn't have come at a better time. I will stay at the hotel with her tonight. I know he will fight to try and change my mind because I would do the same for him.

Thankfully, Jessa is at the dorm when I get there. To buy myself some time, I text the following message to Brady:

Me: Jessa came and got me. I have my mom coming in around 2.

When I get no response, I figure he is still sleeping so I crawl into bed, hoping to get a couple more hours of sleep before dealing with the drama of my mom. I wake up to a text from Brady.

B: Don't ever do that again. ☹. I would have driven you back. You scared the shit out of me. What? No 'love you'?

Me: Sorry! ☹ After last night, I wanted you to sleep. Love you...so much.

B: You sure you don't want me to come with you and your mom?

Me: No, I have it handled.

B: I know that but I could be moral support. ☺

Me: That's ok but thank you. I love you, Brady!

B: I love you beautiful! Call me when you're done.

I leave it at that. I don't want to give him any ideas regarding what I'm about to do. I shower and get ready, and at around two my mom texts me, saying she's outside.

I walk to the entrance of the dorm to let her in and she's smiling through the window at me. When I open the door, I can't believe it.

"Grandma Ida!" I exclaim and give her a hug. The tears start flowing down my face and she slowly runs her hand over my hair, asking what's wrong.

My mom comes over, embracing both of us. "What's wrong, Sadie?" she asks and it's all I can do to breathe, much less talk. "Did you and Brady break up?" my mom questions and I break down into sobs.

"Let's get you to your room, darling." My grandma keeps an arm around me while I open the door to my dorm. My breathing becomes calmer as we walk down the hall. Concerned girls ask if I'm okay and my mom assures them that she will make sure of it.

"Sadie!" Jessa yells down from her loft as we enter the room and starts to climb down. "What's wrong?" She comes over to my side, leading me to my chair.

"I'm her mom, Maggie, and this is her grandma, Ida," my mom informs Jessa. "She became hysterical when she saw us."

"When she left the room, she was okay," Jessa tells them. I hear them talking but I can't say anything yet. "Let me call Brady," she says.

"NO!" I scream.

"Why?" she asks, concerned. "Did something happen? Is this about last night?" she questions me.

"What happened last night?" my grandma asks, taking Jessa's chair while my mom kneels on the ground next to me.

Jessa looks at me, silently asking permission to tell them and I nod my head. "Well, Brady's band was playing at a fraternity house. At the end of the night, a fight broke out between Brady and a guy from Drayton," she informs them.

"Sadie," my mom sighs. "Who was it?"

"Mi..Mi..Miles Jacobs," I stutter.

"From Theo's fraternity, right?" she clarifies and I nod.

"That boy and his father are jackasses. Do we even want to know what he said?" she asks and I shake my head no.

"So, Brady was right to kick his ass," Jessa confirms.

"Darling, I assume Sadie knows that. Does this have to do with Theo?" my grandma asks.

"Yes…no," I manage to get out.

"Does Brady know?" my grandma asks.

"Yes, he knows everything that happened to Sadie. I do, too. He loves her besides all that, probably more for having gone through it." Jessa stands up and gets bottles of water for everyone.

"I know how crazy that boy is over my granddaughter. That's why I'm so confused. Why is she crying just because some dipshit from Drayton started crap at a party and Brady protected her, kicking his well-deserved ass?" All three of them turn to me for an answer.

"Because…I can't have him," I admit.

"Nonsense," my grandma says.

"I love him too much to put him through it. I thought I could move on, but Miles reminded me who I really am." I undo the cap to my water bottle, taking a few sips.

"Who you really are?" Jessa sarcastically asks. "I can tell you who he is…a self-centered, egotistical asshole," she spouts.

"I like you," my grandma says to her. "I like her," she then informs me as though I didn't hear her.

"Don't do this, Sadie." Jessa kneels in front of me. "Don't doubt this," she begs me, placing her hands on my legs. "That guy last night is a piece of shit. Don't let him ruin what you and Brady have. Don't let him win," Her voice becomes increasingly angrier.

"Jessa, I don't want Brady to have to deal with guys telling him how I was or filling his head with thoughts of me sleeping with others. Jesus, look what happened last night because of me. I put Theo in bad situations, making him protect me. I won't do the same with Brady," I argue.

"Sweetie, what happened to Theo wasn't your fault. Theo was always a fighter, you didn't make him into one. It was a horrible thing with Theo...but it wasn't your fault. Brady isn't Theo and Miles isn't Craig. Brady only fought to protect your honor, that's it," my mom says, grabbing my hand in hers.

"But...what if," I start to speak but can't even complete the sentence.

"What if, nothing," my grandma chimes in. "Sadie, I refuse to let you do this to yourself. You are too smart of a girl not to know how much Brady cares for you. I'm pretty sure he would beat up a line of guys for you to prove how worthy you are."

"Damn right I would, Ida," Brady's voice calls out from across the room. How did he get in without me hearing him? I glance at Jessa and she smiles.

"Oh thank god. Talk some sense into my granddaughter, Hot Stuff," she says and Brady nods, coming directly to me.

Bending down on his knees between my legs, he grabs my hands, clasping our fingers. I cringe when I see his swollen knuckles. "I knew something was wrong when I woke up this morning and you weren't there." He looks at my mom and grandma, an apology written across his face for this confession that we were sleeping together. I will have to tell him that they know I'm not a saint. Then he turns back to me. "I don't give a shit about that douche last night. Your grandma's right. I will be happy to beat the shit out of every guy who says anything disrespectful to you, but at the same time, I shouldn't have done it. I'm sorry, Sadie. I should have known to walk away with you. Please forgive me." He stares up at me and my eyes fixate on his soft brown eyes.

"How could you stand there and hear someone say things about me and not do anything about it? I don't like your hands like this, but I can't expect you to stand by and do nothing. It's a lose-lose situation, Brady. I love you too much to let anything happen to you, and if you stay with me, something bad will happen," I admit with tears in my eyes.

"What happens to me if you leave me? I'll beat the shit of every guy that crosses me the wrong way because I'll be a miserable bastard without you." He inches closer to me and ducks his head down to meet my face.

"Aww…" my mom, grandma, and Jessa say in unison.

"Please, Sadie. You told me last night that I was it for you, game over. Is that still true?"

"This was never about me wanting anyone else, Brady." I rest my hands on his forearms. There is no way I can deny this. I knew I didn't stand a chance if he fought for me.

"I can't promise you it won't be a bumpy road for us, Sadie. But my love for you will never waver and will only become stronger each day. With you by my side, we will get through anything that's thrown our way. But only on one condition," he states, moving his hands to my cheeks.

"What?" I whisper.

"You never let me go, because I'll never let you go," he says and I melt instantly. "Promise me?" he insists.

"I promise," I respond and his lips capture mine. He leans forward, keeping my face in his hands to hold me in place while he explores my mouth.

"Please never leave me again. I hated waking up with you missing this morning." He kisses me again and grabs my hands to stand up. "Now that our drama is over ladies, let me take you all to lunch," Brady jokes and my grandma comes over to give him a hug, followed by my mom.

Brady drives my mom's rental car so we can all fit, even though I would have been happy to drive with him alone. I happily instruct my grandma to sit up front, leaving me in the back with Jessa on one side and my mom on the other. Brady's eyes keep finding mine through the rearview mirror. He still doesn't seem completely himself. I can't help but think he is upset with me for leaving this morning, not that I blame him. I meant what I said; I will never walk away from him again. I'm going to follow my heart and pray like hell it doesn't get broken.

We enter a small Italian restaurant and when we get up to the hostess station, Brady asks to speak to a guy named Tony. The young lady excuses herself and walks through the back doors. A couple minutes later, a tall, larger man comes through the doors. He has a head of salt and pepper hair and is dressed in a silk shirt and black dress pants. When he walks over, I can't help but notice what a strong presence he has.

"Brady!" he exclaims and places his hand out to him.

"Tony, how's it going?" Brady shakes his hand back.

"Can't complain. Business has been good. How is everything with you?" he asks while glancing over to the four of us questioningly.

"I can't complain either. Tony, this is my girlfriend, Sadie Miller," he introduces me, gently pulling me forward to his side.

"I wouldn't be complaining either." He smirks at Brady. "It's nice to meet you, Sadie," he says, shaking my hand.

"And this is her roommate Jessa, her grandma Ida, and her mom, Maggie," Brady says, completing the introductions.

Tony politely shakes everyone's hands, telling them it is nice to meet them, until he reaches my mom. "I can see where your daughter gets her looks from," he compliments her and she turns a nice shade of pink.

"Oh. Thank you," my mom flirts back, making me raise my eyebrows.

"So, Tony," Brady tries to grab his attention away from my mom. Tony slowly turns away from my mom to look at Brady. "Can we borrow the back table?" he asks.

"Of course, I don't have any reservations until this evening." He shuffles over to the hostess stand and grabs the menus. "Follow me."

We file in a line through the restaurant filled with families and couples enjoying their food. "Here you go," Tony says, walking through a curtained-off room. A large chandelier hangs above a round table for eight, and there are dark red curtains that hang from the ceiling to the floor, making the room private and elegant. Brady always knows what we need.

"Thanks, Tony. I wouldn't ask but we need some privacy," Brady says, placing his hand on Tony's back.

"Anything for you, Brady, you know that," he says, winking at him. Tony bows slightly at the waist, saying how nice it was to meet us and he hopes we enjoy our meals. We all thank him in return, but I'm not ignorant to his lingering eyes toward my mom.

"I'm sorry for that episode at the dorms," I apologize after we all take our seats. Brady grabs my hand under the table and squeezes it.

"It's alright, sweetie. I'm just glad it all worked out," my mom says, smiling at Brady.

"Thank god you picked a hottie with a brain," my grandma says and we laugh.

"I hope you aren't mad at me, Sadie, but I knew the only one who could talk some sense into you was Brady," Jessa sheepishly says.

"She texted you?" I ask Brady and he nods his head in confirmation.

"Thank you, Jessa," I graciously say.

A young waiter comes into the room with a busboy who fills our water glasses.

"Hello, my name is Jimmy and I will be your waiter this afternoon. Can I get you anything to drink?" he asks. He explains the daily specials and then retreats from the room, leaving an uncomfortable silence behind him.

Jimmy returns a few minutes later with our drinks and bread. We give him our orders and after he leaves, I figure this is the time to find out why my mother and grandmother are here.

"So Mom, why did you and grandma make the trip here?" I ask and Brady moves his arm around the back of my chair, almost as though he is preparing to comfort me.

She looks at Jessa and then back at me. "Jessa knows everything, you can talk in front of her," I say and my mom nods her head.

"I'm leaving your father," she reveals and I almost spit my water out.

"Why? Mom, if this is about me, it's okay. I'm okay."

"Oh sweetie, that didn't help but it has been in the works for a while now." She takes my hand in hers. "If I'm being honest, we haven't been happy for some time."

"Just tell her Maggie. She's an adult, she can handle it," my grandma chimes in.

"Ida," my mom sighs, staring over at her.

"I love your father. He's my only son, but he's been cheating on your mom for years. And as much as he is my son, I equally consider your mom to be my daughter." Grandma places her hand on top of ours.

"Oh Mom, I'm so sorry."

"Aren't guys just a bunch of jackasses?" Jessa speaks up and we giggle. I stare at her, suddenly wondering why she was home this morning and not with Rob.

"I'm moving in with your grandma until I can figure something out," my mom says before I have any more time to consider that thought. "That's not the only reason your grandma and I are here though."

"Why then?" I ask curiously.

"Your father might have cut you off but I didn't," she admits. Then, looking at Brady she says, "I think you are a wonderful man and my Sadie is lucky to have found you. On behalf of my husband, I apologize."

"No need, Maggie," Brady responds.

274

"I don't need your money, Mom. I already have my plan," I tell her. I know first-hand what my dad will do when she leaves. He will fight her for everything, leaving her with nothing. His vengeance will never let up.

"My dad was a smart businessman. He might have left your dad his company, but he left me other things. I'll be just fine."

"Like what, Mom?" I ask.

"He left me a trust that only I can access. It's money I had originally planned to leave you and Theo after I died. Your father signed papers when my dad gave him the company, stating that the money was mine and it was my choice what happens to it."

I remember overhearing my mom in my dad's office that morning, telling a man to put a trust in my name only.

"Still, Mom. You will need that to live off of now. I know Dad won't give you anything," I admit.

"Believe me, Sadie, it's more than enough for me to live off of and still leave you plenty when I die," she says and I sigh, not wanting to think about that. "I want to give you some now. We might not be able to live like we did with your father, but I can pay for your last semester, get you a car, and pay for your dorm."

Brady squeezes my shoulder and draws me into him, kissing my head. "Mom," I sigh.

"It's the end of the discussion, Sadie. I have already paid the university for your tuition," she admits and I stand up, giving her a huge hug.

"Thank you, Mom...thank you so much," I say with tears flowing from my eyes.

"I'm your mother, Sadie. This is what we do." She squeezes me hard, crying as well.

I eventually go back to my seat and cuddle up to Brady. After such a horrible night, I'm ecstatic to have the worry of paying tuition off my plate. But I think I'm still in shock over my mom leaving my dad and his extracurricular activities. I never thought my dad was cheating on my mom. She had been changing ever since Theo died, but I thought it was just because she had lost a child, causing her to cling closer to her last living one. Looking at her now, she does seem more carefree, smiling and laughing more than I have seen her in awhile.

Tony comes in, insisting to Brady he is covering the bill. We thank him and make our way out of the restaurant, but when we get to the curb, I notice my mom isn't with us. Turning around, I see her in the doorway talking with Tony. He raises her hand, kissing it before she graciously thanks him again.

Brady drives us over to his house and we sit in the living room having coffee while we talk. Jessa disappears up to Rob's room and I don't see her for the rest of the night. When everyone grows tired, my mom and grandma go back to their hotel and Brady and I make our way up to his room. He makes me promise again that when he wakes up, I will be there. I agree without hesitation. I change into his t-shirt, snuggling into his arms. For once in my life, everything seems to be on track. I might not have my dad, but if I'm honest with myself, he has never been a major part of life. I have Brady, my mom, my grandma, and Jessa.

Chapter 27

I don't know why I haven't agreed to move in with Brady since I practically live here. I am rarely at the dorms, which means I haven't run into Vince lately. Brady and I went to visit him after my mom left that Sunday, but since then, Brady has gone by himself. He also took me to his sister's for dinner, which was nice and relaxing. Her husband and children were welcoming and friendly, just like her. Brady and Maura are very similar in their joking, carefree personalities.

My mom called last night from my grandma's. My dad has already hired his lawyer to fight my mom for everything they have. She tries to keep it from me, but my grandma fills me in. My dad hasn't tried to contact me since the night I left the house and I prefer it that way.

I worry because Brady has had to go out a couple nights to pick Vince up from the police station. The situation seems to be getting worse, which is making Brady more reserved and quiet. Vince is fortunate that he was such a distinguished professor at the university, where they do everything they can to help Brady and Maura handle the situation. Brady usually picks Vince up, and then takes him to a friend's house to sleep it off. Vince is adamant that he won't come back to the house. I see the toll it is taking on Brady and he is starting to pull away. His body slumps every time his phone rings, fearing the worst. He has started having nightmares and talking in his sleep. Usually they are just mumbles that I don't understand, but last night he called out 'Dad' in a panic. I quickly woke him up and he instantly wrapped his arms around me tight, burying his head in the crook of my neck. He didn't say anything, just held me close until he fell back asleep.

Brady and Maura talk a couple times a day to discuss the situation and what they should do. I often find Brady in the studio, strumming his guitar and singing quietly. Tonight is one of those nights. It's three in the morning and I woke up without Brady, which has been the norm recently. When I open the door to the basement, I see the lights on so I venture downstairs.

Staring through the glass, I admire Brady playing his music. I sometimes wonder why he isn't pursuing a career in that since it seems to calm him. In pajama pants and no shirt with his guitar resting in his lap, the burn of having him inside of me grows. He looks up, notices me, and waves me into the room.

"You should be sleeping, beautiful," he says, continuing to strum a few chords.

"So should you." I make my way over to him.

He shrugs his shoulders.

"Talk to me," I request and he opens his arms, moving me between him and the guitar.

"How about I teach you?" He changes the subject and places my hands on the guitar.

"Brady," I sigh, letting him place his hands over mine.

"Press this string and strum with this hand," he instructs, ignoring my pleas to talk.

After a few chords, Brady starts to kiss the back of my neck and I feel his hard bulge on my back. I tip my head back, enjoying his lips and tongue on me. In turn, Brady props his guitar against the wall and his hands instantly plant themselves on each one of my breasts, massaging them. My hands rest on his firm thighs and I push my ass into his crotch, feeling his erection.

I continue to circle my hips while his hands roam up my tank top and pinch my nipples. I moan in bliss as Brady stands up, pushing me against the window. He slowly runs his hand down my back and then pulls my boxers down around my ankles.

When I try to step out of them, he says, "No baby, just like this." He pulls my tank up, exposing my breasts. Then he lifts my arms, pressing my palms against the glass. I stand there with my back to him, sprawled across the glass panel with my shorts around my ankles and my shirt scrunched up around my neck.

"So fucking hot," he whispers in my ear.

I have never seen this side of Brady, but I'm immensely enjoying it.

I can feel how aroused I already am and I need him inside of me.

"I'm going to fuck you just like this, Sadie," he states and I wait in anticipation.

"Please, Brady," I plea.

He starts kissing my shoulder blades, making his way down my backside before coming back up. Placing his hands on my hips, he pulls me back into him. I feel his cock at my entrance and I relish the moment.

"Ready, baby?" he asks.

"Yes," I desperately answer.

Before I can prepare myself, he is inside of me, thrusting into me deeper with every push. He's never been rough like this, so I'm surprised what an arousing effect it has on me.

"You feel so fucking good," he breathlessly speaks into my ear.

I moan as my body gets smashed against the glass and Brady reaches around, playing with my clit as I scream his name and roll over the edge. A second later, Brady pumps into me twice before he grabs my hips, holding them in place.

"Fuck, Sadie," he shouts, stilling inside of me. Then he picks me up so I'm straddling him and throws our clothes in between our bodies. "Now I want you in my bed," he whispers, kissing my lips.

His lips remain on mine while he carries me up the two flights of stairs. He places me in his bed, positioning me on top of him while his fingers flow through my hair. "I didn't hurt you, did I?" his shaky voice asks.

"No, of course not," I answer and turn my head up to him as he cups my cheek with his hand.

"Good. You know how much I love you." There are tears in his eyes.

"And I love you." I smile up to him. I know what he is doing, I did it myself. If sex makes him forget, I will happily oblige, but eventually I will have to find a healthy way to help him deal with his dad.

I jolt awake with Brady's body shifting under me. I glance at his clock and see it's only been an hour since we fell asleep. "Shit! I'm on my way," Brady says into the phone and climbs out of bed. I sit up, refusing to take a back seat any longer. He didn't when it came to my issues and I won't when it comes to his.

"Let me get dressed," I say, swinging my legs over the bed, ready to get out when he steps toward me.

"No, Sadie, I'll be right back." He keeps his hand on my shoulder, keeping me on the bed but I stand up.

"It's not a choice, Brady, I'm coming." I get up from the bed and grab my yoga pants and sweatshirt.

"You don't need to see this," he says, running his fingers through his hair. "Please," he begs.

I walk over to him and place my hand in his. "They were your words, Brady. You said you would never let go, but I feel you slipping away. Every night you disappear and every night I find you downstairs. And every day when I wake up to your sad eyes, we slowly become more disconnected." I lean in closer. "You have to let me in, Brady."

"It's pathetic and sad, Sadie. He isn't the man you know on these nights." He puts his head down, staring at the ground.

"Brady, what are you afraid of?" I question, bending down to meet his eyes.

"That you can't handle it..." he admits.

"And what?" I pry.

"You'll leave," he says, finally divulging the whole truth. I can work with this.

"Did you leave me?" I ask him back and he shakes his head. "No, and I'm not going to leave you," I tell him. I grab his hand, "Let's go." I lead us out of the room.

Brady doesn't say anything on our way out to the car but keeps my hand in his.

We pull up to the police station and an officer walks up to the car before we can even get out, informing Brady that they had to send Vince to the hospital for what they believe is alcohol poisoning. On the drive to the hospital, Brady calls Maura to let her know and she says she is on her way.

He parks in the visitor parking and I entwine our fingers as we walk into the emergency room entrance. I give him a squeeze right before the sliding doors open and he looks over at me. Fear fills his eyes and I hope he will let me in.

Brady walks up to the nurse's station, giving his name and she tells him to take a seat and someone will be out. We sit in the plastic chairs, not paying attention to the infomercial on the television. Brady impatiently shakes his leg while groans flow out of his mouth. Clearly, he doesn't want to be here and I can't help but think maybe my presence is making this worse. He hasn't even glanced my way since we walked into the hospital.

Finally, a nurse comes in, calling Brady's name. Brady stands up and then turns to me, "Just please stay here? At least until I can see what is going on." Seeing the anguish in his eyes, I nod my head and sit back down, watching him walk out of the room.

I try to distract myself by flipping through magazines or watching an infomercial about some skin care regime. I'm thankful when Maura comes into the room.

"Oh Sadie, I'm glad he brought you," she says, obviously out of breath from rushing here.

"I didn't really give him a choice," I comment and she embraces me.

"He's lucky to have you. He won't take to you witnessing this easily so just remember, he loves you," she warns me and I can't help thinking that she's the second person close to him that has told me this.

"I don't plan on leaving," I assure her and she smiles my way, taking my hands in hers.

"I knew I liked you that day in spin." She turns around and makes her way to the nurse's station. After talking friendly with the nurses, she walks toward the rooms in the emergency area.

I sit back down, waiting for some news. About fifteen minutes later, Grant walks in and takes the seat next to me.

"Any news?" he asks and I shake my head.

"Who called you?" I question, noticing his clearly sleepy face. He's wearing sweatpants and a sweatshirt, and a baseball cap covers what I assume is his bedhead.

"Maura." He takes his ball cap off, repositioning it. "I'm surprised to see you," he states, still staring straight ahead.

"Sorry to disappoint you," I snap.

"Oh Sadie, I just meant because of Brady. I didn't mean…"

"I'm sorry, Grant, I'm just touchy. I know what you meant." I place my hand on his knee when Brady walks into the room.

"Am I interrupting something?" he asks, anger evident in his voice.

"Of course not." I stand up and walk toward him and Grant follows my lead.

"It's not good. Alcohol poisoning," he says directly to Grant and he nods his head back. I guess they have been here before. "Can you take Sadie home?" he asks.

"No, I'm not leaving," I declare to him.

"There isn't a reason to be here, Sadie," he says, releasing an exasperated breath.

"I'm here for you, Brady." I touch his arm in reassurance.

"I don't need you," he bitterly responds and I quickly remove my arm. "That's not what I meant...just go, Sadie." He runs his hands through his hair.

"No." I stand there, not moving.

"Sadie..." he trails off.

"I'll stay in the waiting room if you want, but I refuse to leave here without you," I demand.

"Fine," he deadpans, clearly annoyed with this conversation. "Grant, can I have a word outside?" He motions with his head for him to follow. Brady doesn't hug or kiss me before he leaves. This is a very different Brady than I have ever known, and for the first time, I wonder if we will get through this.

"Sure," Grant says, looking at me before exiting the room.

Sitting down in the uncomfortable chairs, I feel the tears welling up behind my eyes but I will not let them fall. *Be strong, for Brady*, I tell myself over and over. Grant comes in a couple minutes later and sits down in his previous seat. I don't ask what Brady was talking to him about and Grant doesn't divulge it either. The uneasy silence between us fills the empty room until Kara walks in. *What the hell?*

"Oh Grant, I came as soon as John told me." She rushes in, taking the seat next to him.

My eyes glare toward her and then to Grant. This little threesome of theirs is starting to piss me off.

"You didn't need to come, Kara. You know he won't want you here." Grant continues to thumb through a sports magazine.

"She's here," she spats, nodding her head in my direction.

"I'm his girlfriend," I leer and put my magazine down on the table.

"Only because you slid your way in past me," she continues, positioning her body to face me completely.

"There was no sliding, Kara. You need to get over it." I lean back in my chair and cross my legs, picking up my magazine again.

"Girls, let's remember why we are here," Grant chimes in and Kara turns her back to both of us, thumbing through her phone.

She's dressed in yoga pants and a sweatshirt and her hair is pulled up in a messy bun. Obviously, she just rolled out of bed and I wonder who John is, why he knew about Vince, and how often Kara has been here with Brady when I haven't. The more questions that run through my mind, the angrier I'm becoming. I decide to go for a walk. Grant tries to come with me but I'm able to divert him.

I make my way over to a vending machine and purchase a coffee. Although I usually take it black, I decide on cream and sugar, hoping it might camouflage the bad taste. Just as I start back down the hall, I spot Brady and Maura heading into the waiting room. By the time I get there, Kara is hanging on Brady and he isn't pushing her away. The four of them abruptly stop talking and stare at me when I walk in the room. Suddenly, I feel like an outsider and maybe Brady was right, I should leave.

"Hey, Sadie," Maura says. She walks up to me and puts her arm around my shoulders, bringing me into the group.

"How's everything?" I ask, my voice shaky and unnerved by what I just witnessed.

"It will be just fine," Maura assures me, and Brady continues looking at the ground while Kara still has her arm hooked through his. In all our time together, Brady has never made me feel so out of place. He has always assured people he was with me, but if a stranger walked into this room right now, they would think Kara was his girlfriend. "Brady and I are going to stay for the night. We were thinking Grant could take you home." She looks at me when she says it, and I think about how, just a few hours ago she told me I should stay and not leave Brady's side.

"Um..." I look at Brady, who continues to look anywhere but my direction. "Alright," I agree and his eyes finally land on me. I glance at Kara's arm and then back to his eyes, making sure he knows I see what is happening. He quickly releases her arm, as though he didn't know it was there and walks toward me.

"Can I talk to you first?" he asks.

"It's fine, Brady...we should get going." I look at Grant, who digs his keys out of his pocket. "I'm sorry." I kiss his cheek before walking away.

"I'll call you in a bit," he says.

"Okay," I respond and walk out the doors. When I get on the other side, the tears start escaping and I can't stop them. I brace myself against the wall to quickly try to swipe them away before Grant comes out. I swore I was going to fight for him, but he just won't let me. I thought Maura was on my side, but she was the one who suggested I leave. And here I am leaving and that bitch Kara is still in there.

"Ready?" Grant asks, relieving me from my thoughts.

"Sure," I say and start walking down the hall.

"It's not you, Sadie, it's just Brady. He can't let people in."

"Obviously not everyone," I spat.

"Believe me...he doesn't want her there either. It's just that she won't leave. I think he has just grown used to her being there since she has always weaseled her way in." The sliding doors open and the cold air hits my face, the tears now chilled against my cheeks.

I don't know what to say so I remain silent, but the tears keep coming. Grant has been kind enough to ignore my sniffles. I instruct him to take me to the dorm instead of Brady's house. The streets are dark and empty, void of any college students. Grant walks me to my door, and I thank him. He has tried to give Brady the benefit of the doubt the whole ride over. I appreciate his attempt but right now, I just need some time to myself.

Jessa is asleep when I enter the room, so I tiptoe into my bed. No need to change into pajamas since I'm already wearing sweatpants and a t-shirt. The smell of Brady, embedded into his shirt, fills my nostrils as I lie in bed awake. I check my phone, nothing.

I replay everything that's happened throughout the last few weeks. The longer I lie there, the farther away I feel from him. I put my ear buds in, listening to The Invisibles album he put on there for me. The slow songs that I thought were about a special girl in his life that broke his heart start playing. They all hold the common theme of someone being lost, alone, and walking away.

I bolt up in bed, almost hitting my head on the ceiling. I rush down my steps, throwing my shoes back on. Jessa's keys are sitting on the dresser so I jot down a quick note and grab them.

Chapter 28

The ten minute drive seems like an hour. Everything I want to say overflows in my brain. I consistently change and revise my speech, making sure I use the right words. I park next to Brady's Camaro, so I know he is still here.

I practically run into the sliding doors before they open, and am finally where I should have never left an hour ago. My squeaky footsteps echo in the hallway as I swiftly walk toward the waiting room.

When I enter the small area, I'm thankful they're there and not in Vince's hospital room. Maura is fiddling with her phone next to Grant, while Brady's head is tipped back with his eyes closed. Kara is right next to him with her head on his shoulder, and I want to scream at her to get the fuck off my man. A huge sigh comes out of my mouth before I realize it and Brady's head pops up. Maura and Grant look up, while Kara continues to sleep on Brady.

"Sadie," he says and rises to his feet. Kara's head falls with a thud down onto the chair when he walks toward me, waking her up.

"What the fuck?" she questions, holding her head with her hand.

"I'm not going anywhere, Brady," I tell him.

"Let's go, guys. Give them some privacy," Maura instructs, standing up. She and Grant both start to leave the room but Kara stays put.

"Kara?" Grant turns around, waiting for her. She reluctantly gets up and follows them out.

Once they are all gone, I grab his hand, leading him over to a chair. I kneel down between his legs and place my hands on his face. "I'm here to stay. I will wait in this waiting room if you want, but I will not leave this hospital without you. I love you and whatever you go through, I go through. We will do this together, Brady. You no longer have the option to do this alone," I lecture. His eyes are on mine but my Brady isn't there, it's a hollow man in front of me. "You can ignore me, push me away, and yell at me, but I will come back to you every time to stand by your side. I will hold your hand, hug your body, and soothe your worries, but I will not walk away. I will not leave you," I finish speaking and a tear rolls off his cheek. He stares down at me and a horrible feeling flows through me that maybe this was a terrible idea. Maybe he doesn't want me anymore.

I lean up, softly kissing his lips, tasting the salt from his tears. He doesn't respond to my affection so I slowly pull away, embarrassed. Then Brady puts his hands on the back of my head, drawing me to him. He gives me a gentle kiss on my lips, raising me up and pulling me into his lap. Kissing his way to my ear he whispers, "Thank you."

I stay in his lap with his arms around me and mine around him. The three others make their way in eventually, quietly sitting on the other side of the room. A doctor comes in a little while later and informs Brady and Maura that they can go in and see their father. Maura puts everything in her purse and walks out of the room. I take my seat next to Grant but Brady walks over to me, holding his hand out. I look up into his eyes and I see no sign of the angst that filled them moments ago. Placing my hand in his, he lifts me off the chair and leads me toward the door.

Vince looks comfortable lying in the bed beside the IV attached to his arm. Maura and Brady walk to either side of the bed and I keep my distance in the back of the room. I don't want to push too much; this was a big step for Brady. Maura takes her father's hand, squeezing it while talking to him. Brady leans back in the chair, staring at his dad. With all three of them in the room, the similarities are uncanny. I can't believe I knew all three of them separately but never realized they were related.

The doctor tells us that he should be okay but needs to be closely monitored. Then he hands some pamphlets to Maura regarding rehabilitation facilities. The nurses come in and insist we all go home and come back in the morning. They say there is nothing anyone can do; he just needs his rest.

The five of us file out of the hospital. Brady follows me to my dorm to drop Jessa's car off and then we go back to his place. It's early morning when we finally crawl into bed. Brady positions me on top of his chest again, undoing my ponytail and letting his fingers seep through my blonde hair.

"I'm sorry for tonight, Sadie," he whispers, and I slowly pick up my head.

"I know," I say in return.

"It might take some time for me," he admits.

"That's okay," I reassure him. "I'm not going anywhere." I lay my head back down on his chiseled chest.

"I didn't know it was possible to love you even more," he says casually, continuing to play with my hair.

Picking up my head, I stare into those caramel eyes that have given me so much in such a short amount of time. "Me either," I say in return, grazing his chest with small kisses.

Brady and I are on our way back to the hospital. Maura is meeting us there with her husband. The three of them want to confront Vince about admitting himself into a rehab facility again. I opt to stay in the hall, out of courtesy for Vince. Brady is actually smiling when he comes out, telling me he agreed to go. I wrap my arms around him, happy for all of them. Then he tells me the bad news. He has to leave right after finals to take him up to a facility in Michigan and he will be gone for four days, returning Christmas Eve. Although I'm going to miss him, I think I have an idea that will keep me busy. I just need to find some recruits to help me out.

One week later, I'm anxiously awaiting Brady's return. He expects me here since we will have a full house tomorrow. We are hosting my mom and grandma, Maura and her family, Grant, and Jessa, along with her family. Jessa's family came here to visit her for the holidays. Rob went home a few days ago and he invited Jessa but she declined, wanting to be with her family.

I hear the Camaro pull in the driveway and it takes all my self-control not to run down the steps and jump into his arms. Instead, I scramble around the room, making sure everything is in its place. I toss a few pillows on the bed and re-position his guitar in the corner and a picture of me and Theo on the dresser.

Grant and Jessa have been a huge help these past few days helping me re-decorate the third-floor master suite for Brady and me. We have painted it a misty blue and I bought a brand new white comforter, along with white and black drapes. Although I can't change the memories of this room for Brady, I hope by us making new ones in it, he will be able to move on.

"Sadie!" he calls up from downstairs but I stick to my plan, keeping quiet. His footsteps make their way up the stairs as I bite my lip in anticipation. God, I have missed him these last four days. It is the longest we have been apart since we got together, and I honestly don't remember what it was like not having him in my life.

I hear him stop at his bedroom door, "What the..." he says. Surely he is confused seeing all of Jessa's stuff in there. His footsteps quickly turn toward the second staircase.

I lay myself on the bed and strike my best sexy pose, even though I'm still wearing jeans and a t-shirt. As his steps become louder and closer, my heart wells in dire need and desire. When his face reaches the top and I see the faux-hawk, brown hair of my boyfriend, an ache fills inside of me.

"What's this?" he cautiously asks. "No...really?" he questions as his eyes search the room. He walks toward the closet, seeing my clothes on one side and his on the other. Then he ventures into the bathroom and sees my toothbrush alongside his.

Coming out of the bathroom, he looks at me again. He silently asks me with his eyes and I give him a small nod of my head, making him smile widely. Finally, Brady jumps on the bed and kisses me. "You sure?" He backs away from me a little.

"I've never been more sure of anything," I respond, pulling him down to me.

Epilogue

Grant

It feels weird being back at this house after so many years, but I'm glad I could get used to it again with Sadie here first. I laugh when I think about how I thought she was the girl for me that day in the library. We seemed to fit, like two peas in a pod, but she was already taken. And not by just anyone...it had to be my arch nemesis, Brady Carsen.

We used to be best of friends, Brady and I, but when my asshole dad took away his mom, he couldn't forgive me. I couldn't blame him; I hated myself just as much. But when I moved in with Kara's family, I missed him. Feeling more alone since my mother had died, I comforted myself with girls. Whichever girl showed interest had a chance with me. That's when things went completely disastrous between Brady and me.

He was dating this girl, Jen Kramer. They had only been on a few dates but at a party, she showed some interest in me and I took her upstairs, only to have Brady walk in on us. Jen and I were completely naked in the middle of having sex so there was no denying what was going on. Brady stormed toward me and I let him hit me as many times as he wanted. I deserved every punch. Not only for what I did with Jen but because of my dad, too.

Once we started college, he joined The Invisibles and I joined a fraternity, sealing our separate ways for good. Last year, when I started seeing Mr. Carsen asleep on the park benches and passed out in alleyways, I knew I had to take care of him. Don't get me wrong, Mr. Carsen always loved his drinks. They used to have the most amazing parties when we were little. Brady, Maura, Kara, and I would run around playing tag and hide-n-seek while our parents got trashed.

I never thought about it then, but Mr. Carsen always seemed to be passed out on the couch at some point before the end of the night. But after my dad took away his wife, Mr. Carsen drank all the time. When I moved in with them, I remember Brady sleeping in the chair next to his bed to make sure he didn't get sick or calling the university, informing them he was ill. That's why I left to go live with Kara's family; I couldn't handle seeing what my father had caused.

"Hey you." Jessa nudges her shoulder into mine, interrupting my journey down memory lane.

"Hey," I respond, gently nudging her back. The smile she gives me takes all of my control not to throw her over my shoulder and stomp upstairs. I have to keep reminding myself she is taken and I will never again take another guy's girl, even if I hate the asshole. "They kind of make me sick," I joke, nodding my head toward Sadie and Brady, who are currently wrapped in each other's arms while kissing. God, I'm a jealous bastard.

"Yeah, I don't know what I'm going to do when I live here. Maybe I should have stayed in the dorms for my last semester," she laughs, flashing that one dimple in her right cheek that has been driving me crazy for days.

From the moment I saw Jessa at my fraternity party, she has consumed my every thought. When Sadie asked if I would help her paint the third floor, I jumped at the chance when she told me Jessa would be helping as well.

As we walk over to the table to sit for dinner, I casually act like it was a coincidence we ended up next together, when in fact I have been thinking about how I was going to maneuver it most of the day. I pull the chair out for her and she smiles at me, clearly taken back by the kind gesture and my heart breaks, knowing she's never been cared for like she deserves. I push it back in and stare at her exposed neck, where the small scripted words 'free' are tattooed along with black birds flying around it. I'm curious if she just liked it or it means something, but from what I know of her, I think it's the latter. Her ear piercings up and down her right earlobe are clearly visible with her pixie-cut hair style. We couldn't be more different in appearance, but then I look at Sadie and Brady and they are just as different. I don't remember ever wanting someone like I want Jessa. I sit down next to her and grip my napkin so my hand doesn't disobey and grab hers.

Luckily, Brady starts talking, alleviating me from this pain for a short time. "Hey, everyone. Sadie and I want to thank you all for coming." He stares down at her and she smiles warmly back up to him. "We want to play a little game and I hope that you all don't mind, but we feel like we have so much to be thankful for this year, we want to hear yours. I'll start," he says and I want to kick his ass for this impromptu game. "I'm thankful that I am no longer am alone. That I have my one and only by my side forever and always. Never let go, babe," he says, bending down and kissing Sadie. Can this get any cornier? Do they have to keep flaunting their newfound love?

Sadie stands up. "Never, Brady," she says to him, grabbing his hand. "I want to thank Jessa for dragging me to that god-awful bar where my white knight with an edge saved me. I know I ran away that night but never again. I'm here, forever and always," she says and Jessa smiles toward them. I didn't know that's how they met.

Everyone at the table starts standing up, thanking other loved ones or events that have happened. It's getting closer to my turn and my stomach is filled with butterflies. I'm not usually shy to talk in front of people, but the way Jessa glances at me every time someone says what they are thankful for, I worry I will fumble over my words. Maura's five year-old son knocks me with his elbow, telling me it's my turn. I have no idea what that little man is thankful for since my head has been everywhere but at this table.

I nervously scoot my chair out from the table. "I'm thankful to have an old friend back in my life." I stare at Brady who nods his head, smiling. Then I pull out Jessa's chair for her and she stands up.

She looks around the table before her eyes land on me. "I'm thankful for new friends," she says, winking at me.

My heart races at the thought she might want me as much as I want her. Too bad we have two things against us: she has a boyfriend and ever since Lizzy, I don't do relationships.

MICHELLE LYNN

Let Me In (The Invisibles #3) Available Now

Amazon

Amazon UK

More from The Invisibles

Don't Let Go playlist on Spotify

Join The Invisibles Discussion Group on Facebook

Don't Let Go Book Trailer

My Thanks

I could not be a writer if it wasn't for the support of my husband and kids. So they will always be first on my list since they have to deal with the daily struggles of having a wife and mother who is also an aspiring author. Thank you for your patience and understanding during the days that I stayed cooped up with my laptop at the dining room table. I appreciate you not complaining when I ask you to repeat yourself numerous times since my full attention isn't always there. Please remember that I love you all...you're my life.

Next would be my parents, who constantly encourage me to continue toward my dreams. My dad who kept nagging in my ear all these years telling me how I'm always talking about writing a book, so why don't I get to it.

My savior, S.G. Thomas, my editor. You did it again. Swooping down like the angel you are, "polishing" my novel. I can't wait to work with you again, but I promise I'll give you more time the next go around!

Heather Davenport, I don't know what to say, except you ROCK. Thank you for answering my zillion questions and not only beta reading Don't Let Go once but twice. You have been an awesome guide through this process and I'm truly grateful to have met you. To Natalie Given Catalano and the rest of the Love Between the Sheets team. I've loved working with you during my cover reveal, book blitz and blog tour for not only Don't Let Go but Love Me Back as well. You girls are wonderful at what you do!

All my beta readers, Michelle Hereford, Heather Davenport,

Jennelyn Tabios Carrion, Colleen Lee, Crystal Taylor, Lynne Fellows, Keri Anderson-Gilson. I valued the feedback from each one of you for Don't Let Go.

Lastly all the book bloggers. I apologize about my incessant messages asking to share teasers and links. You are all the ones that get the word out about the books and authors. I'm astonished everyday how kind and welcoming you are to help us first time indie authors out. Without you, I'm not sure where my books would be!

Most of all, thank you to all the readers who take a chance on indie authors everyday—this book would have most likely never been written much less published if it weren't for you. Thank you from the bottom of my heart.

Please reach out. Whether you enjoyed this book or not, I would greatly appreciate if you could take some time and leave a review, thank you.

Michelle Lynn

www.michellelynnbooks.com

Facebook

Goodreads

@michellelynnbks

michellelynnbooks@gmail.com

S.G. Thomas (Editor)

perfectproofandpolish@gmail.com

Sommer Stein (Cover Designer)
Perfect Pear Creative

Facebook

Books by Michelle Lynn

<u>Love Me Back (Keep scrolling for a sneak peek)</u>

Growing up in small-town Belcrest, Maddy Jennings always thought she was destined to be with her childhood sweetheart, Trent Basso. Throughout the complicated road she has traveled with Trent, someone else has had a strong presence in Maddy's life. Trent's older brother Gabe has always been someone she could count on, therefore neither of them can be blamed when lines blur from friendship to something more. However, promises made between brothers threaten to ensure that neither of them will have a permanent place in her life.

When Maddy returns to her hometown for her brother's wedding, she is forced to face both Trent and Gabe for the first time in two years. While the two Basso brothers fight to win her heart, she is busy struggling with a past that won't seem to let her go. Whether she wants to or not, Maddy must decide to either forfeit her own happiness or forever tear a family apart.

Amazon

Amazon UK

<u>Let Me In (The Invisibles #2)</u>

Grant is damaged, selfish, and undeserving of love...or so he thinks.

Jessa is happy, in love, and has overcome her past...or so she thinks.

Grant and Jessa can't stop thinking about one another since being introduced at a party a month ago. And despite their differences, they can't seem to stay away from each other either. However, both are hiding secrets of less-than-perfect pasts, fearing what will happen when those mistakes come to light. As they grow closer, they each battle their own insecurities, and neither believes that they are worthy of the kind of love that they both still want. So if it's true that opposites attract, what happens when the similarities begin to surface?

Amazon

Amazon UK

Collaboration

This is not your typical rock star romance. For one, the "rock star" is a rapper. And not just any rapper. Trace is the hottest ticket in the music industry right now, regardless of which definition of 'hot' you choose.

Taryn Starr is not the girl-next-door who unknowingly meets a celebrity. Known as "America's Sweetheart," the reigning country music princess and world-renowned superstar knows exactly who Trace is...or does she?

Their worlds collide when the musicians whose paths were never destined to cross are forced by their joint record label to collaborate on a song. The sparks fly and ignite a fire that blazes hotter with every minute they spend together—for better or worse. One thing's for certain, the two media magnets can't deny their explosive chemistry, but will life in the spotlight ultimately bring Trace and Taryn together or force them apart?

Amazon

Amazon UK

Excerpt from *Love Me Back* by Michelle Lynn's

Chapter 1 — 11 years old

"Madeline Dolores Jennings!" Bryan yells teasingly at me from the bottom of the hill.

"What do you want, Bryan Otto Edwards?"

"Hey, I'm just joking, Maddy." Bryan runs up the hill, throwing his arm around me. "You knew it had to be coming; I have been holding it in all day since Kenna slipped at lunch."

I hate the days my mom "works late". It entails me having to walk up the grassy hill from my grade school to my brother Jack's football practice with the other latchkey brothers and sisters of the football heroes of our small town. There are four of us that make the trek every day.

Mackenna Ross is my best friend and our polar opposite personalities only enhance our different qualities. She is free-spirited, whereas I am more conservative. She speaks her mind and I keep my thoughts to myself. We share a love for tennis, swimming, and the game MASH (mansion, apartment, shack or house), where we try to map out our perfect lives.

Our brothers are teammates but not the best of friends. In fact, they have been known to fight with each other on several occasions. The most recent battle is over a girl... Cindy Rydel. I don't see what is so intriguing about her, but I am not a seventeen year-old hormone-induced boy either. It doesn't matter to Kenna and me that they don't get along, so long as it doesn't keep us away from one another.

Jack glances up to the bleachers on his way to the field, giving me a wave as he checks to make sure that I made it safely across the hill from our school. I wave back and take my seat next to MacKenna. She already has her notebook out, wanting to go first. We keep all of our MASH games in a binder, marking stars next to the lives we want. I grab her notebook, flipping to the next blank page.

"Alright Kenna, four boys?" I ask.

"Let's do five today. I can't decide who to leave out, Jackson or Tyler," she says, tapping her lips with her finger.

"Fine, five," I reply. Mackenna never changes the cars she desires or where she wants to live, but the boys' list is forever rotating between the boys in our school.

"Ok, well my usual four boys and..." she pauses, glancing over to the field next to us where the latchkey boys are tossing a football around. "Bryan," she says, spitting it out so fast I barely catch what she said.

"What?" I scream at her. Two days ago, Bryan told her that her butt is big, and now she is picking him to be her future husband?

"Maddy! Shhh...it's my choice. Write it down," she says, pointing to the paper with her neon-green painted fingernail.

"Alright, but I don't understand you at all." I shake my head back and forth, writing it down and hoping that the rotation eliminates him. I love Mackenna but Bryan is a jerk; I would not let her marry him.

Luckily, Mackenna ends up married to Tyler, living in a shack in California with eight kids, and driving a Range Rover. I am happy Bryan was eliminated in the third round.

"Not my best life but I'll take it. I got my Range Rover." Mackenna shrugs her shoulders, moving her eyes toward the grassy area again but quickly turning back toward me. "Your turn, hand it over," she says, holding her hand out.

I dig through my bag and pull out my purple binder, handing it over to her.

"Maddy, this time you cannot put Trent down four times; you have to choose other boys." She starts writing MASH across the white sheet of paper.

"I only did that once, Kenna." I look over at Trent throwing the ball to Bryan. "Plus, I don't like him anymore," I say, trying to convince myself as much as Mackenna.

"I've heard that before," she says, tapping the pen on the paper.

I have known Trent my whole life. His brother, Doug, is Jack's best friend. We have been thrown together during our brothers' t-ball and football practices and games, as well as too many Cub Scout events to count. We would play together when we were little, but as we get older we tend to ignore each other, doing our own thing when forced to be around one another.

Mackenna is right though. If I am being honest with myself, I have had a crush on him my whole life. I have written "Mrs. Trent Basso" millions of times and scribbled over it a zillion more. Regardless of my current feelings toward Trent, he is always on my MASH list for a future husband.

Today I hate Trent because, during recess, Evan Graham said that Trent asked him to ask me if Mackenna liked him. I tried to act as though it didn't bother me, but I wanted to march over to Trent and kick him in the shin. I told Evan I would ask and get back to him tomorrow. I already knew her answer without having to ask her; she would never do that to me. I am so mad at Trent Basso today that I knock him down from his number one spot to my fourth option for future husband. Baby steps.

At the end of my MASH, I am married to Jimmy Schmidt, the class clown, and drive a minivan around Alaska with only one child. Not even close to my best life. I throw my binder on the bench in front of me, leaning back to enjoy the sunshine.

"Let's do it again," Mackenna says eagerly.

"No, I'm tired. Let's just relax." I don't open my eyes. I want to empty my mind and enjoy the peace, knowing it will end when Jack and I go home.

"You go ahead and relax; I am going to play some football."

Mackenna walks down the bleachers over to Bryan, Trent, and the other boys.

I open one eye, peering down at her. I am jealous of her confidence. She just walks right up to the guys, grabs the football from Trent, and throws it to Bryan. The boys seem annoyed that she is interrupting their game but they let her join in. I see Trent trying to show her how to throw a football, but she just pushes him away and takes the ball again. I love that girl.

About fifteen minutes later, Mackenna comes running up the stairs and grabs her bag. Practice is over and the football team is making their way to the gates that enclose the field.

"Move your asses, Littles," Trent's brother Doug yells over to us. All the latchkey younger siblings are called "the Littles". MacKenna is 'Little Ross', Trent is 'Little Basso', Bryan is 'Little Edwards', and I'm 'Little Jennings'.

None of us say anything as we venture down to the end of the gates to meet our older siblings.

"Let's go Mad; we're going over to the Basso's for dinner," Jack says, motioning for me to hurry up.

"I'll be right there." I hold up my finger and give Mackenna a hug, even though I will probably talk to her in a couple of hours. I walk over to where Jack is already climbing into his Mustang, and see that Doug and Trent are already waiting for me. Doug pushes the front seat forward so I can climb in the back next to Trent.

"Hey, Maddy," Trent says, turning his head to stare out the window.

"Hi, Trent," I respond, staring out of my own window. That pretty much sums up our friendship lately. I have tried to figure out what happened to us but have come up with nothing.

We arrive at the Basso's ten minutes later. They live on the outskirts of town and have acres of land with horses. Their house has a wraparound porch with flower baskets hanging out of every opening. It looks like something out of a *Better Homes and Gardens* magazine. As the Mustang comes to a stop at the top of their gravel driveway, their yellow lab greets us the second we open the door.

I bend down, letting Dixon climb on me while I pet him with both of my hands. I stand up and Dixon follows me to the front porch and into the house. I know this house as well as my own, since I have probably eaten dinner here more than mine. As soon as we walk in, Trent goes up the stairs to his room, Jack and Doug head to the basement to play pool, and I venture into the kitchen.

"I was wondering when you guys were going to get here," Mrs. Basso says to me over her shoulder while she prepares dinner.

I sit on the stool at the breakfast bar, taking out my homework. "Hi, Mrs. Basso. Thank you for having us for dinner." I am grateful that I didn't have to make it myself tonight.

"Oh Maddy, you are always welcome. You know that." Mrs. Basso turns around, smiling at me. She is the epitome of the perfect mom. She works at the local library, always has dinner on the table for her husband and boys, and she volunteers for all of the school functions and fundraisers.

"I know," I say, and then begin to focus on my homework.

I am able to finish all of my homework while Mrs. Basso finishes dinner, humming to herself. She is always happy. I wonder what she knows that my mom doesn't.

"Dinner, boys!" Mrs. Basso calls, taking out her ponytail and shaking her golden blond hair back and forth. She is a beautiful woman and doesn't look her age at all.

Four boys come running in while I am setting out the plates and silverware.

"Hey, Madgirl. Long time no see," Trent's older brother, Gabe, says as he messes with my hair.

"Hi, Gabe," I softly say. Gabe is fourteen and is a freshman at the high school. He doesn't have to wait for Doug at practices because he is old enough to come home by himself.

"Where's dad?" Doug asks, while stealing a roll out of the basket and devouring it. I can't imagine how much food they must go through in this house with three boys.

I wonder why Mrs. Basso stays at home when her husband isn't around. Not like my mom, who is gone as soon as my dad leaves town for a couple of days. They couldn't be more different.

We eat the chicken and rice with broccoli, while the three older boys fight over the food. Trent is quiet, never looking up from his plate. I don't know what I did to make him hate me so much? After dinner, Jack says that he wants to play one more game, so I go into the family room to watch television. Trent and Gabe are already in there. I decide to sit down on the opposite end of the couch as Trent. A couple of minutes later, Gabe leaves, mumbling something about homework.

I take this as my chance to find out what Trent's problem is and why he is so set on ignoring me lately.

"So, you like Kenna?" I ask, not turning my head from the television.

"I don't know," he says with a shrug.

"You don't know? Well, why did you ask Evan to ask me to ask her then?" I ask, looking at him out of the corner of my eye to try and read his expression.

He sighs and says, "I wanted to see what you would say."

"What do you mean? If you like her, go ahead and ask her out," I say, even though my heart is screaming at me to say something else.

"I don't like Kenna." He moves closer to me on the couch. I am totally confused by this boy.

"Then why did you have Evan ask me that?" I repeat, turning to face him on the couch. We have been friends since we were in diapers. Why is everything so awkward now?

"I wanted to see if you would be jealous," he says quietly, taking my hand and entwining our fingers.

"Did you get the reaction you wanted?" I ask, not removing my hand with his.

"No, I thought you liked me. Am I wrong?" He is staring at me now, his crystal blue eyes boring into mine. I couldn't look away if I tried.

"You are right, I do like you." I bite my lower lip, unsure of what happens now.

"I like you too," Trent whispers and turns around to watch television, never letting go of my hand.

Chapter 2 — Present Day 25 years old

The plane dips down and both of my hands clutch the armrests. I have never liked flying but I am extra on edge this trip. I don't want to go back home but I have no choice. My brother has decided to finally marry his college sweetheart, Lindsey Jacobson.

Don't get me wrong. I love Lindsey and I couldn't ask for a better sister-in-law. The problem is that they planned a week-long wedding extravaganza and, like every other wedding of the Bigs and Littles over the years, everyone is involved. Therefore, I'm not only spending a week with Jack and Lindsey and their wedding party, but I'll also be seeing Bryan, Mackenna, and, from what I heard last night, Trent.

A hand squeezes mine gently. "It's alright sweetie, just some turbulence," Ian Fisher, my best friend, says quietly.

"I know. I hate flying," I say. Ian and I became best friends our senior year of college when we worked together at the rec center. We both lusted over the same guy but unfortunately for me, the object of our mutual affection swung Ian's way, not mine.

I made Ian take a week off work to come with me, and since he already knows most of the people, it will make things easier. I need him there with me to face everyone again.

"It's going to be fine Maddy, just relax." Ian looks at me, squeezes my hand, and then goes back to reading his magazine. We both know he isn't talking about the flight, and we also both know that things won't be fine.

The plane lands five minutes early. I am torn with wanting to get off or not, but I know I have to. Ian and I make our way to baggage claim and he stops on the way to get one of the luggage carts.

"Why do we need that?" I ask sharply.

"For our bags. I can't carry them all," he snaps back to me.

"How many bags to do you have?" I met him at the gate this morning so both of us had already checked our luggage.

"I don't know," he says, tilting his head down to look at me.

"Oh God, you probably have more than me," I gripe.

"Probably. Now help me pull this through," Ian says, yanking at the cart corral.

"Here, let me help," a deep voice says from behind us.

I see the tanned forearm easily guide the cart out of the corral. My eyes roam upward, taking in a firm bicep, strong shoulders, and when my eyes reach the face attached to all of the above, I gasp.

"Hey Madgirl, long time no see," Gabe Basso says, smirking at me.

"Gabe," I say stunned. I'm not ready to face him so soon.

"I know, I caught a break at work in order to get here early." His eyes leave mine, focusing on Ian. "Hi, I'm Gabe," he says, extending his hand out toward Ian.

Ian looks as dumbfounded as I probably do, but puts his hand out to shake Gabe's.

"Sorry, Ian this is Gabe Basso. Gabe, this is Ian Fisher." I motion my finger back and forth between the two of them.

"Nice to meet you," Ian says.

Gabe nods his head to him. "What baggage claim are you guys at?" he asks.

"Five, you?" Ian takes charge of the conversation, since apparently I have been struck mute. If I am this bad in front of Gabe, how will I make it through everyone else?

Gabe's eyes shift to me and I see the concern in his eyes. "Six," he answers. "Is anyone picking you guys up?" he asks, still looking at me. I can't believe how much he looks like Trent, or more accurately, how much Trent looks like him.

"I rented a car. I didn't want to rely on anyone for rides the whole week," I say, divulging more information than necessary.

"Do you mind if I hitch a ride? I was going to catch a cab, but since you guys are here...." he says, his sentence trailing off.

"Sure, no problem," I say with a shrug.

The three of us walk over to our respective baggage claims. I can see Gabe's has already started moving, but ours is still quiet. A minute later, Gabe jogs over to us, holding a garment bag in his hand.

Although it's only June, Gabe is already tan, which I assume has to do with living in Florida instead of the Midwest. I'd heard that Gabe moved down there after college with a couple of buddies, going in together on some real estate deals. I also heard that he's doing pretty well for himself, especially for only being twenty-eight.

My bag is the first to come off, and I hope that's a sign that this week won't be too bad. Ian is waiting next to his cart; he has pulled off two bags already and is going for a third. His matching plaid faux designer-print luggage is a set of five and I assume he brought every piece.

"How much luggage did he bring?" Gabe asks, motioning his head toward Ian.

"I have no idea, but I bet he comes home with even more than he brought," I say, smiling.

"I guess he'll be prepared for whatever is going on. From what Doug told me, it's going to be quite a week."

"Yeah, I haven't heard much of anything," I respond, raising my shoulders and looking down at my feet.

"Knowing Jack, I'm sure he's planned a fun time."

"That's my brother, party planner extraordinaire," I say, smiling back up at him, noticing how perfect and white his teeth are.

"I'm looking forward to it; it has been a killer summer. All of our houses are booked for the season and we have been working like crazy getting everything ready. It was all I could do to get the time off," he explains. "How about you, Maddy? What's the decorating business like?"

"Hard to get into. I do most of my work for free, just to get my foot in the door. I tried to work as an assistant for another decorator, but they just want to boss you around and do their personal errands," I confess. I have actually thought about switching careers lately, but I don't want to go back to school.

"Yeah, I have heard that. I had a friend who graduated in fashion design and she had a hard time too."

"What happened? Did she finally break through?" I cross my fingers, praying his answer is 'yes'. I could use some hope to continue with my dream.

"Unfortunately, no. She ended up getting married to some investment banker she met and now lives in Connecticut with two kids," he says, giving me a lopsided smile.

"Oh," I murmur, deflated. I knew going into design that few people were able to really succeed in it, but since it's my passion, I went for it anyway.

"But," he says, nudging his shoulder with mine, "she wasn't half as talented as you, Madeline Jennings." He smiles down at me sweetly.

"Thank you," I grin back, "but you have never seen my work."

"Yes, I have," he answers. Before I can question him further, we see Ian coming over with his cart overflowing with luggage.

"About time, Ian." I turn around, towing my suitcase behind me.

Suddenly, I feel my suitcase jerk to a stop behind me.

Gabe is there grabbing it. "You might as well take advantage of the cart," he says, taking the suitcase from my hands and placing it on the cart. Ian huffs as though it is too much to push, but Gabe and I both chuckle as we walk to the rental car counter.

As soon as we get there, the young boy behind the counter motions for me to step forward so I walk over to him. I am surprised to see Gabe step up next to me.

"Can I help you?" the young kid asks.

"Reservation for Madeline Jennings." I place my ID and credit card on the counter.

"Okay, we have you down for a compact this week." The kid moves to take my ID and credit card, but a hand quickly covers them both.

"Can we upgrade to an SUV?" Gabe asks.

"What?" I ask, raising my eyebrows at him.

"His luggage isn't going to fit in a compact," he says, pointing to an exhausted Ian who is making his way over to the rental car place with all of the luggage in tow.

"We will have to strap it to the roof. I can't afford to upgrade," I admit, nodding to the young man to continue with the previously agreed upon transaction.

"First of all, I don't think a compact has a rack you can strap luggage to," he says, laughing. "Second, I would never make you pay. Let me get an SUV, and we can share it all week. We will be going to the same places anyway," he adds, awaiting my answer.

I bite my bottom lip, contemplating my options. "I can't let you do that, Gabe. Not to mention, the reason I'm getting a rental car is so that I don't have to rely on anyone this week."

He pulls out his wallet, handing the kid his ID and credit card. "Go ahead and book us an SUV and put both of our names on it." He grabs my credit card and hands it back to me. "You can keep the truck and come get me when we are doing something," he says with finality.

Did I miss something? Since when is he in charge of me? The problem is, I knew Ian's luggage might be a problem. I guess I will just go ahead with Gabe's plan and then drop the truck off later for him to use. I don't need or want his charity.

We lug all of Ian's bags onto the shuttle van that will take us to the rental car lot. When we arrive, Gabe makes me pick out the SUV we are going to use. Of course, Gabe doesn't just get a regular SUV; he has to get a full-sized one. I pick a nice blue Chevy Tahoe, but it is huge and I don't really want to drive it. After living in New York for the past two years, I've gotten used to not driving, and to go from taxi cabs to this monster of a truck is too much for me to take. When Gabe tries to give me the keys, I tell him to keep them.

Gabe raises his eyebrows, but begins loading the SUV with luggage. When the last bag is in the back, I am astonished to see that it is jam-packed with luggage. *Does he always have to be right?*

We head down the freeway toward our town, which is about an hour outside of Chicago. I can't stop nibbling on my lower lip. I don't know what to expect when I get there. I have heard Gabe's phone buzz a few times with text messages, and I wonder who they are from.

By the time we pass the sign "Welcome to Belcrest: population 1,531", my lip is raw and I am starting to sweat. I can't believe I am back in the one place I swore I would never return.

"Holy shit. You weren't kidding when you said you came from a small town," Ian remarks from the backseat.

"Belcrest is small but mighty. Right, Madgirl?" Gabe playfully nudges me with his elbow. That is how the football team has always been described, 'small but mighty'. We've never had as many guys as the other teams, but we were still state champions five years in a row when my brother and Gabe played. By the time I graduated, the run ended.

I remain quiet, nervous about seeing everyone. We pull up to Gabe's house, which still has the same white porch with hanging flower baskets. I get out, stretching my legs and Mrs. Basso comes walking out with a chocolate lab behind her. Dixon passed away when we were in high school and they got a new pup, Kisses, which was affectionately named by Mrs. Basso. She said she was outnumbered for years and it was time she had a girl around the house. Since all of the boys were pretty much out of the house by then, there wasn't really a fight.

"Gabe, it's so good to have you home," she says, embracing him in a tight hug.

"It's good to be home, Mom," he responds, squeezing her back. I know he has always had a close relationship to his family, unlike me.

"Anyone else here yet?" he asks.

I freeze, not wanting to know whether or not Trent is here.

"Doug is out back with your dad," she says and then turns towards me, doing a double take. She looks back and forth between Gabe and me, though whether she is confused or upset, I can't really tell.

"Madeline?" she asks curtly.

"Hello, Mrs. Basso," I say.

"I assumed you would be in town this week," she says, coming over to give me a brief hug. Cold compared to how she used to hug me.

"Why are you guys driving together?" she asks, seeming irritated.

"We ran into each other at the airport and thought we would share a rental car this week." Gabe tosses the keys in my direction.

Catching them, I hear Ian clear his throat behind me.

"Oh, I'm sorry. Mrs. Basso this is my friend, Ian. Ian this is Gabe's mom, Mrs. Basso," I motion back and forth.

She eyes him up and down. "Please, call me Wendy," she says, extending her hand.

"Nice to meet you...Wendy," Ian says, shaking her hand.

"Alright then, let's go," I say to Ian. "Nice to see you again, Mrs. Basso. Gabe, let me know if you want the car." I turn around before either one of them can say anything, heading back to the driver's side of the blue monster.

"Wait, Maddy!" Gabe calls, jogging over to me.

"What's up?" I say, trying to keep the impatience out of my voice.

"I don't have your number. Give me your phone," he demands.

I dig it out of my purse and hand it to him. He programs his number and then calls himself. After he hands it back to me, I see that he stored himself as the 'Hot Basso Brother'.

"Nice," I smirk up to him.

"It's not my fault my brothers got stuck at the shallow end of the gene pool." He holds his hands out, waiting for me to disagree. I don't.

We pull out of the driveway from the place that I once considered my home, and I want to cry for all that has happened between me and the Bassos. I promised myself that I wouldn't let myself get dragged into it again. I see Mrs. Basso giving Gabe the third-degree, probably about why he would show up with me, and I watch him shaking his head back and forth.

"She's a trip," Ian says. "What is her problem with you?"

"She used to be nice. I was like a daughter to her," I say, staring at the road ahead of me.

"What happened?" he asks.

I don't answer. I don't want to talk about it. I can't tell him that I took something from her that I could never replace.

AVAILABLE NOW!

MICHELLE LYNN